Sudden Response: An EMS Novel

by

R.L. MathewsonThis is a work of fiction. All of the characters, organizations and events described in this novel are either products of the author's imagination or are used fictitiously.

ISBN-13: 978-1479338788
ebook ISBN 978-0-9832125-7-7

http://www.rlmathewson.com
Rerum Publishing House

Other books by R.L. Mathewson:

Tall, Dark & Lonely: A Pyte Series Novel
Without Regret: A Sentinel Novel
A Humble Heart: A Hollywood Hearts Novel
A Reclusive Heart: A Hollywood Hearts Novel
Playing for Keeps: A Neighbor From Hell Novel
Perfection: A Neighbor From Hell Novel

This book is dedicated to all the men and women who put their lives on the line in our time of need. It doesn't matter if you work on a 911 system or work every day to make sure your patient makes it to their dialysis appointment on time you are all heroes in my book.

Thank you.

A special thank you to the EMTs who took care of my son after he decided to play superman one day and nearly took ten years off my life.

As always a special thank you to Rhonda Valverde and all my forum buddies at http://www.vampireromancebooks.com

And of course to my children who will always be my inspiration and my little buddies.

I love you, Kayley and Shane....

Even if you do frighten me from time to time.

Chapter 1

"Fresh meat," Eric read the sign with a chuckle as he pulled his light blue uniform shirt on over his white tee shirt. "I guess you must be Greg."

The man nodded frantically as Eric looked over the boys' recent work. They had Greg strapped to a long board in nothing but his boxers. Greg's mouth was taped shut with a piece of two inch white medical tape. Someone, probably Johnson, drew a big happy face on the man's stomach. To top it off they leaned Greg against the chain link fence with the sign tapped across his hips for the entire world to see.

Eric put his bag down on the sidewalk and worked on tidying his uniform. "The name's Eric. I'm really sorry about this, Greg. I meant to get here sooner, but I got a little held up."

Greg tried to shrug against his restraints.

"I gotta tell you that I'm a little embarrassed to work with these guys." He gestured to Greg's predicament. Greg nodded slightly. "So juvenile." He shook his head in disgust and bent down in front of Greg. Greg tried to look down to see what Eric was doing, probably hoping that he was getting a pair of scissors to cut him down.

Eric stood up with an aerosol can in his hand, absently shaking it. "I tell the boys if they're going to do something, do it right the first time. We take a lot of pride in our work around here, but this," he gestured lazily towards Greg, "has amateur written all over it. I'm sorry, Greg, but I have a reputation to protect." With that Eric sprayed green spray-paint on Greg's brown hair.

After a few minutes Eric stepped back to examine his work. "Hmm, better, but not quite what I'm looking for." He shook his head and bent down to retrieve something else from the bag. This time he stood up holding a red marker.

Greg watched as the marker came closer to his face until his eyes crossed. He felt the pen press against the tape covering his lips. He looked up to see Eric smile. “There, that’s much better.” He stepped back to examine his work. The green hair and full pouty red lips worked for him.

He picked up his bag and gave Greg a smile. “Welcome to the 707, Greg. I’m your training officer tonight. I’ll see you inside.” Eric walked away while Greg tried to scream against the tape.

Eric walked into the fire house. “What’s up, Eric?” a man asked.

“Not much.” He made his way upstairs to find the rest of the men watching the game.

“Eric!” they shouted in unison.

“Gentlemen, I see you greeted my third rider," a new EMT who rode along on a shift to train, "Very disappointing work, gentlemen, very disappointing,” he said, shaking his head in disgust.

Ethan ran a hand over his bald head as he said, “Come on, man, we had to rush it. The game was coming on.”

Eric looked at the large television. The Yankees were playing Boston at Fenway. “Sorry, my apologies.” He held up his hands and made his way back to the sleeping quarters. He walked to the last room on the right and threw his bag on the bed to the left. The one to the right was empty, letting him know his partner wasn't here yet. He would make the bed later. That is if it was a slow night otherwise he would be working all night on rig and wouldn't have a chance to grab some sleep.

He wasn’t supposed to be working tonight, but the lieutenant called him at home a few hours ago and asked if he could come in and train a third rider. Eric jumped at the chance since his social life had been shit for months and he could always use the money.

“Eric, you have a call!” one of the men yelled.

Eric walked back out into the living room of the three level fire house and passed the guys now watching him instead of the game. Jeff held his hand over the phone. "A woman, damn she sounds sexy as hell!" He handed the phone over to Eric.

"Hello?" he said, having no clue as to who would be calling him at work.

"Hi, sweetie!"

Eric sighed, looking back at the men, not really all that surprised to see them laughing. He promptly gave them a one finger salute, eliciting more laughter. His love life was a joke to them. They couldn't understand how any man could go months without a girlfriend or, at the very least, get laid.

"Hey, mom, what's going on?" he asked.

"I'm just making sure that you're coming tomorrow night for dinner. Your brother will be here with his new girlfriend."

"That's great, mom," he said, not really caring at all. This was his mother's way of bringing up a possible match for him. According to his mother it didn't matter that he was a thirty year old man, she had a responsibility to make sure he was happy and of course to her that meant finding a wife.

"I wanted to tell you about this lovely girl I met at the grocery store yesterday."

"Oh, Mom, you didn't," he said, feeling a headache coming on.

She ignored him and continued. "She's pretty, single, young and did I mention head cashier?"

"Mom, call her up and cancel. I'm not interested."

"I don't see why I should. I offered the poor girl a homemade meal and I intend to keep that promise. Now, since you'll be here you can help keep her company."

"Mom, I might not be able to come tomorrow night. I might have to pick up another shift." Even as he said it he knew his mother already dismissed the idea and expected him there.

She sighed into the phone. "I'll expect you by six. Oh, and make sure you tell Joe to come, too."

"Bye, Mom." He hung up, wondering how the hell he was going to get out of going.

"So, who was she trying to hook you up with this time?" Jeff asked.

"A cashier," he muttered, ignoring their laughter. "Anyone seen Teddy?" he asked, wondering where his partner for the night was. If he wasn't so damned bored he would never have taken this shift.

Working as an EMT was probably the best job he'd ever had. It was great. The hours were good, better than good, the pay was incredible and every day was new and exciting. The only thing that could really make or break your day besides a really fucked up call was your partner.

Eight to twenty-four hours shifts working with someone in what really came down to a box on wheels could either be a hell of a good time or have you coming to blows. Imagine being stuck in a small box with someone who didn't bathe or worse wore what seemed like a gallon of cheap perfume or cologne. He'd found himself standing out in the rain, blizzard, or sweltering heat many times in order to get away from the stench. Worse was being partnered with some annoying asshole or an outright bitch that you couldn't stand.

He was lucky that his full time partner was also his best friend. They'd been best friends since they were eight. Joe was a hell of a partner. Never complained, always had a joke, and was easy to get along with, unlike his partner for tonight. He really lucked out with Joe.

Teddy on the other hand was a Class A prick. He hit on anything with breasts and didn't take rejection well. The guy had more write ups than the entire squad put together, but thanks to the Union he couldn't be fired. Tonight was going to be a true test of his patience. Besides being an arrogant asshole, the guy didn't know what the hell he was doing and was a lazy bastard. Why in the hell did he agree to come in tonight?

"Don't get all choked up, but Teddy won't be in tonight. He banged out," Jeff said as he grabbed a bottle of water from the fridge.

"No shit?" Eric asked, hoping the man wasn't fucking with him.

"I shit you not. Seems a stripper broke his nose when he tried to ignore the 'no touch' rule," Jeff said, chuckling.

Eric shook his head, laughing. Leave it to that pervert to get his ass kicked by a stripper. "Who am I working with then?"

"Not sure. Bill's been on the phone for the past hour trying to get you someone to work with," Jeff said, leaning against the counter.

"If one of you gentlemen would be so kind as to go release my third rider and tell him to clean up I'll go check out the rig," he said, heading towards the garage.

"Do we have to?" one of the men whined, making him laugh.

Eric walked over to the board to grab the keys for ambulance seventy-nine only to find the hook empty. No doubt the last crew left the keys in the ignition, he hoped at least. He walked past several of the box ambulances towards the van style ambulances and sighed with relief when he spotted ambulance seventy-nine with its back doors wide open.

Whoever his partner was for the night was already in the ambulance checking it out. He walked over and paused when he spotted the very luscious figure bent over inside his rig. He ran his eyes over the familiar figure and he groaned inwardly. His eyes went from the long honey blond hair pulled back into a no-nonsense ponytail to the small waist, flared hips and perfect bottom that was pointed his way.

Damn.

He couldn't think of a better sight to start the night off with. It was too damn bad there wasn't a chance in hell he would ever find out how those lush curves would feel beneath him.

"I thought the restraining order stated that you couldn't come within a hundred yards of me?" he demanded.

* * * *

Joe bit back a smile at the familiar deep voice. He was the only man on earth who could make her smile without fail. It had always been that way ever since they were kids.

She still remembered the first time she met him. It was her first day in a new school. Her mother, who decided this time was going to be different, decided to shove eight year old tomboy Josephine, Joe for short, into a overly frilly dress that was too short and in her opinion too ugly to be seen in public. She'd never been so embarrassed in her life. During recess she tried to hide from the rest of the kids, but that only managed to draw more attention. When one little boy came over and shoved a handful of worms down her dress she made that boy eat every single one of them.

An hour later they both sat in the principal's office, filthy, clothes torn, and mutually angry at Tyler Mathews for tattling on their little fight. They made a pact then and there to get Tyler back and had been best friends ever since.

Their friendship had survived the cootie stage and continued on into middle school, high school and then EMT training. Many people, including Eric's mother, thought they were cute and would end up married one day. That little pipe dream faded away when everyone realized they were best friends and nothing more.

She'd lost track over the number of women who got pissed over their relationship. Most of them foolishly tried to give Eric an ultimatum because they couldn't handle her place in his life. Eric never batted an eye when he dumped them flat on their asses seconds later. Hell, he even broke up with his fiancé three years ago when she tried the same thing.

There had only been a few men who tried that nonsense with her. They quickly learned that her loyalty belonged to Eric. That little problem had been the cause for many break ups over the years. Not that she or Eric ever made it an issue. They didn't. They just went on as they always had. It's not like they purposely tried to push people away, but sometimes it was hard for other people to handle their friendship. She never understood their problem. If anything it should make them feel more comfortable that they were both more than capable of loyalty. Plus, and let's be honest here, if they wanted to have sex they would have done it a long time ago.

She felt the back of the ambulance dip as Eric climbed in behind her. "I can appreciate a woman who's willing to turn her nose up at a judicial order to be with me," he said in his deep sexy voice that had Joe rolling her eyes.

Joe turned and smoothly shoved several bags of expired saline in his arms. "You know a piece of paper will never stand in the way of our love," she said in a sweet teasing voice while she batted her eyes up at him.

Eric chuckled softly. "I see you missed me."

She nodded solemnly. "I did. I really did. When Bill called up and *begged* me to come in even though we just got off a twenty-four hour shift this morning I jumped at the chance." She ran her eyes down his lean well defined body back up to meet his mischievous green eyes. "You know I can never stay away from you." She reached up with both hands and pinched his cheeks, hard. "You're just so darn cute," she said, pursing up her lips.

"I'm studly, baby, get it right," he sighed heavily as if it were a burden to remind her yet again.

She placed her hands on her hips. "You're absolutely right. What was I thinking?"

Eric jumped out of the ambulance. "It's okay. I forgive you," he said as he made his way to the trash can to dump the saline. He was going to have to post something to remind crews to double check supplies when they picked them up at the hospital.

He grabbed a bottle of sanitizer and some rags before heading back to the ambulance. Joe was already completing their check list. He tossed a rag onto her clipboard. She looked up to stick her tongue out at him and went back to her paperwork.

"Did I mention that we have a third rider today?" he asked as he sprayed down the stretcher and began wiping it down.

"Great," she said, stretching out the word.

He paused mid-swipe to look over at her. "What's that supposed to mean?"

"It means I have to play babysitter the entire shift," she answered.

Eric frowned. "I don't think he's going to be much of a problem. He looked capable."

Joe rolled her eyes. "I wasn't talking about him."

Chapter 2

"Everything okay back there, Greg?" Eric yelled into the back of the ambulance.

Greg turned around in the tech seat to answer him. "Yeah, everything's fine. Um, when are we going to get a call?" Greg asked, trying to feign casualness. Eric and Joe shared a look. No doubt the kid was a whacker.

A whacker was a term they used for someone in the field that took the job too seriously and thought of themselves as Superman. They got too excited about the job and focused way too much on it when they weren't working. Most new EMTs were guaranteed whackers who came in overeager, too confident and full of their own bullshit. As entertaining as it was to seasoned EMTs, and a little annoying, it could also be dangerous in the field.

"Cause I'm ready you know. I don't really need to third ride, because I have some experience, but Bill said it was policy. He said it was up to you to sign me off early so I can get off the initial probation period. So, if you want to do that you know I wouldn't mind. I don't want to waste your night or anything," Greg rambled on.

Joe covered her mouth to keep from laughing and leaned into the steering wheel while Eric glanced around the convenient store parking lot they were stationed at.

"I, um," he forced himself not to laugh and keep a straight face, "I really appreciate the offer, Greg. Thank you, but don't worry about wasting my time. We really like the company."

Joe shook with silent laughter against the wheel. Yup, they'd been training officers for six of the twelve years they'd worked as EMTs and heard it all from their third riders. A few were honest about being nervous, the others hid it well until their first call and a few like Greg liked to bullshit their experience right from the start. Definitely a whacker, Eric thought.

"I've been working as a lifeguard at a resort since I was sixteen," Greg offered.

"Is that so?" Eric said with false interest. This was the point where Greg would brag, trying to convince the two of them that they didn't need to train him and that he knew what he was doing. It never failed to be entertaining when a third rider thought they were seasoned pros just because of one or two experiences from their past.

They had one guy outright refuse to listen to them while they were extricating a man from an overturned car and tried to correct *them* because he'd seen an episode of ER where they did it completely different, and wrong. Eric ended up having to punch the guy out before he paralyzed the poor bastard in the car. The jerk tried to yank the patient out of the car by his head. That patient actually thanked Eric and lied to a cop later, covering Eric's ass. Again, whackers could be very dangerous in the field.

"Yeah," Greg said, nodding to himself. "Did that for almost ten years now. I've been teaching CPR and first aid for two years as well."

Great. He taught people how to watch a video and pass a written test so he thought he was king shit now. This was going to be an interesting night.

"Ever have to use your skills?" Joe asked, twisting in her seat to look back.

The guy averted his eyes as he said cockily, "Oh yeah, you wouldn't believe the shit I saw on that job." Which no doubt meant he hadn't so much as applied a band-aid to some kid's skinned knee.

Joe gave him a smile. Her beautiful baby blue eyes sparkled. "That's good. It means you'll probably pick up on the way we do things around here quickly."

Eric had to hold back a snort. Joe was always too nice. Well, right now she was. If this guy's bullshit got in the way of patient care even he wouldn't want to get in her way. She'd go apeshit on this guy if he caused one of their patients any problems.

Greg nodded thoughtfully. "True."

"Great. I'm going to run inside and grab a drink. I'll be right back," she said, still smiling.

Eric watched her walk into the store and wasn't aware that Greg moved out of his seat to lean in the front and do the same until he heard the man mutter, "Nice."

More annoyed that the man was getting a little too close to him, he shoved him back with his elbow. "I don't swing that way, cupcake."

"Oh," Greg said, moving back. "Didn't mean to crowd you."

Eric leaned back as he kept an eye on the store's entrance. This wasn't the best neighborhood, but Joe would kick his ass six ways to Sunday if he tried pulling any of that chauvinistic shit on her. As far as Joe was concerned she was one of the guys. He knew she could handle herself and would tear his head off if she even suspected for a second that he doubted her, which is why he kept his mouth shut and didn't offer to go get that drink for her. He liked his balls right where they were.

"Hey, um, Eric?"

"Yeah?" he said, already fearing the guy would try to convince him to let him drive.

"Joe, is she seeing anyone?" Greg asked as he ran his fingers through his greenish brown hair. The five minutes he shoved his head under the sink faucet hadn't helped.

"Nope," Eric said, making the word pop.

"So, you and Joe aren't....," he said leadingly.

"Nope."

"Do you mind if I go for it?"

"Nope," he said, knowing the guy would be shot down and how pissed it would make Joe. Joe didn't date doctors or whackers. Yup, this should be very entertaining indeed.

* * * *

"Such a tough choice," Joe mumbled as she looked from the Snickers bar to Reese's Peanut Butter Cups.

"You should get them both," a low voice said.

Joe looked over her shoulder and forced a smile as Greg gave her what he probably thought was a sexy grin. Great. This was going to be a fun night. She looked past Greg to find Eric leaning against the door frame, grinning hugely. The bastard set her up. She was so going to kick his ass later.

It was only the knowledge that she'd done worse to him that kept her from chucking one of the candy bars at his head. He better hope they weren't sent to the Sunflower nursing home tonight. Judy was working and that cougar was completely hot for Eric, much to his horror. She was barely five feet tall and definitely five feet wide, wore more makeup than a drag queen and had no shame when it came to Eric.

"Shouldn't you guys be in the rig in case we get a call?" she asked casually.

Eric held up a portable radio. Damn technology! "Got it covered. Already told dispatch we were stepping out," he said cheerfully.

"So, Joe," Greg said as he picked up a candy bar to study it. "How long have you been an EMT?"

"About twelve years now," she said, shooting a glare at Eric who had the nerve to wink at her.

"Wow, twelve years. You must have some pretty amazing stories to tell. Maybe sometime we should get a drink and talk about them?"

Before she could answer, Eric spoke up. "That sounds like fun. She really likes that bar over on Madison. They have karaoke there every Thursday and Saturday night."

Greg's smile widened. The poor bastard probably thought Eric was helping him. "Really? You like karaoke?"

"She loves it," Eric said, wiggling his eyebrows. "You should hear her rendition of 'War,' she totally kicks ass."

Joe sucked in a breath. That rat bastard! The one time she made the mistake of getting drunk at a frat party and danced on a table taking requests and he was going to throw it in her face? Unbelievable! He was the one that requested that song!

"So, what do you say?" Greg asked, giving her a cocky grin that he probably thought was irresistible. There was only one man she knew who could pull that grin off without fail and right now he was a rat bastard.

"Say about what?" she asked, returning her attention back to the candy bars. If she was going to survive this night she was going to need chocolate.

She heard Eric's soft laughter and discretely flipped him off, making him laugh harder.

"Tomorrow night? You, me, dinner, dancing, and maybe a little karaoke?" Greg asked smoothly.

"Not gonna happen tomorrow night, spanky. She has plans with me," Eric announced. Joe wasn't foolish enough to think he was coming to her rescue. Oh no, not Eric. He just didn't want to get stuck with whatever bimbo his mother was throwing his way and had no problem with using her as a shield. If she didn't love Alice, Eric's mother, so much or really love her cooking she'd ditch his ass in a heartbeat.

"Well, what about this weekend?" Greg asked, sounding a little unsure of himself.

Oh, this was perfect. She smiled sweetly when she answered, making sure she could see Eric's expression. "I'm sorry. I already have plans for this weekend. I'm going deep sea fishing for three days." She was not disappointed by Eric's reaction.

"You betraying bitch!" he hissed.

She winked at him. "You got that right." There were really only a few things in this world that Eric really loved and lived for and deep sea fishing was one of them. His Uncle Brian and grandfather used to take them out several times a year when they were kids and they both loved it. Still did.

"*Echo seventeen*?" dispatch called.

Eric leveled a glare on her as he brought the portable radio up to his mouth. "I'm going," he announced.

"Nope," she said, loving the power she held over him. Ah, it looked like she was finally going to get some help painting her garage. There wasn't much Eric wouldn't do for a weekend of deep sea fishing.

"Watch me," he said, before he keyed in. "Echo seventeen."

"*What's your location, echo seventeen*?" dispatch asked.

"East side," Eric answered.

"Echo seventeen, take a priority one call at 258 Lawson for an assault. Police are already in route."

"Echo seventeen received, 258 Lawson."

"Oh my god!" Greg said, shaking. "Oh my god!" He dropped the candy bar, ran for the door, tripped over his own feet, stumbled, but didn't let that stop him from sprinting towards the ambulance and diving in.

With a pained sigh, Joe put her candy bar back and walked to the door. Eric held it open for her. As they walked towards the ambulance Eric asked, "Where are you going?"

"Cape Cod."

"That's a six hour drive," he pointed out.

"Yup, I'm leaving around four in the morning Friday. I won't be back until late Sunday night, but don't worry I'm sure you'll have fun without me," she said, smiling.

"Bullshit, I'm going and we both know it," he said, climbing into the passenger seat.

"Oh my god, oh my god," Greg mumbled from the back.

Joe climbed in behind the wheel and started the rig. She flicked on the emergency lights and pulled out. She kept one hand on the wheel and the other on the emergency switchboard, switching the sirens from the fog horn to the wailing sound.

Eric pulled out an emergency run sheet and attached it to his clipboard, ignoring Greg's "oh my gods," which had now turned to pure excitement. The kid was about to start operating on pure adrenaline. No doubt it would make the call more interesting.

"I'm going," he stated as he filled in the date and their names.

She maneuvered in and out of traffic with the grace of a pro. "Nope, you're really not."

"Why not?" he asked.

"Probably because I didn't invite you?" she said. She really enjoyed messing with him.

He snorted. "And you think that means something to me? I'm going. End of story."

"We'll see," she said.

"Yeah, we will, won't we?" he said confidently as they pulled in behind two police cruisers in front a small yellow house that had seen better days.

"Echo seventeen on scene," he informed dispatch.

They stepped out of the ambulance the same time the front door flew open and a naked man wielding a knife ran out. "Fuck you, pigs!" the man yelled as he ran towards them.

"I'm so going," Eric said before he launched himself at the guy. He grabbed the man's hand and twisted it behind his back, making him drop the knife.

Joe ignored the man's screams and threats of violence as she kicked the knife away and helped Eric take the guy to the ground. She held the man's legs down while Eric restrained him to the ground.

Two cops came running towards them from behind the house as an older officer came out of the house, leading two cuffed, bleeding men towards them. The cops spotted them and grinned.

"Oh look, Eric and Joe brought us a present," Bret, a cop ten years their senior, said as he shoved the two men in front of him. "Don't worry we brought you something, too," he said, gesturing to the two men under arrest.

"Oh, Bret, you are just the sweetest man alive," Joe said, giving him a sweet smile that made the older man chuckle.

"I do what I can. Do you want to look these two over for us?" Bret asked.

"Sure thing," Eric said. "Just as soon as you take tiny here off our hands."

The two officers quickly took over. Eric helped Joe to her feet. She pulled out a small bottle of hand sanitizer and squirted some in Eric's waiting hand before taking some for herself.

"Hey, isn't that your third rider puking?" Jeff, one of the younger cops asked.

Joe and Eric stilled. Slowly, they turned around and sure enough there was Greg vomiting all over a dead bush.

Joe sighed heavily as Eric asked on a drawn out sigh, "Why must you embarrass us? At least aim for the perp on the ground."

Chapter 3

"How's your stomach?" Joe asked. Eric didn't miss the slight twitch of her lips.

Greg' face reddened. "It's fine. Just something I ate I think," he said quickly.

"Uh huh," Eric said, trying not to laugh. The guy puked at all six calls they had. Five hours on the job and the kid still hadn't said one word to a patient. He ended up vomiting every single time they arrived on scene. Then he'd sit up front for the drive to the hospital and remain there sipping a water or ginger ale.

It would suck for Greg, but there was no way Eric or Joe could sign off on this ride along. The kid wouldn't be getting any credit for this. No doubt Greg would try and argue it to death, but Eric wasn't budging. Yeah it sucked to have to do more ride alongs, but it couldn't be helped. Eric wasn't about to put some patient's life on the line for anything.

"Alright, gentlemen," she looked at Eric, "and I use that term loosely. I'm going to catch a few winks." She stepped around them and headed into the fire house.

"I think I should lie down, too," Greg said. Eric didn't miss the look the guy was sending Joe's ass. It also hadn't escaped his notice that Greg swore up and down that he wasn't tired and was going to hang out with the guys until he found out that the three of them shared a bunk room. Once he knew he'd be sleeping in the same room with Joe the guy started up with the fake yawns.

Joe might be one of the toughest woman he'd ever known, but that didn't mean he stood by and left her to handle shit like this. He never had and never would. As much as it got Joe's panties in a bunch when he stepped in and played her protector, he wouldn't stop.

She might think of herself as one of the guys, but she wasn't. Joe was a beautiful woman with beautiful hair, killer eyes, and a sexy little smile that drove men nuts. It didn't hurt that she had a killer body, not that she thought so. It really killed him that she didn't know how hot she was. If you tried to tell her she'd laugh her ass off. She was the most down to earth woman he'd ever known. If she wasn't his best friend......

There really was no point in finishing that thought. She was and it was his job as the man in her life to kick the living shit out of any asshole that hurt her. With that in mind he followed the overeager puppy as he drooled after Joe to the back rooms.

"There are only two beds, Greg. You'll have to throw some blankets on the floor between the beds or go see if there's a spot on the couch," Joe explained apologetically as she unlaced her black boots.

Greg eyed the small space between the two beds and fought a smile. He'd be sleeping inches from Joe. Not fucking happening. Eric eyed his unmade bed with his old sleeping bag thrown on top of it and then Joe's. He smiled. Ah, god love her, Joe always put comfort first. There was no sleeping bag for Joe, oh no, not for his Joe. Her bed was already made with what he knew were clean high count cotton sheets, a down comforter and an extra firm pillow.

Joe pulled off her light blue uniform shirt, leaving her in a very tight white tank top. He could easily see the light baby pink sports bra she wore underneath. Out of the corner of his eyes he caught Greg licking his lips as he stared at her chest and as usual Joe was completely oblivious.

Why did she have to make his job so fucking difficult?

"Greg, you can have my bunk," he said.

"Really?" Greg said, looking even more excited. No doubt the man thought he was about to be left alone with Joe all night, in the dark.

"Yup, it's all yours," he said.

"Cool. Thanks," Greg said quickly, taking his boots off and then he chucked his shirt, making sure to flex to show off his flat stomach and slight build.

Joe mumbled goodnight around a yawn and climbed onto her bed. Greg climbed onto the other bed, keeping his gaze firmly locked on Joe.

"What happens if we get a call?" he asked absently.

Eric gestured to the white phone on the wall above Joe's bed. "A really annoying sound will go off and that phone will ring."

"Oh, okay. If we don't hear it will you come wake us up?" Greg asked, still staring at Joe.

"Oh, that won't be necessary," Eric said, pulling off his boots.

"What are you doing?" Greg asked.

"Getting ready for bed. What does it look like?" Eric asked, not bothering to hide his smile at the man's obvious disappointment.

"But...but....."

He yanked his shirt up over his head and made sure he flexed his much larger muscles. Stupid, but it was a guy thing. He needed to put the scrawny little bastard in his place.

"Where are you sleeping?" Greg asked nervously.

"We're double bunking of course," he said, grinning.

Greg' eyes widened and Eric could have sworn the man was ready to bolt. He reached out and flicked off the light, leaving them in total darkness.

"Ah," Greg swallowed loudly, "that's really not necessary I don't mind taking the floor."

"Oh, I don't mind," Eric said. Just for shits and giggles he pressed his foot on Greg' mattress and pushed down, making the guy think he was about to have company.

The guy actually squealed. In ten seconds flat Greg was off the bed, the door was thrown open, and he was making a mad dash to safety, leaving Eric laughing his ass off.

"Oh, that wasn't very nice," Joe said, her voice thick with humor.

He sighed heavily. "Yeah, but it sure did put a smile on my face." He closed the door and walked over to Joe's bed and climbed in behind her.

"And just what do you think you're doing?" Joe demanded even as she scooted forward to make room for him.

"Going to bed. What does it look like?" he asked, throwing an arm over her waist.

"There's a freshly vacated bed right over there," she said sleepily.

"I like this one better. It's comfy," he said, snuggling up against her.

She groaned. "Eric, we're not kids anymore. Go sleep in your own bed."

"Ah, too late, I'm already drifting off," he said, biting back a chuckle as she poked him.

"Jerk."

"Yup."

"If you snore in my ear I'm gonna have to kill you," she pointed out.

"Duly noted," he said, closing his eyes and snuggling closer to her. He knew she was only busting his balls. Ever since they were kids they'd been very touchy feely. They snuggled, they cuddled, she sat on his lap, he normally threw his arm over her shoulders when they were just sitting around or walking, hell they even skinny dipped a few times.

More than once he had some woman he was dating flip out over it. Hell, his date to the prom dumped his ass on the dance floor when he refused to dance with her instead of Joe. He didn't care. This was his best friend, his Joe. They were close and he didn't give a damn if anyone had a problem with it. Joe kept him happy, kept him grounded, and had been there for him for everything in his life without question. Her shoulder was the one he cried on when his father died. She was the person who cheered him on at his football games. She was the one that he went to when anything big or small happened in his life and she would most likely be there when he took his last breath.

"That better not be what I think it is," Joe mumbled in the dark.

It was. "It's not. Jeez, woman, someone's paranoid. It's my pocket light," he said, wincing. Ah, he was only human after all. It wasn't the first time she got him hard nor would it be the last time. The physical discomfort was a small price to pay to have her in his arms.

"Well, then your flashlight is growing. Jeez, Eric, put a leash on that thing before it stabs me!" she teased.

"But it likes you," he pouted.

She giggled. "I seem to remember a certain tenth grade math class where it liked standing up in front of the entire class."

He sucked in a breath. "Hey, that traumatized me!"

"Uh huh," she said around another yawn. "I bet it did."

"It did," he readily agreed as he leaned in and inhaled her vanilla scent. He pressed a kiss to the back of her neck. She sighed contently.

"Night, Joe,"

"Good night, John boy," she said.

"Smart ass."

Chapter 4

Joe whimpered pathetically as her really annoying and loud alarm clock went off, letting her know it was two in the afternoon. She blindly reached out and started slapping her hand down, knowing it was only a matter of time before she hit that damn alarm clock. A minute later pure beautiful silence surrounded her once again.

Deciding another hour of sleep was just the ticket she rolled over and closed her eyes. What felt like moments later her cell phone went off. Muttering a few choice curses she rolled over and answered the phone without opening her eyes.

"Hello?"

"Hi, sweetie. Did I wake you?" Alice Parish, her surrogate mother, asked. Since the grand old age of eight when Eric took a mud covered Joe home Alice had been her mother. Her own mother, Pamela, adored the situation and happily relinquished all control and decisions to Alice.

Of course this was not an agreement Alice made with Pamela. Pamela just decided that she no longer had to do anything for Joe, because she found another sucker in her life to push her responsibilities onto. It didn't really surprise anyone when Pamela suddenly packed up and left town when Joe was sixteen. It hadn't mattered by then, because she'd already been living with Alice and the boys for two years by that point.

"Hey, mom, yeah I guess I dozed back off again," she said, trying to stifle a yawn. She'd only slept for a half hour this morning with Eric before they had a call and after that the calls kept coming. Then they ended up staying an extra three hours over their shift this morning.

"I'm sorry I woke you, sweetie," Alice said. It made Joe smile knowing that if she'd been Eric, Alice would tell him to get his lazy buns up. Sometimes it was nice being the favorite. Everyone in town knew Alice Parish utterly adored her boys, but Joe was the little girl she always wanted. That and Alice was always trying to make up for Pamela abandoning her. The boys didn't mind and she'd gotten used to it by now.

Joe glanced at her much hated alarm clock and groaned. It was half past four. She'd over slept. "What can I do for you, mom?"

"Oh, I was wondering if you could pick up some ice cream to go along with the cake I made for dessert."

She sat up, swinging her legs over the side of the bed, wishing she could go back to sleep. "That's fine, mom."

"Dinner's at six," she reminded her.

"I'll get there before that and help out," Joe said, trying not yawn. Oh, she was really looking forward to three days on the boat where she would be rocked to sleep.

"Thanks, sweetie. I'll see you later," Alice said before hanging up.

Joe dragged her feet to the bathroom. After a quick shower she blow-dried her hair, applied a small amount of make-up before yanking on her form fitting low riding jeans and blouse that ended above her belly button. Going to work looking plain was one thing. She was there to work, but any other time she left the house she dressed up a bit. Well, at least make it more obvious that she was a woman. Anything more than that was just way too much work.

Feeling refreshed and somewhat more alert she got into her car and headed towards Clement's Market. She grabbed the French vanilla ice cream she knew Alice wanted. She grabbed a half gallon of chocolate fudge swirl for Nathan, Alice's oldest son and the brother of Joe's heart, and then a half gallon of M & M ice cream for herself and Eric. Nathan's girlfriend and whoever Alice was trying to set up with Eric would have plenty of flavors to choose from.

Ten minutes later she was pulling up to the small white Victorian house that she still referred to as home. There were three extra cars in the driveway, two she recognized. She hated being the last one to arrive anywhere. She grabbed the bags and headed inside without knocking. If she tried to knock Alice would get insulted. Joe was family and god help her if she didn't act it.

She walked into the house, surprised when she didn't spot anyone in the living room. The smell of pot roast immediately hit her as she headed towards the kitchen. "Mom?" she called out.

"We're in the kitchen, sweetie!" Alice yelled back.

"Yeah, *sweetie*, we're in the kitchen!" Nathan added mockingly.

Smart ass.

She walked into the kitchen to find Nathan, tall with blond hair instead of Eric's dark brown hair, and blue eyes sitting at the table, holding hands with a very pretty plump woman. That was one thing she always loved about Nathan, he cared more about the woman on the inside rather than what she looked like. No doubt Joe would like her.

She found Eric sitting on the counter, looking uncomfortable under the gaze of a woman with long wavy red hair and a bit too much make up and too thin to be healthy. She looked to be mid twenties and really into fashion, judging by her overdone dress and amount of costume jewelry she wore. Joe doubted her bone thin arm was strong enough to move under the weight of the insane amount of bracelets she wore.

Joe didn't think she'd ever understand why Alice took it as her personal mission in life to find a girlfriend for her youngest son. He was incredibly good looking if you liked the bad boy look mixed with a touch of adorable, which she did, but that was neither here nor there. He never lacked options. They couldn't go anywhere without some woman shoving her number at him. So, why Alice thought he needed help she'd never know.

"About time you got your lazy ass here," Eric said with a wink.

"Eric Parish!" Alice said, sounding more shocked than she really should at this point.

"Yeah, Eric," she said, sticking her tongue out like a two year old.

As she passed him on the way to the fridge he swatted her on the ass. Hard.

"Eric!" Alice snapped.

"What?" he asked, looking and sounding innocent.

Joe just barely resisted the urge to rub her ass. Damn that stung, but she wouldn't give him the satisfaction of knowing it did. Their relationship was complicated and admittedly very weird.

She put the ice cream away and palmed an ice cube.

"Sweetie, this is Nathan's girlfriend, Caitlyn and this is my friend Camie," she said, not mentioning Camie was meant to be Eric's date. No doubt the man would outright bolt if she did. He didn't want to date anyone right now or at least hadn't found anyone he liked.

"It's very nice to meet both of you," Joe said as she casually walked behind Eric. Quickly and discretely, she shoved the ice cube down the back of his pants.

She heard him suck in a breath and had to smile. Immediate retribution was always nice.

"Camie, Caitlyn, this is our Joe," Alice said, gesturing towards Joe before she gave her a quick hug and a kiss.

Joe walked past Eric just barely missing another swat on the ass as he stood up to rid himself of the ice. She walked over and gave Nathan a big hug and a kiss and shook Caitlyn's hand.

"So, you're their sister?" Camie asked, eying Joe up and down.

Nathan chuckled. "She's mom's favorite brat, my pain in the ass sister, and Eric's bitch."

Caitlyn covered her mouth to hide a giggle. No doubt she already knew the whole story behind their family. Camie looked really confused and mom's face went completely red.

"Nathan Parish!"

"What?" Nathan asked, still laughing. Joe playfully swatted him.

Eric shrugged unconcerned. "It's true," he said simply. He pursed his lips up thoughtfully. "Actually, if anything I'm her bitch."

Joe sighed and nodded. "That's true. You are my bitch."

"Josephine!" Alice said, obviously fighting back a smile. "You're going to make them think I raised you like this!"

Nathan blinked. "You did."

"I did not!"

"Oh, come on, mom. No need to pretend. Everyone knows you raised the three of us to be foul mouthed little bastards," Eric said, egging his mother on.

Caitlyn laughed while Camie looked utterly confused. If Joe had to guess the woman didn't have a clue they were all joking. It only took two minutes after meeting Alice to know she was a down to earth wholesome woman. She raised the three of them with more love than anyone could ever hope for.

"So...." Camie began. "I'm really confused."

Nathan and Eric sighed at the same time. Joe decided to set the table and leave it up to the guys to explain their odd little family.

"Okay, I'll explain our little family dynamic since I get a kick out of it," Nathan said cheerfully.

"Oh, brother," Alice muttered with a fond smile.

* * * *

Eric settled into a chair safely away from the woman his mother was trying to throw at him. He seriously had to question her mental status on this one. Not one single woman he dated, not even Beth, the woman he'd been engaged to, was anything like this. This woman was too focused on her clothes and appearance to know anyone else existed. She'd already sent Caitlyn a dismissive look and a look to his mother he didn't particular like. To top it off she wouldn't stop staring at him like she owned him. It was really annoying and a bit frightening. He was half afraid that if he turned his back on her that she'd brand his ass.

He sat back in his chair and let his eyes roam over Joe. He definitely hadn't missed the nasty look Camie sent Joe when she walked into the kitchen. His upbringing was the only thing that prevented him from tossing her out on her ass at the moment.

Women could be such bitches sometimes. Not all of them, but women like this one definitely were. It just pissed him off when women gave Joe a dismissive look because she wasn't dressed in the latest fashion and didn't pray at the altar of cosmetics. Joe was beautiful, hell, she was sexy in her own right. She was distinctly female and perfectly curved in his book. She might not wear the latest fashions, but she always managed to make his blood boil, probably always would.

He let his eyes roam over her hair that she left loose, it teased her shoulder blades as she moved. He nearly cursed when she took out an elastic and put it up in a messy bun, but she still looked good. He let his eyes run down her slender neck to the tight black blouse she wore that ended above her belly button. He liked that flat athletic stomach of hers. It was perfectly defined with a hint of muscle thanks to their job.

When she faced him, smiling, he licked his lips as his eyes took in her high firm breasts, perfect for his hands, not that it would happen. He took in her figure, just perfect. Absolutely perfect. It really was no wonder women hated her. She was magnificent.

"Earth to Eric," Nathan said, pulling him out of his thoughts. Great, was he drooling? He sure as hell hoped not.

"Yeah?" he said, looking at his brother who simply rolled his eyes. "You want me to tell the story?"

"Knock yourself out," Eric said, dropping his head back to stare at the ceiling. No need to get caught ogling Joe again. She'd tease him mercilessly and tell him he needed to get laid. No doubt he did. It had been too long. Way too long.

After what happened the last time it was going to be a long time before he tried again, a really long time. That kind of shit really messed with a man's head.

"So, one day when Eric was eight, dad gets a call that some bully had not only beaten up his baby boy, but that bully made Eric eat a handful of worms," Nathan started.

"That's awful!" Camie said, looking thoroughly disgusted. It had been pretty gross, he had to admit. The worms weren't too bad, but all that dirt had been nasty.

Joe laughed once again, drawing his attention. He liked her laugh. It always soothed him.

"It gets better," Nathan promised. "I'm a year older so dad had me dragged out of class with the intention of having me beat the snot out of the bully. We walk into the office, looking for this big bad bully only to find these two scraped up and covered in mud. Dad demands to see the little boy who beat up his son and talk to his parents only to be told that this adorable little girl was the culprit."

"Hey! He started it by shoving the worms down my dress!" Joe argued, laughing.

"I had to do something to improve that ugly ass dress you were wearing. It looked like you were wearing a couch," Eric teased. Joe rewarded him by throwing a hot roll at his head which he caught and happily ate.

"Anyway," Nathan said, drawing back everyone's attention. "I, being the good brother that I am, offered to beat her up. Dad was at a loss, but still somehow managed to slap me upside the head when I offered."

"You did not!" Alice sounded horrified.

"He did," Joe agreed.

"Anyway, once dad decided I wasn't going to kick her butt we hung around, waiting for Joe's mother so he could talk to her. We waited two hours and she never showed. By then dad fell in love with the little brat," Nathan said teasingly.

"So did you, big guy," Joe said, sorting through the silverware.

Nathan chuckled. "Of course I did. I knew right off the bat that you were good sister material. So dad who was at a total loss and this big baby," he jerked a thumb towards Eric, "decided she should come home with us where everything could be straightened out. Mom gets one look at her and gushed and decided she was keeping her."

"So, you like, all adopted her?" Camie guessed.

Everyone except Caitlyn shook their heads. "Not exactly. Even though I think Dad mentioned more than once before he passed away that he was going to kidnap Joe and adopt her we never made it official."

"He would have to," Alice said with a watery smile.

"It didn't matter what the law says we all heard him referring to Joe as his little girl so it didn't matter," Eric said, earning a sad smile from Joe.

"So she never lived with you?" Camie asked, seeming determined to find out exactly what Joe's role was.

"She became an instant fixture in the house. She went with us everywhere, did her homework here, had chores here, but her mother wouldn't let her move in with us which was okay until she was about fourteen and then she started to sleep over here more often until she was living here and mom told us to go get her stuff. She stayed here until after she'd been working on the ambulance for a while and could afford to live on her own. I think she was nineteen at the time?"

"Yes," Joe said as she finished setting the table and started placing bowls of food on the table. "I moved out a month or two before Eric did."

"Only because you stole the apartment I wanted," Eric pointed out, stealing another roll.

Joe simply shrugged.

"Okay," Camie said slowly. "So Eric and Joe are like brother and sister?"

Eric and Joe shared a look of horror. Nathan winced and even Alice shook her head, looking like she might be ill.

"That's a seriously horrifying thought," Joe muttered. "Kind of disgusting actually."

"Damn straight," Eric said, saluting her with his half eating roll.

Chapter 5

"Eric, why don't you sit over here?" Alice asked, gesturing towards the empty seat next to Camie.

Eric kept his smile pleasant. "I'm fine where I am. Besides, I wouldn't want to interfere with your time with your friend."

His mother scowled in his direction. He didn't care. He came here to spend with his family and meet his brother's new girlfriend, not be set up with an ice bitch, who was now sending glares at Joe every time she thought no one was looking.

Seriously where the hell did his mother find these women? The last one she brought over had just separated from her husband and wouldn't stop bawling throughout the entire meal. Did she really think he was desperate?

"But-" Alice started to argue their seating arrangements.

"I'm already settled, mom. Everyone is. Let's just eat, shall we? This smells too good to let get cold," he said, gesturing to the platter of pot roast and large serving bowls of side dishes.

Camie smiled coyly as she stood up. "I can just move over there if you want. I'm sure your mother just wants to have a chance to sit next to Joe," she said, starting around the table to his side.

His smile became tight as he reached out and snagged Joe's arm just as she set down the large pitchers of water and ice tea on the table.

"Hey!" she said, slightly stumbling under his grip.

Eric ignored her squeaks of protest and yanked her ass down in the seat next to him. Camie paused mid-step, throwing Joe a glare that by all rights should have killed her on the spot.

Joe took one look at his expression and smiled sweetly, too damn sweetly. "You know what, if you want this seat I don't mind. I'd love to catch up with Nathan and Caitlyn," she said, starting to get up.

He put his arm around her and hauled her back down, keeping her firmly in place. Keeping his tone and expression light he said, "But you and I really need to talk."

"No we don't," she said, trying to get up again. She really was enjoying screwing with him too much, but after what he tried to pull with Greg last night she didn't feel too bad.

"Sure we do," he said, holding her firmly in place with one arm while he started spooning food onto their plates. "We really should discuss our trip tomorrow."

Caitlyn smiled. "You're going on a trip tomorrow?"

Eric said, "Yes," the same time Joe said, "No."

"*I'm* going on a trip tomorrow. Eric's inviting himself along," Joe clarified.

Nathan snorted. "Since when does he need an invite? You guys go everywhere and do everything together. I think it's pretty much assumed at this point that where one of you goes the other will follow."

Camie looked murderous. Joe seriously wondered where Alice found these women and thanked god that she never tried to set her up. The prospects were truly frightening.

Joe scoffed as Eric ladled gravy on her potatoes the way she liked it, perfectly in the middle with none of it spilling over. "That's not even remotely true. We have lives outside of our friendship."

Nathan scooped mashed potatoes onto his plate as he said, "Name one major thing either one of you did without the other present or a vacation or even a small trip you took without the other."

Eric chuckled lightly. "I've done plenty of things without Joe there and I can assure you I haven't been with her for everything she did either."

"Name one thing and I will give you each a hundred dollars," Nathan said smugly.

Joe and Eric shared a look as they both thought it over. Joe started with the big events in life, the simple things to remember. There was the time she lost her virginity, but Eric had been in the car several spots over doing the same thing so that didn't technically count. First kiss was out too since Eric was the one to give it to her on a dare. Driver's license? Graduation? EMT training? First job?

Shit!

"Oh, I got one!" Eric announced. "The night I got engaged," he said, looking at Nathan with his hand out.

Joe winced.

Nathan laughed.

Alice sighed.

Camie looked pissed at the mention of Eric being engaged to another woman, which was seriously getting creepy since she'd only met him less than an hour ago.

Caitlyn smiled sweetly.

"Pay up, sucker."

"Ah, Eric?" Joe said.

"What? We won," he said, looking victorious.

Nathan chuckled. "Oh, no you didn't."

"What the hell are you talking about? Of course I did," Eric said, looking and sounding confused.

"Ah, Eric, he's right. I was there. Remember?"

He didn't look like he did.

She sighed. "Remember the three of us were at the club over on Wilmington and you and I were dancing and Beth kind of had a meltdown about that and you jokingly offered to marry her to shut her up. Remember?"

Alice gasped. "You proposed as a joke?"

He shrugged. "I would have gone through with it I guess. She was a good cook."

"You guess?" Alice repeated in shock. "I thought you loved her?"

He winced.

"Eric Parish, do not tell me you were going to marry some poor girl because she was a good cook."

"Why else?" he said with a cocky grin. Joe rolled her eyes. The man really enjoyed teasing his mother too much. Not that it wasn't the truth. Eric didn't believe in romantic love, lust? Yes, but not the kind of love that lasted forever.

Joe thought of something. "Oh wait, when their engagement ended I wasn't there, so we win."

His wince deepened. "Ah, Joe? You kind of were."

She frowned as she thought it over. "No, I wasn't. Yeah, you guys were fighting while we were up at the ski resort, but you broke up after you dropped me off at my house. So there, that's one major event at least, even though I'm sure there are more that I just don't remember right now."

Nathan kept chuckling.

Bastard.

"What?" she asked, looking at Eric as he bowed his head over his plate, shoveling food in his mouth like there was no tomorrow.

"You were there alright," Nathan said.

Okay, now she was seriously confused. She narrowed her eyes on Eric who was shoveling his food in faster, obviously trying to avoid the question.

"*What did you do*?" she demanded as she narrowed her eyes on him. She was very sure that she wouldn't forget being in the room when her best friend broke off his engagement. Call her crazy, but that kind of thing should be memorable.

No answer.

"Maybe we should talk about something else," Alice said nervously.

Joe turned her glare onto Nathan whose smile grew wider. "Well, it seemed good old Beth, whom I like to point out I never liked, tried to put her foot down where the two of you were concerned. Seems she didn't like all the touchy feely crap between the two of you that we all long ago accepted as normal, at least where you two are concerned. She wanted him to start treating her the way he treats you."

She nodded slowly. "Yeah, I know she had a problem with that and I understood it and apologized if it made her uncomfortable. Hell, I even spent the entire second day by myself, giving them time alone."

"Well, you may have spent the entire day apart, however......" Nathan said leadingly.

"What?" she demanded.

"Oh, brother," Alice mumbled. She sighed softly as she grabbed another biscuit. Camie still glared, probably about the engagement news. That really was seriously freaky. Caitlyn smiled shyly as she ate small bites, obviously uncomfortable and Joe couldn't blame her since she was starting to feel little uncomfortable herself.

"What the hell don't I know about?" Joe demanded, glancing between Eric and Nathan.

Eric groaned loudly as he dropped his fork on his plate and sat up straight. "Fine! You want to know what happened? I'll tell you. She made demands on me all day, hung on me all day, talked all goddamn day, everywhere I went there she was. Every time I tried to shake her off she was there. Finally it was late at night and I wanted some sleep so I was going to go sleep on the couch since there were only two rooms. She tried to demand that I sleep with her and I put my foot down."

Joe nodded. She knew about that. Eric hated sharing a bed with anyone. The few times he tried to spend the entire night in bed with a woman he freaked out. He was very particular about his sleep. He hated snoring, bed hogs, people who shifted in their sleep or made any sounds. For some reason he didn't object to sharing her bed and doing all those things to *her*.

"You had a problem sharing a bed with your fiancé?" Camie asked, looking unsure whether that news should please her or anger her.

"I'm a light sleeper, damn it!" Eric said defensively. "Everyone knows that."

"Uh huh," Nathan said absently, still smiling. Bastard. "Tell her the rest."

"If you don't tell me what you did to cost me a hundred bucks I swear to god I am going to strap your ass to a backboard on Monday morning and let the guys shave your ass from head to toe." she threatened, knowing the guys would happily do it.

"Fine, my little drama queen, if you must know. The couch was too damn lumpy so I went to your room to get some sleep."

"Wait. If you wouldn't sleep in the same bed with your fiancé then why would you sleep with her?" Camie asked with a suspicious scowl.

Nathan sighed dramatically. "Because she's his bitch. You really need to pay attention."

"Nathan!" Alice gasped, smiling.

Caitlyn chuckled softly. Joe was really going to like Caitlyn, she could tell.

"Anyway," Eric said, stretching out the word. "I fell asleep and sometime after two, Beth woke up and decided to come looking for me. When she didn't find me on the couch she went straight to Joe's room and that's where she found me."

Joe held up her hand. "Wait a minute. I seriously don't remember any of this and I'm pretty sure since she was incapable of talking without screeching that she would have woken me up."

Eric cringed as he looked away.

Nathan laughed long and loud.

Alice sighed, taking a sip of the wine she somehow managed to get without Joe noticing during this weird little conversation.

Camie put her fork down and crossed her arms defiantly over her chest while glaring at her and Eric. Was anyone else freaked out by this?

Caitlyn smiled sweetly.

"Well?" Joe said, sounding as irritated as she felt.

Eric cleared his throat uncomfortably. "It's really no big deal."

That sent Nathan into a fresh round of laughter.

Oh, she had a strong feeling that she wasn't going to like this. Not one bit.

"Care to explain how I was in the room with the two of you while you broke off your engagement without getting woken up by a woman who never said anything below a shriek?"

Nathan grabbed his chest as tears rolled down his cheeks. He started laughing so hard that he actually fell out of his chair and hit the floor with a loud thud.

"Oh, brother," Alice sighed, taking another large sip of wine.

"How?" she demanded.

Eric gave her his best charming smile. "I made sure you wouldn't wake up."

"*How*?"

He picked up his fork and started pushing around his food, keeping his gaze off of her. "I, uh,....I may have," he cleared his throat, "had to um, place a pillow over your head just for a little bit there."

She gasped. "You smothered me?"

"Yes!" Nathan somehow managed to say through his uncontrollable laughter.

"You bastard," she breathed.

"Oh, come on! I made sure you were still breathing! You only turned blue once and that was because I was too busy defending you to notice!"

"Oh, gee, I guess that makes it okay then," she said dryly.

Chapter 6

"Thanks a lot, asshole," Eric said, snatching the cake knife out of Nathan's hands.

"Hey!" Nathan made a grab for it and missed.

Eric glared at his older brother as he made short work of cutting a huge slice of their mother's triple layered double chocolate cake with fudge and peanut butter frosting. He plopped the huge slice of cake in a bowl and tossed the knife behind him into the sink.

Nathan rolled his eyes. "Real mature, dip shit." He made a move to steal Eric's cake only to have his hand slapped away. "Ow! What the hell?"

"What is going on in here?" Alice asked in the same exasperated tone she used when they were teenagers and she caught them smoking. At least she didn't look like she was about to make them smoke an entire carton of cigarettes this time.

"Nothing," both men grumbled.

"Uh huh," Alice said absently as she walked around the counter and grabbed a clean knife out of a drawer. She looked at Nathan and frowned. "Sweetie, shouldn't you be getting Caitlyn a slice of cake?"

"I was trying to," Nathan bit out as he rubbed the back of his hand, scowling at Eric.

Their mother let out a pained sigh as she grabbed several plates. She raised an eyebrow as she glanced at Eric. "I'm assuming you're getting Joe a plate."

Eric gestured towards the large slice of cake with his chin as he scooped out some M & M ice cream.

"Are you getting Camie a slice as well?" she asked, sounding hopeful.

He snorted. "What? And encourage her stalker tendencies?" He shook his head.

Nathan chuckled softly as he looked quickly over his shoulder to make sure the three of them were still alone in the kitchen.

"Seriously, mom, what were you thinking? That woman is frightening," Nathan said, feigning a shudder.

Eric sucked ice cream off his finger. "Thank god, I thought it was just me," he said with a sigh. "Seriously, mom, what the hell were you thinking?"

"I was thinking," she said as she expertly sliced and placed four slices of cake onto small plates, "that it would be nice to see my youngest son settle down and give me some grandchildren before I die."

"Jeez, ma, I'm only thirty. Besides I don't see you getting all desperate about Nathan. He's not married either."

"I don't have to set Nathan up-"

"Something I truly appreciate by the way," Nathan muttered.

"-because he puts himself out there and doesn't have a problem keeping a steady girlfriend," she finished as she began scooping ice cream onto the plates, making sure to give Nathan an extra scoop of chocolate swirl.

"Fine, but you don't do this to Joe either. Only me, why?" he asked as he grabbed two spoons and stabbed them into the large slice of cake.

She waved his comment off like it was nothing. "I'm not worried about Joe. She dates when she wants to. When she's ready to settle down she will."

Eric gaped at her. "How exactly is that different from what I'm doing?"

"Because you, my baby boy, have never had a steady girlfriend." She held up her hand to stop his protests. "Beth doesn't count, sweetie. You dated for maybe a month before you got engaged and then were together for another two weeks and I don't think I heard or saw you treat even her anything other than just a friend. You keep all your relationships casual, sweetie. It's past time you had a serious girlfriend. Then we can work on getting you married off," she said with a hopeful smile.

"I just haven't met anyone that I want to get serious about. Has that occurred to you?' he asked.

She smiled. "That is exactly why I invite woman over so that you have a chance to meet someone."

"Mom," he growled softly. "I meet new people every day."

"It doesn't kill you to meet more people," she said, placing two plates into Nathan's hands.

"Well, maybe he'd be more receptive to your matchmaking if,....gee, I don't know, maybe if they weren't nut jobs and frightening as hell," Nathan said wryly.

Alice gasped. "She's not that bad.....is she?"

Both men stared at her.

She nibbled her lip. "Well, she seemed so nice at the grocery store. We talked a few times and she expressed that she would like to meet a nice guy, so," she shrugged her shoulders, "I thought I'd introduce the two of you." She gave him a sheepish smile.

"I'm touched," Eric said dryly.

She sighed warily. "Here." She thrust one of the plates in his direction. "Bring this to Camie so I can get coffee."

Reluctantly he took it, hoping she didn't think this meant they were engaged. The thought made him inwardly cringe.

Grumbling to himself, he carried the two plates into the living room. He found Camie sitting on the love seat, glaring at him like he'd just forgotten their anniversary or something. Without a word he handed, well, more like thrust, a plate into her hand. He ignored her gasp of outrage and walked over to one of the two large overstuffed grey couches, wondering where the hell Joe was.

It had been a good twenty minutes since she discovered he sort of smothered her with a pillow. You'd think she'd be over it by now. Such a drama queen, he thought as he plopped down on the couch.

"Where'd Joe go?" he asked around a huge spoonful of cake and ice cream.

Caitlyn cleared her throat. "She left," she said, sounding on the verge of laughter.

"Left?" he demanded, placing his dessert on the coffee table. His eyes shot over to Camie who was glaring at him. Oh, he was going to spank Joe's ass raw for this. He couldn't believe she'd leave him with this nut because he may have inadvertently smothered her and encouraged Greg to hound her this morning. Nothing he'd done to her warranted this. Oh, when he got his hands on her-

"You should have just said you were gay instead of wasting my time," Camie snapped angrily as Nathan and his mother walked into the room. She got to her feet. Eric couldn't move as her words registered in his mind. What the hell? Gay? Him? Not a chance.

All four of them silently watched her leave. Three pairs of eyes turned on him as the sound of the front door slamming shut echoed throughout the suddenly quiet house.

He forced himself to remain calm as he asked, "Why does she think I'm gay?"

"You mean you're not?" Nathan asked, feigning innocence.

Their mother sighed heavily as she reached up and slapped her oldest son upside the head.

"Ow!"

"Would you people focus? Why does that lunatic think I'm gay?"

"Joe may have led her to believe that," Caitlyn said quietly, drawing everyone's attention.

Eric thought over that little revelation and after a few minutes shrugged. As long as the psycho was gone he really could care less how it was done. He sat back down with his dessert and dug in. He ignored his brother's teasing remarks while he enjoyed his cake lunatic free.

Besides, being accused of being gay was a small price to pay for weekend of deep sea fishing. He considered this little episode as payment in full. Although he may decide to make her life a living hell on the boat for a couple days, it really depended on if he was bored or not. For Joe's sake she better hope the fish were biting this weekend.

Chapter 7

"That's my Coke, woman!"

"Not anymore," Joe said, finishing off the last few ounces of the cold beverage that he desperately needed.

Eric glared. "You owe me a drink."

"Nope."

"What do you mean, 'nope'?" he demanded. "You just finished my soda and I'm thirsty."

"You should have thought about that before you pulled your shit this weekend," she said as she leaned back against the passenger seat.

He felt his lips twitch. "I have no idea what you're talking about," he said, trying to sound innocent and probably failed since he couldn't wipe the shit eating grin off his face.

She turned her head and glared at him, just glared.

He cleared his throat in an attempt not to laugh out loud.

"You pushed me over the side of the boat a grand total of fifteen times!" she shouted, throwing the empty soda bottle at his head.

He easily ducked out of the way. "They were all accidents," he said with a straight face, "I swear."

Of course they hadn't been. Well, maybe that first time was. He couldn't recall if he'd meant to knock her over the side of the boat into the ocean or not. At the time he was only trying to get that prick from Vermont away from her. If he had to watch that asshole try to "show" Joe how to hold her pole one more time he would have killed the bastard and left the body at sea.

Eric maneuvered between the two of them when the bastard went to put his arms around Joe, again. Somehow during his little rescue he accidentally knocked Joe into the ocean. At least he was pretty sure that time was accidental. The fourteen times that followed were definitely intentional, mostly because they brought a smile to his face. Her wet clothes clinging to every curve of her body was just an added bonus. A very nice bonus that currently had him shifting in his seat.

Something in his expression must have clued her into where his thoughts had wandered. Glaring, she reached to unbuckle her seat belt, probably to kick his ass, when the radio went off.

"*Echo seventeen,*" dispatch said over the radio.

Joe swore softly under her breath at the interruption. Eric sent her a triumphant grin as he grabbed the microphone.

"Echo seventeen," Eric said in his deep rich voice. Joe mentally kicked herself for noticing. These little moments were really starting to creep her out.

"*What's your location*?"

"West side."

"*Echo seventeen, I need you to respond to an unknown emergency at 278 Slade Street.*"

"Received," Eric said as Joe righted herself in her seat and buckled her seat belt.

"What do you think? Prank call?" Joe asked, all business now, as she pulled out an emergency run sheet and attached it the clipboard.

Eric put on his sunglasses, giving him the ultimate bad boy look that made her mouth go surprisingly dry in seconds.

"Probably," he said as he flicked on the emergency lights.

Two minutes later they were pulling up in front of a small townhouse. Joe jumped out of the ambulance and opened the backdoors. Eric was there instantly, helping her unload the stretcher. As they pushed the stretcher up the driveway of the small townhouse a woman in her early thirties with tightly curled mousy brown hair came running out, holding her cell phone against her chest.

"Thank god you're here!" she cried out, tears ran down her cheeks as she raced towards them.

"Where's the emergency, ma'am?" Eric asked as he pulled on a pair purple nitro gloves as Joe continued to push the stretcher. As soon as he was done he took over pulling the stretcher so she could do the same. After twelve years they were at the point where words were unnecessary. Working together was like a well coordinated dance. They could anticipate each other's needs without a word.

She gestured frantically with the cell phone towards the house. "He's in the bathroom! He won't open the door, but he told me to call 911 and he won't tell me what's wrong! It's gotta be bad....oh god!" She put a hand over her mouth and sobbed loudly.

"We'll have a look and see what we can do to help," Joe said softly. She could promise that everything was okay and that they'd take care of it, but only if she wanted to face a huge lawsuit. It was always best to avoid making promises and watch each other's backs. They'd come across their share of disgruntled patients and family members looking to get back at someone or make a quick buck and knew all the key words to avoid by heart.

The woman nodded in jerky motions. "T-that stretcher won't fit down the hall," she said between sobs.

Without a word they pushed the stretcher against the house. "That's fine, ma'am. Can you show us where he is now?" Eric asked, throwing the tech bag over his shoulder.

They followed the woman into a small foyer that led to a narrow hallway with a light lavender door at the end. Before they reached the door they could hear a man grunting and swearing.

"Sean?" the woman said, knocking on the door. "The ambulance is here!"

"Thank god," the man said, gasping.

Joe reached out and tried the doorknob only to find it locked. "Sir? We need you to unlock the door if you want help."

There was a slight pause before he said, "Marie?"

"Yes?" Marie said, sobbing softly.

"I need you to go find my insurance card. It's in my office," he said, sounding distressed.

The woman looked confused, but did as she was asked. "O-kay, Sean."

A minute later they heard the lock click. "Okay, come in," Sean said, sounding in pain. "Just shut the door behind you."

Joe and Eric shared a look before stepping inside, Eric first. It was a bit of a squeeze as they stepped inside the small bathroom and shut the door behind them. They found a man in his late thirties wearing a gray tee shirt and nothing else, kneeling on the floor, bent over the edge of the tub and looking incredibly uncomfortable. Of course she'd be uncomfortable with two strangers in the room and her bare ass pointing out for all to see.

She quickly looked around for blood or any obvious signs of trauma and found nothing but his discarded pants on the floor and a small tube of personal lube on the counter in the rather tidy bathroom. She was about to ask him what was wrong when a vibrating sound reached her ears. She frowned and looked at his pants.

"Is that your phone going off, sir?" she asked.

"No," he said softly.

"What seems to be the problem today, sir?" Eric asked as he quickly assessed the situation. He looked just as confused as she felt.

"I-I had an accident," the man stammered.

"Okay," Eric said slowly. "Where are you injured?" As he asked, Joe ran her eyes over the man again and couldn't see anything wrong.

The man averted his eyes and sucked in a deep breath. "I slipped on something," he said and Joe again wondered where the hell that phone was.

Eric nodded sympathetically. "Okay, do you think you broke anything when you slipped?" he asked, setting down the tech bag on the narrow counter.

Sean shook his head. "No.....I...." He licked his lips nervously. "It's inside me," he whispered hoarsely.

As if on cue their eyes dropped to his exposed ass.

"I see," they both murmured.

Joe cleared her throat. "And that vibrating sound....." she prompted.

"Is coming from me," Sean said tightly.

"What is-" Eric started only to be cut off by Sean.

"It's a vibrator. My wife's. S-she must have left it out on the floor because..because I came in here to take a shower and slipped and landed on it. I tried to pull it out, but I can't reach it," the man rambled on.

"I see," Eric said and Joe could tell he was struggling just as hard as she was not to laugh. Laughing at patients was bad she learned her first year. It could set them off into violence, a shouting match or worse, a write up. "So, um, you slipped on the floor and landed on it causing it to impale you?" Eric asked in his most professional tone, making it harder for her not to laugh.

"Yes, that's exactly what happened," Sean said, sounding relieved that they were at least pretending to buy his story.

"Can you stand up?" Joe asked.

Sean shook his head. "No, it's eight inches long. Every time I try to stand it really really hurts!" he cried.

Eight inches, pretty impressive, she thought and could definitely be a problem moving him, but they were going to have to do it.

"Please don't tell my wife," he said, sounding mortified.

"Our only concern right now is getting you to the hospital. What you tell your wife is your business," Eric said casually, but she didn't miss the humor in his eyes.

"Do you think...do you think one of you could possibly get it out?" Sean asked, sounding hopeful.

Eric threw her a horrified look as he shook his head frantically. She had to agree. There just wasn't enough money on earth to make her want to put her fingers up some guy's ass and retrieve an eight inch vibrator. Nope, not going to happen.

"I'm sorry, sir, but we can't extricate something embedded in your body," she said smoothly, inwardly thanking OEMS then and there for that little rule. The only time they could attempt to remove something from the body was if it was blocking the airway. Since his ass wasn't required for breathing they were good to go.

The man nodded solemnly. "I understand." He swallowed hard. "Can we go now?"

"Yes, we have a few options here, Sean. We can get you back into your pants to protect your privacy-"

"That's fine. Please, let's just get going I want to get the most embarrassing event of my life over with," he said, panting.

"Okay," Eric said, nodding. "We're going to help you stand then one of us will help you pull your pants up."

"I can't stand up," Sean pointed out.

"You can remain bent over, but you should be able to use your legs to stand. We'll help you take it slow," Joe said.

"Okay," Sean said with a small whimpering sound.

Without a word they moved into position and carefully helped him stand up by pulling him up by his arms. Once they stood they stared across the man's back at each other. Eric gestured with his eyes for her to get the pants. Joe adamantly shook her head. He gestured again, harder this time. Nope, wasn't going to happen.

"Eric, I'll hold him so you can help him with his pants," she said, giving him a shit eating grin. Yup, she trapped him into it, but she wasn't feeling guilty about it. Not in the least. Not after this weekend.

He glared at her, mouthing, "Bitch".

"Hurry, please!" the man sounded like he was in extreme pain.

"Sir, is this hurting you?" she asked, concerned.

He moaned softly before saying in a strained voice, "Not exactly."

Eric got into position with the pants. "Step into them," he said.

The man shuffled his feet, moaning softly as he did it. He began panting, causing Eric to send Joe a nervous look. Eric pulled up the pants and stood up behind him just as the man groaned loudly. His body shook beneath Joe's grip.

She bit her lip to stop from laughing. Eric turned his head quickly away, making choking sounds. He was having a hell of a time not laughing. Sean seemed oblivious to it as he continued to moan and shake. Joe glanced down at her pants and boots, making sure the man hadn't just made a deposit on her. If he did they were going in the trash. It was one thing to get puked on or bled on in her job, but quite another to have some guy with a sex toy fetish come on her shoes. She sighed with relief when she spotted the white mess on the bottom of the mauve shower curtain.

"I'm sorry...didn't mean to," Sean said, panting softly.

"Don't worry about it," Joe said, knowing Eric was beyond speaking at the moment. He threw the bag over his shoulder and grabbed Sean's other arm.

"Time to do the shuffle," Eric said as he avoided her eyes. It was a good thing too because she knew one look from him and the damn would burst open.

Chapter 8

"I'm hungry," Eric announced as he plopped down heavily on the couch near Joe, well more like practically fell on her. He threw his arm around her shoulders as he leaned back against the faded material of the overstuffed couch. "Go cook for me."

She snorted. "I'm not your bitch."

Eric sighed heavily as he leaned into her even more. "It's really not healthy to live in denial."

"Uh huh," Joe said absently as she flicked through the channels of the station's large flat screen television. It figured the one time the station was empty and she had control of the remote there would be nothing on.

"Why are you not seeing to my needs?" Eric demanded as he stole the remote from her.

Normally she would steal it back on principal, but right now she really didn't care. They'd already been held over on their shift by four hours to cover two downed trucks. Also, thanks to three bang outs, people calling in sick, they'd been going all day and hadn't had a chance to grab food. In fact, they'd just got back to the station a half hour ago. After cleaning out the truck and replacing supplies she crashed on the couch, counting down the minutes until she could go home, order a pizza, shower, get her laundry done and hopefully crash early for the night, knowing she would be back here bright and early tomorrow morning.

Just as she was picturing her big comfortable bed and imagining how good that first moment when her head touched the pillow would feel the station phone rang, shattering her little fantasy.

Eric groaned as he got to his feet and made his way, unhappily, to the phone on the old rickety desk everyone was supposed to use to write up their reports, but didn't. With a resigned sigh he picked up the phone and leaned against the desk.

"Hello," he said as dread filled Joe.

Dispatch wouldn't screw them over again, would they? When she saw Eric's jaw clench she knew her answer. Yes, yes they would.

Eric rubbed the back of his neck as he tried to reason with dispatch. "We were supposed to be off four hours ago.....Yeah, I know you guys are short staffed, but we've been going all day." He stood up and began pacing around the area as far as the long tangled chord would allow. "We don't mind doing emergencies, but-" Whatever dispatch said had him closing his eyes and dropping his head back. "They called 911 because he refused to take his pills?" he asked in disbelief.

With a lovely mixture of softly spoken swears, Joe stood up and made her way back to their freshly stocked and cleaned ambulance, knowing there was absolutely no way they could refuse this call since it came in as an emergency and they were still on duty. Well, they technically could, but she actually wanted to keep her job.

Even though it was her turn to drive she climbed into the passenger seat and pulled out an emergency run sheet. Not even thirty seconds later Eric yanked the driver's side door open, jumped in and slammed the door shut, rocking the ambulance violently.

"This fucking sucks," he said as he maneuvered the ambulance out of the parking bay. "Next time they ask us to come in and cover their asses we're saying no," he snapped as he flipped on the emergency lights with a little more force than necessary.

She gave a noncommittal "uh huh" as she started to fill in the paperwork with their information, knowing that by the next time dispatch asked them to fill in they'd be over this bullshit call.

* * * *

Eric sighed dramatically as he tossed the soft restraints out the back of the ambulance onto the stretcher. "Fine, if you insist," he said, sounding put out.

Joe quickly looked over the restraints as she frowned. "If I insist about what?"

He jumped out the back of the ambulance and closed the doors as Joe took the front position on the stretcher. "On making me spaghetti for dinner," he said innocently, hoping she'd just give in and do it. He was a starving man after all.

Joe snorted as she guided them to the front door of Nicholson House, the shit hole residential program that decided to call 911 because one of its residents decided to refuse his meds tonight. This was a purely bullshit call.

Over the years they'd seen their share of fucked up nursing homes that hadn't known when one of their residents had been dead for two days, bed sores that turned into five inch craters on patients' backs and legs, patients left tied to chairs in the middle of a hall for days with huge puddles of piss and shit around their feet, but residential programs in his mind were the absolute winners in the incompetency category.

Most residential programs were run by bleeding hearts, at least in his opinion. They were more concerned about the patient's "feelings" then they were about their staff's safety and well-being. Dangerous work conditions, flax rules, and piss poor treatment caused high turnovers in most of the residential programs he'd come across. It was just common sense that if you always took the patient's side on everything without question and fucked over your employee for doing his job that you're going to piss off a lot of good employees and be left with the ones who could care less, and more often than not didn't bother to do their jobs.

Nicholson House in his opinion was a prime example of a fucked up residential program. Twelve years ago when they started out as EMTs, Nicholson House had been ruled with an iron fist. The seasoned staff was well trained and took no bullshit from the patients. They did their jobs without fear and were fair with the patients. Every shift was run smoothly. They knew where the patients were, what they were doing, and if a patient stepped out of line there wasn't any hesitation to bring them back into the program.

Now.......

Now whenever they got a call for Nicholson House they usually found the staff smoking outside by their cars, watching television, or drinking coffee in the kitchen while bitching about their jobs. The patients? Well, in his mind a residential program that catered to violent, mentally unstable patients might want to know where their patients were. Call him crazy, but if he worked eight hours in a two level home with sixteen dangerous individuals, some of whom really did listen to the voices in their heads, he'd make it a point to know exactly where they were and what they were doing and damn well make sure all the sharp objects in the house were locked up.

He bit back a choice word or two as they pulled the stretcher up the cracked walkway of the dimly lit yard and past a group of five employees smoking. One of the employees acknowledged them with a small wave, but other than that they were pretty much ignored.

"Hold on," Eric said as Joe raised her hand to knock on the door. "I have a feeling about something," he said, stepping past her and opening the unlocked door. He shoved the stretcher to the side of the walkway, not wanting to leave it unsupervised in the house or scare the hell out of the residents with it. The sight of their stretcher had set off more than one fight in programs like this in the past. Since mental patients, the ones known to be difficult, were usually the last to find out they were being transferred to another psychiatric facility they usually got a little paranoid when they saw EMTs and a stretcher suddenly appear. Since he liked to avoid helping restrain a patient that wasn't even his, he'd leave the stretcher outside until they needed it.

They walked into the large house and shut the door behind them. Joe gestured to a sign above the alarm that read, "Door must remain locked and armed. No excuses!"

"Nice," he grunted as they walked past a large living room with three patients playing a video game.

A young guy the size of a linebacker suddenly stood up, glaring at them. "You fucking better hope you're not here for me!" He took a menacing step towards Joe.

"Take another step towards my partner and I will be," Eric promised as he smoothly slid in front of Joe who muttered an exasperated, "puhlease" probably at his protective posturing since she rarely took threats from patients seriously, no matter their size, which really pissed him off most of the time. Kind of like now.

The man hesitated, shifting nervously. Not that Eric blamed him. He'd hate having no say in his life, never mind being the last one to find out a major life decision had been made for him without his input. Not that he didn't understand the reasoning behind it.

As the person who usually had the misfortune of being the bearer of the Section 12, the legal document that pretty much took away all of a person's rights, he knew the reasoning behind not telling the patient the news until the last minute. Some patients did not take it well, he sure as hell wouldn't, and they went through several predictable stages, denial, acceptance, outrage, and violence. Then again a large percentage of the patients accepted their fate without striking the messenger. He knew it wasn't always easy to tell how a person would react to a Section 12 and for shit pay he'd probably pass the buck off onto someone else, too. Then again he wasn't a pussy and didn't believe in bullshitting people.

"Oh thank god you're here!" a man with a serious lisp announced a little too dramatically for Eric's comfort. With a bad feeling Eric turned to see the new comer and had to bite back a curse or two as the guy pressed his hand to his heart. The guy was at least four inches shorter than Joe and was basically skin and bone. Eric quickly glanced at the guy who could easily pass as a linebacker for the Raiders and back to the guy who was being paid to keep him in line.

Yeah, right.........

Whatever happened to hiring the right person for the job? Eric wondered. This twig of a guy might be the nicest guy on earth, but he had no business working in this particular residential program. Granted he'd known some really small guys that could kick ass when it came down to it, but judging by the way this man kept sending the patients nervous glances and shifting away from them, Eric really doubted that was the case with this guy.

"Are they here for me, Donny?" the linebacker demanded.

The twig named Donny noticeably swallowed and stepped back as he tried to wave it off. "No, they're not here for you, John."

The linebacker glared at Donny for another moment before nodding firmly and returning to his game. No doubt if the man was lying John would break him in two.

"What's going on today?" Joe asked Donny.

Donny bit his lip nervously. "We're having problems getting one of our patients to take his medication tonight," he admitted.

Eric shared a look with Joe as he ran a frustrated hand through his short hair. "Has the patient attacked anyone? Threatened to hurt himself or been requested by his doctor to be removed from the property?" he asked, trying to keep the frustration he was feeling out of his tone. There had better be a damn good reason for them being held over.

A damn good one.

Donny sighed dramatically. "We're hoping your presence will scare him into taking his pills."

Even though Joe was a good two feet away from him now he felt her go absolutely still the same time he did.

"You called 911 to scare a resident?" Joe choked out in disbelief.

"The pills are important," Donny said, frowning as if this should be obvious. "If he doesn't take his pills he becomes violent and then we have to call you. So we're just saving you the trouble now."

Eric felt like pointing out that they did not have to call 911 if a patient became violent. It was his job to keep the patient under control, not theirs.

"Where is he now?" Joe asked, sounding as impatient as he felt.

Donny gestured lazily towards the stairs that led to the second floor. "Oh, he's asleep."

"You called 911 for a patient who's fast asleep? A patient that posed no threat to anyone at the moment because he refused his pills?" Eric snapped.

Donny shifted nervously as he took a step away from them as if they were crazy.

"Sir, do you realize that when you call 911 for a nonemergency that you're taking away resources that might be needed elsewhere?" Joe demanded in an all business-like tone. Eric wouldn't have bothered with the niceties. He would have just called the guy a fucking moron and accepted the write up.

"It is an emergency," Donny muttered pathetically.

"Actually, we're not sure whether he took his pills or not," a woman said.

Joe and Eric looked past Donny to find a rather rotund middle aged woman walking towards them with a thick black binder and several prescription bottles.

Donny huffed at the woman. "I know he didn't take his pills tonight."

The woman held up the binder. "Tom marked the sheet that he gave the pills tonight."

"He did not, because he left five hours before the pills were due so he obviously messed up," Donny snapped at the woman whose face was turning bright red with embarrassment.

"The pill count doesn't add up either," the woman mumbled.

Donny rolled his eyes. "You're new here. You still don't know how this works."

The woman looked like she was about to cry and really if they didn't get the hell out of here soon so he could go home he would, too. "Do you mind if I look?" he asked the woman with patience he wasn't feeling.

She nodded as she handed him the binder with her thumb bookmarking a section. "That's for Adam. He's supposed to take three pills, three times a day, but when I counted the pills there are ten too many in each bottle. I don't think he's been taking them."

"Let me see those," Donny snapped, grabbing the bottles and quickly counting the contents of the first bottle. After the first count he counted again and his face went pale. "This can't be right."

Great, so they had no fucking clue when the guy took his pills last.

"Police," a familiar voice announced with a loud knock at the door. A few seconds later Tyler, a cop they'd run into from time to time stepped into the house.

"Hey, Tyler," Joe said with a warm smile.

"Hi, Joe."

Call him crazy, but Eric really didn't think the smile and look Tyler was giving Joe was something a happily engaged man should be doing. It was certainly doing a great job of pissing him off though. He was already pissed about this bullshit call and having a cop devour Joe with his eyes was not helping.

"They want us to play the boogie man and scare a patient into taking his meds," Eric said brusquely, drawing Tyler's attention back to him.

Tyler frowned. "Are you fucking kidding me?"

"Nope," Joe said, biting back a yawn.

"He's, um, he's very dangerous without his meds," Donny stammered defensively.

"Considering no one seems to know the last time he took his pills maybe you should have called his doctor instead of 911," Eric pointed out.

Donny opened his mouth probably to argue, but then sighed and nodded his head. "You're right. I'm really sorry about this, but could you please give us a hand since you are here?" he asked, sounding close to crying. When Eric and Joe shared a look with Tyler, Donny quickly added. "Adam's upstairs right now if you want to talk to him."

Joe opened her mouth to say something only to be cut off by the linebacker now gawking at them. "You're here for Adam?" he asked in disbelief. "Good luck with that. That guy's a crazy son of a bitch!" The rest of the patients quickly nodded their agreement.

Oh, that couldn't be good, Eric thought dryly. When all the psychiatric patients could agree on what patient should scare you shitless it was never a good sign.

Apparently Joe agreed if the glare she sent him was any indication. "You are so buying me dinner tonight. Don't even *think* about arguing," she said in the same tone she used one week every month when she couldn't get enough chocolate and everything he did seemed to piss her right the hell off. Was it the twenty-third already, he idly wondered. Nah, he still had another two weeks before he had to wear a cup.

"Fine, but I hope you like ordering your meal through a clown's mouth," he snapped back.

Shaking her head in disgust, Joe gestured for Donny to show them to the patient. After a pregnant pause the man reluctantly started up the stairs, followed by Joe and him at eye level with her perfectly rounded ass. Hey, if he was stuck doing a bullshit call he was going to enjoy the perks.

"You're buying me a steak dinner," Joe hissed softly to him so she wouldn't startle their soon-to-be unhappy patient.

He snorted. "The only steak dinner you'll get out of me tonight is a burnt hamburger patty covered in canned gravy."

"You cheap bastard!" she hissed, making him grin. That is until the bastard trailing after them that he'd forgotten all about opened his big mouth.

"I'd be more than happy to make this call up to you, Joe, with a steak dinner," Tyler announced eagerly.

Without pausing Joe looked back at Tyler and gave him the sweetest smile. "Aw, you're so sweet, Tyler," she whispered as she turned to watch where she was going, but not before she stuck her tongue out at him.

Eric glared over his shoulder at the other man. "You betraying bastard!" he whispered, more like hissed.

Tyler grinned triumphantly as he mouthed, "I know."

Chapter 9

Joe bit back a yawn as she watched Donny cautiously approach the small sleeping figure curled up on one of the two twin beds in the small and rather depressing room. Her eyes darted to the other twin bed and noted that it was stripped. No roommate in her opinion was a good thing since they usually got in the way. She really hated it when they tried to "help."

"He's engaged," Eric whispered in her ear as they waited for Donny to grow a pair of balls and wake the guy up. He was adding way too much drama to the situation and was bound to agitate the patient.

"So?" she whispered softly, keeping her eyes on the patient.

She could practically feel Eric roll his eyes behind her. "So, I don't think his *fiancé* would appreciate you going out for a steak dinner with him," he explained softly near her ear.

Now it was her turn to roll her eyes. "He's not buying me a steak dinner tonight."

"Good."

"You are."

His answer was an amused snort. "Good luck with that, sweetheart."

"Keep it up and I'll be adding an appetizer and a dessert to my list of demands," she whispered softly back.

He was quiet for a moment. She assumed that he was probably wondering when this guy was going to get around to talking to the patient instead of standing there shifting nervously near the bed.

"Are you planning to put out?" he whispered, his warm breath teasing her ear and neck, sending goose bumps racing along her skin.

It was a little unnerving that she almost shouted, *god yes*. Her reactions to him were seriously starting to creep her out a bit. This was Eric, her best friend, the guy she'd grown up with and most likely the guy she'd fight with over the last tapioca pudding in fifty years at whatever nursing home was stupid enough to accept both of them.

She needed a real vacation, some rest and she definitely needed to start dating again. That was the only explanation for her reactions to him. It had been way too long since the last time she'd been with a man. Was it May or June of last year that she ended things with that cop from Northville? A year and a half without sex was obviously making her crazy.

Okay, so in all fairness she'd been aware of Eric that way for far longer than a year and a half. What heterosexual woman in her right mind wouldn't be? He was devastatingly handsome in that bad boy way that she really liked. He was also smart, funny and great to be around. If he wasn't her best friend she would-

There was no use finishing that train of thought. The fact was he was her best friend and nothing more. Not that she wanted things to change. She didn't. She loved that they were comfortable with each other and could tell each other everything. He was her rock and if he was anything more than her best friend she'd be lost. He was the guy she bitched to, not about.

"Only if you let me get ice cream with my dessert," she countered back softly, forcing her mind to jump back into the rhythm of their relationship and stay there.

Eric let out a disappointed sigh. "Damn, if only you weren't a little gold digger."

"If only," she mumbled distractedly as she watched Donny finally grow a pair and approach the patient. Of course his willingness to get it over with might have something to do with Tyler standing next to him looking pissed. No doubt he was.

"Adam, you need to wake up and take your pills," Donny said nervously.

"No," Adam said firmly as he rolled over to glare at Donny.

One look at the man that instilled fear in everyone in the house left her a little confused. He was small, smaller than her and thin. Granted she knew that didn't always mean the person was weak, but seriously this guy had a man the size of a football player quaking in his drawers.

Did he have a history with weapons? Fire? Mutilation? It really would have been nice if they'd given them a little heads up, but then again the patient wasn't technically their patient yet and that meant they had no legal rights to his medical records. Apparently they were just here to scare the hell out of him into taking his pills and hope he didn't flip out in the process.

This plan sucked.

"Adam-"

"I SAID GO AWAY!" Adam bellowed as he jumped to his feet on his bed and swung at Donny, who thankfully stumbled back in surprise seconds earlier.

"Oh my god!" Donny cried as he ran from the room, leaving the three of them to deal with him.

Great. Just great.

"Relax," Tyler said in a soothing tone.

Adam looked like he was about to say something when his eyes landed on them. He gestured at them wildly as he shifted from foot to foot on his bed. "I'm not going with you!" he screeched.

Without a word they both stepped forward and broke off to flank the officer. Joe moved to Tyler's right, keeping her hands loose by her sides and visible and without looking she knew Eric was doing the same.

They learned long ago that approaching a combative patient with your palms up was a bad idea. Most people probably thought the gesture was placating, but in reality it usually put people on the defensive pretty quickly. In a stressful situation like this one it could be taken as a defensive stance and the last thing any of them wanted at the moment was to make this guy feel like he needed to protect himself.

"Adam?" she said, keeping her tone friendly. "My name's Joe. Do you know why we were called tonight?"

Adam's eyes darted cautiously over the two men. "You're here to take me back to the hospital. I'm not going! I haven't done anything wrong!" he said, shifting again.

She shook her head. "No, we weren't called to transport you."

"You're lying!"

"I promise you that we were not called to transport you tonight. We were actually called because the staff here isn't sure if you've been taking your pills."

His eyes shifted to her quickly before shifting back to Tyler and Eric. "They're lying. I've been taking my pills."

"Did you take them tonight?" Eric asked.

"Yes!" Adam said without any hesitation.

"No, you didn't, Adam," Donny scolded from the doorway, obviously feeling braver with the three of them separating him from Adam. "You refused your pills tonight."

"Shut up!" Adam screamed, taking a threatening step towards Donny. Joe automatically shifted to the right to block the man. "I took my pills!"

"No, you didn't take your pills, Adam, and if you don't take them they're going to-"

"Stop," Joe said firmly, cutting off Donny's threat. She kept her eyes locked on Adam who now looked tensed and ready for an attack. "We're not going to do anything. We were simply asked to come here and see if you've taken your pills."

Adam snorted. "They don't send the police or an ambulance over pills."

"You're right. They shouldn't have called us over this," Eric said, no doubt giving Donny a pointed look.

"Why don't we go downstairs and sit down and talk this through?" Tyler offered.

Adam looked like he was considering it when Donny opened his mouth. "He's not allowed out of his room. He's on room restriction because of the pills," he pointed out.

"I took my pills!" Adam screeched, leaping from the bed to attack Tyler. It took Joe a few seconds to react. She honestly hadn't seen this coming. She'd been prepared to take him to the ground, but for an attack on Donny who couldn't seem to shut the hell up.

"Shit!" Eric snapped as he attempted to pull Adam away from Tyler, but the much smaller man wouldn't give up his hold. He swung, kicked, and bit Tyler while Eric struggled to pull him off.

Joe moved low and grabbed Adam's legs, hugging them close, ignoring the brutal kicks to her ribs and stomach. "Get him down!" she yelled, squeezing Adam's legs together before she dropped her weight to help bring him down, but only managed to anchor his legs against her.

"Oh my God, he's got a gun!" Donny screeched from the hallway.

Her eyes shot to the doorway in time to see Donny running down the hall, shoving patients and staff out of his way while he made a mad dash to safety. The rest of their audience wasn't too far behind.

"Someone call for backup!" Tyler demanded above her. She turned her head and felt her eyes widen as she watched both Tyler and Eric struggle to pull Adam's hands away from Tyler's holstered gun.

"Get out of here, Joe!" Eric yelled as he struggled to take Adam to the ground and away from the gun.

Joe would have rolled her eyes at his over protectiveness if they weren't busy at the moment.

"Let go!" Tyler groaned as he worked at tearing Adam's hands off his gun.

Somehow over the loud grunts and panting she heard the snap of Tyler's gun holster giving.

"Shit!"

"Run, Joe!" Eric yelled again, sending her a pleading look as he fought to keep Adam's fingers away from the trigger as he started to pull the gun away from the holster.

She couldn't run and leave him. At that moment she was more afraid of what would happen to Eric if she let go of Adam's legs and ran.

"Get the fuck out of here, Joe!" Eric bellowed.

Holding Adam's legs down was the only thing stopping him from kicking away and getting his hands on the gun sooner, but Joe knew it was only a matter of time before he managed to pull the trigger and shoot someone. He was out of control, acting feral, and the two large well trained men above her were having a hell of a time getting him under control. If they didn't do something soon he was going to get that gun clear and pull the trigger.

"Please, Joe, let go!" Eric pleaded, breaking her heart.

She knew he wanted her to run and save herself, but she couldn't do it. She wasn't on some bravery kick. No, she was absolutely terrified. She couldn't leave this room and leave *him* behind. Joe was scared out of her mind that if she left now she would never see him again and she couldn't risk that. She didn't know much, but she knew she couldn't live without Eric.

Taking a deep breath, she did what she had to do. She let go and in the next second she shoved to her feet, hard. Adam hadn't been prepared for her sudden movement and Joe used his surprise to break his hold on the gun with her head and shoulders, slightly cringing when her head slammed into the butt of the gun, but she didn't stop until she broke Adam's hold.

Then all hell broke loose.

As Tyler stumbled back, Adam turned his anger on her. With a feral screech he pulled back his fist and slammed it into the side of her face, knocking her back onto the ground.

Just as she prepared herself for another strike Adam released a cry of pain and was slammed down to the ground with his arms twisted behind his back. She absently wiped at the hot liquid dripping near her eye as she watched Eric place a knee in the middle of Adam's back, ignoring the smaller man's cry of pain he leaned in to whisper near his ear.

"If you *ever* touch her again I will fucking kill you," he said in a cold lethal tone that sent chills down her back. "You so much as look at her and I will kill you."

Adam squeezed his eyes shut so he wasn't looking at her. She might have laughed if she wasn't truly frightened. She'd never seen Eric like this before and was a little worried about what he might do.

"I got him," Tyler said, gesturing for Eric to move over. After a slight hesitation he moved off Adam, but held his arms back so he couldn't move. He looked over at her and frowned.

"Joe?"

"Huh?" she said in a daze. When had she closed her eyes? And when exactly had her head started to pound?

"Gets a couple of head injuries and she passes out," she heard Eric mumble. "Such a girl."

Chapter 10

"I want him written up!" the social worker demanded, again.

Eric ignored her as Bill tried to calm her down. He didn't give a rat's ass what they did to him. The only thing he cared about at the moment was behind those double gray doors, being examined.

He rubbed a shaky hand over his face. She'd really scared the hell out of him tonight. Over the years they'd been in more fucked up situations than he could count, but none of them like tonights.

When that little bastard went after Tyler's gun he swore his heart stopped. The only thing he could think of was getting Joe out of there before he pulled the trigger. Any other woman would have made a run for it, but had Joe?

Oh hell no, not miss, "I'm one of the guys." She not only stayed, but she just had to risk her life. That damn gun could have easily gone off when she decided to use her body to knock Adam's hands away.

He dropped his face into his hands. He did not want to think about how close he came to losing her. What in the hell had she been thinking? It had been sheer luck that the gun hadn't gone off when she slammed into Adam's hands.

It was fucking selfish, that's what it was. She could have gotten herself killed and left him all alone. Did she even think about what her dying would do to him?

No.

It was so fucking important to her to be one of the guys that she never once stopped to think how it would affect him if something happened to her. If something happened to her he would-

"The three of them attacked him! He was forced to defend himself," the social worker declared loudly, drawing the attention of everyone in the crowded waiting room.

"Ma'am, you don't know the full story," Bill said, keeping his tone polite, but Eric knew the man was pissed. Not even an hour ago he'd been in the nurses' break room when Bill stormed into the room after seeing Joe and slammed the door shut. Then for good measure he kicked a few chairs across the room.

After a rather loud shouting match between them and two nurses running away from the room in a panic they calmed down enough for him to tell Bill what went down. Hearing what happened only seemed to enrage the man more and set off another bout of chair kicking.

Eric would have joined him if a doctor hadn't shown up at that moment to ask about Joe's closest relative, nearly taking twenty years off his life. After explaining that they needed permission to treat her because she was still unconscious he reluctantly explained that she didn't have any relatives.

He certainly didn't count her mother since no one had seen or heard from her in almost fifteen years. When the doctor refused to explain what was wrong or what they needed to do, he of course lied and told him that he was Joe's medical proxy. Although technically it wasn't lying since they had filled out the paperwork, but they forgot to have it notarized.

It took a few minutes of arguing and Bill flat out lying to back him up to convince the doctor, but finally he relented. They'd already ruled out a spinal injury as well as a skull fracture, but he was positive she had a concussion and they required permission to treat the deep gash along her temple. He quickly gave it and obediently followed a nurse to the waiting area to fill out her paperwork.

The paperwork hadn't provided the distraction he needed. In less than five minutes he had it filled out and returned to the triage station. He'd hoped it would take longer so he didn't have to think about Joe being helpless and alone.

"I know that three so called *professionals* took it upon themselves to gang up on a helpless man," she said with an indignant sniff. "Thanks to their brutal tactics that poor man is in there getting his broken arm fixed."

Yeah, he broke the little bastard's arm. Did he care? Not one fucking bit. He knew without a doubt that if the little bastard had gotten his hand on the gun he would have shot them and everyone in that house. Throw in the fact that he'd attacked Joe when she was bleeding and down and would have probably killed her with his bare hands if Eric hadn't grabbed him then he would say the guy had got off pretty lucky.

"If they'd done their jobs properly my client would not be-"

"And if you had done your job," Eric snapped, sick of her bullshit, as he got to his feet, "then you would have known that facility was not providing him with proper care and that he needed a medical intervention. If you had done your fucking job we wouldn't be here right now and my partner and an officer would not be stuck in this hospital getting patched up."

Tyler had suffered dozens of bites, scratches, and punches requiring god only knows how many stitches and shots. By the time backup had arrived he'd looked like he went ten rounds with a tiger.

"Eric," Bill said tightly, "I'll handle this."

"How dare you?" the social worker hissed. "It's not my fault that my client was attacked. He has several neurological problems and you were well aware of that fact. You knew he has bipolar and schizophrenia! Knowing that you should have-"

"I'll be sure to tell his family that you took the time to announce his private medical information to a roomful of strangers. I'm sure they'll appreciate that," Eric drawled, cutting her off. He ignored her outraged sputtering and headed for the double doors of the emergency room. He was tired of waiting.

The double doors abruptly opened just as a nurse called out. "You can't leave!"

Eric sighed long and loud as he watched Joe storm, half stumble, into the ER waiting room with her light blue uniformed shirt untucked and bloodstained, her boots untied and a large white gauze pad taped to her forehead, barely covering the large bruise peeking out to complete the ensemble. He'd like to say he was surprised that she was trying to haul ass A.M.A. (against medical advice) this early in the game, but sadly he wasn't.

Nothing pissed Joe off more than being told what to do, which of course meant he was going to have to resort to lying and manipulation to make sure that her sweet ass never touched the tech bench in the back of an ambulance ever again.

Joe leveled a glare on him when she spotted him. She pointed an accusing finger in his direction, barely righting herself as she stumbled on her own two feet. "Don't think you're getting out of buying me a steak dinner tonight, you cheap bastard!"

* * * *

"I. Hate. You," Joe bit out evenly as she watched Eric savor another bite of the steak that should rightfully be hers.

"Mmmm, this was a really good idea tonight," he said, taking a sip of *her* beer.

"You're dead to me," she groaned just as another wave of nausea took over. Slapping a hand over her mouth, she quickly crawled off her bed and made a mad dash to the bathroom. She just barely made it to the toilet when the ginger ale Eric had forced her to drink ten minutes earlier made another appearance.

Her head pounded, sending a fresh wave of nausea to her stomach. She gripped the sides of the toilet and held on for dear life as she lost the rest of the contents of her stomach. Dizziness took over, from the local anesthesia that had upset her stomach in the first place or the searing pain behind her eyes, she wasn't sure.

"Let's get you into bed before you slam your head and I end up having to bring you back to the hospital for more stitches," Eric said in a soothing voice as he gently picked her up and carried her back to her bed.

She couldn't help but glare at the take out container that held the remains of her juicy steak. "You could have waited until tomorrow night," she mumbled pathetically.

"I believe you requested your steak dinner tonight," Eric reminded her with a smug grin.

"You know I get sick from anesthesia! You could have waited!" she said a little too loudly, causing the pain behind her eyes to explode. She sucked in a breath as she buried her face in her pillow, hoping it would just go away. When it didn't she focused on not crying. No matter what she would never allow herself to cry. Crying was a waste of energy and didn't do anyone a damn bit of good.

From somewhere above her she heard Eric's soft curse followed by his footsteps as he walked away. She forced herself to focus on relaxing her breathing. A moment later the pounding had somewhat dulled, allowing her to curl up on her side, facing away from the television and small lamp near her desk.

A minute later Eric knelt in front of her with what looked like another glass of ginger ale and the bottle of generic aspirin she kept in the kitchen.

"Open up," he said softly. When she grudgingly did as he asked he dropped three pills in her mouth. "Swallow," he said, holding the glass to her mouth. With a roll of her eyes she did just that.

Eric watched her intently as he gently ran his fingers through her hair, pushing it out of her face. After a minute he sighed softly. "You need the pain medication they prescribed to you."

She started to shake her head only to remember that right now that wasn't such a good idea. "I can't take that while I'm working," she pointed out, cringing from the new onslaught of pain that accompanied speaking.

"Since you're not going to work for a few days I don't see the problem," Eric happily announced, cutting off any protests she'd like to make by forcing her to drink more ginger ale. So she just glowered at him.

When he decided she'd drank enough he removed the cup and placed it by her bed. He stood up and pulled the covers over her. "I don't like the idea of leaving you alone to go pick up the pills."

"Then don't. I don't need them. I'm fine," she lied, feeling like someone dropped kicked her in the head. Considering she slammed her head into the butt of a gun it was probably a pretty fair description.

He continued as if she hadn't spoken. "So, I called-"

"If you tell me that you called mom," she said, cutting him off, "I will kick your ass."

Eric picked up an ice pack and gently placed it against her forehead. "It would serve you right if I did," he mumbled, ignoring her frown. "But no, I realized calling mom would only set off that stubborn streak of yours and piss me off when she started barking orders."

Relieved, she laid back and allowed him to place her hand over the ice pack to keep it in place. The last thing she needed was for Alice to come here and fuss over her. As much as she loved the woman, and she did, she tended to turn into a mother hen when one of them was sick.

Then there was her tendency to act like a drill sergeant to everyone around them who wasn't sick. She still cringed when she thought about the time Nathan caught Mono. Alice being Alice of course fussed over him, making sure everyone of his needs was met whether he wanted them met or not. She probably would have found the whole thing funny if she hadn't been regulated to what Alice liked to call, "Disinfectant duty."

For the first day Eric and she were forced to clean anything and everything Nathan might have come into contact with. It hadn't mattered that Mono couldn't be spread by touching the bricks in the fire place. They were scrubbed within an inch of their lives along with everything else in the house. The second day and every day afterwards until Nathan was better, were spent on cleaning his room, bathroom and laundry. The only thing that saved Nathan from getting his ass kicked when they had to wash his dirty underwear and sheets was that he had it worse with Alice fussing all over him for every little thing.

She really didn't want to deal with Alice on top of everything else right now. Not that she would admit it to Eric, but she was still pretty shaken up by what happened earlier tonight. They'd had a lot of close calls over the years, but tonight's experience easily surpassed every single one of them.

On more than one call she'd wondered if they were going to be hurt or maimed, but she'd never actually feared one of them could be killed. There was no doubt in her mind that if the patient had managed to get the gun away from them he would have shot at least one of them and she'd been terrified that it would have been Eric.

"Hey," Eric said softly as he knelt on the floor next to the bed. "What's wrong?"

"Nothing," she said, forcing a weak smile. "I was just thinking of the lecture mom would give me if she found out I left the hospital A.M.A." Which was a lie, because Alice wouldn't lecture her, she'd simply drag her sorry ass back to the hospital, kicking and screaming.

"Don't worry, I called Nathan. He should be here soon," Eric said, running his fingers gingerly along the bruise, careful not to make any real contact. "I could kill that little bastard," he said tightly.

"Nathan?" she asked, trying to lighten the mood. Thankfully it worked. Eric rolled his eyes. "No, not Nathan."

"It's over," she said, hoping he'd let it go. She didn't want to think about tonight or what could have happened if things had gone differently.

Eric stood up and busied himself with cleaning up his dinner mess rather than respond to her. "When Nathan gets here you're taking your pills," he informed her.

She snorted then winced when pain shot through her temple. "Pain medication doesn't work for me," she argued, pressing the tips of her fingers against her temple in hopes that the pressure would soothe the pain. It didn't.

"They'll help you sleep," Eric pointed out, positioning the television so that it once again faced the bed. Joe didn't bother telling him that the glare from the television was hurting her eyes. That would just make him more determined to force the pain pills down her throat and she was not taking them.

They didn't work for her so she didn't see the point in taking them. Besides if she took them then she wouldn't be allowed to return to work tomorrow. Not that she thought anything would happen, but if anything did she could get in trouble for having narcotics in her system.

"No, they won't and I'm not taking them and that's final," she said as firmly as she could manage without pain and turned over onto her side to face away from the television. A few seconds later she could have kissed Eric when he shut off the bedroom light. Some of the pain shooting through her skull faded. Not that she would tell him.

When she felt him climb onto the bed and settle next to her she sighed contently and closed her eyes, more than willing to spend the next three or four hours struggling to fall asleep as long as Eric was with her. Just knowing he was okay helped ease some of her discomfort.

He placed his hand on her blanket clad hip and gave it a gentle squeeze. "Yes, you are."

"No, I'm not," she said in the same stern voice.

"We'll see."

"No, we won't," she promised him, snuggling back against his body.

"I just left in the middle of a date," Nathan suddenly announced, "so you better believe you're taking the pills even if we have to hold you down and shove a tube down your throat!"

Joe rolled over to glare at Nathan as he stalked into the room, loosening his tie. She narrowed her eyes on him. "You wouldn't dare."

Chapter 11

"We didn't kill her, did we?" Nathan asked nervously as he glanced down at Joe.

Eric shifted her in his arms, careful to keep her arms pinned against her sides as he raised one hand to check her carotid artery. "Strong and steady. She's just out," he said, gently pulling away from her so he could lay her on the bed. As he got to his feet Nathan pulled the covers up and tucked her in.

"Thanks for getting the pills," Eric said, rubbing his sore shoulder. She'd put up a hell of a fight. It wasn't because the pills were a waste of time and wouldn't work like she'd claimed the entire time they'd wrestled with her to make her take the damn things. No, the reason that she damn near kneed him in the balls was very simple. She thought she was going to work tomorrow.

Not fucking happening.

She had fifteen stitches in her head for fuck sake and needed to rest, but would she listen to either one of them? Not a chance. She actually pointed out that the injury was on her forehead and wouldn't interfere with her doing her job or lifting a patient.

Joe was too damn stubborn and this little incident just showed him that she needed to get the hell out of the field. She was a young, beautiful woman and it was just so wrong on so many levels that this job was her life.

He knew she'd fight him every inch of the way, but once he had her off the rig for good she'd thank him. She needed to start enjoying her life and he knew she wouldn't allow herself to do that as long as she worked on the ambulance. Once he found her something else to do he knew it would only be a matter of time before she realized it was the best thing for her.

"Mom's going to wring our necks," Nathan unnecessarily pointed out.

It pretty much went without saying that their mother would throttle them when she found out that they kept this from her. The woman truly believed that they were incapable of taking care of themselves when they were sick. It didn't matter that two of them were EMTs with more medical experience than her, she was their mother plain and simple and only she could take care of them.

Eric looked over at his brother and grimaced. The man's obviously tailored suit was now a mass of wrinkles thanks to the ten minute wrestling match Joe insisted upon before they could get her to take the damn pills. In the end they'd been forced to shove the pills in her mouth, clamp a hand over her mouth to stop her from spitting them out again, and pinch her nose shut until she swallowed them.

"You might want to throw your suit in the dryer before you go back to your date," Eric pointed out, fighting back a yawn. Today had been too damn long.

Nate shrugged out of his coat and tossed it on the chair in the corner. "It's already late and I'd rather not have to get dressed and come back here in four hours to do this all over again when she wakes up."

Eric didn't think ten o'clock was too late to go back and finish his date, but if the man was offering to stay and help with the next wrestling match then he wasn't going to be stupid enough to point it out. He was however curious.

"Is everything okay?" he asked, sitting on the edge of the bed to pull off his socks and pants while Nathan did the same on the chair.

"With what?" Nathan asked, yanking off his shoes.

"With Caitlyn," Eric said, wondering if his brother was already starting to pull away from the woman. The man had a nasty habit of dumping women that in Eric's opinion were damn near perfect for his brother.

"Nothing's wrong. She's great."

So were the other women that had come and gone out of his brother's life over the past ten years, but tonight wasn't the night to bring up the sad expression on his brother's face. Tonight he was exhausted.

"I'm going to take a quick shower," Eric said, grabbing a pair of fresh boxer briefs from Joe's bureau. He ignored Nathan's amused expression and went to bathroom where he took a long hot shower. It helped relax his muscles, but it did nothing to calm his nerves.

The only thing that helped was seeing Joe safely curled up in bed sleeping. He wasn't too surprised to discover Nathan lying on top of Joe's old sleeping bag on the floor. Although none of them had a problem sleeping in the same bed together since it had been a necessity on more than one family outing when they were kids, however none of those experiences had ended well for Nathan.

Odd things just seemed to happen to Nathan when the three of them shared a bed. Most of the time he'd end up falling off the bed, but on more than one occasion he'd ended up with a few minor injuries like a bump on the head, a knee to the groin, a few broken fingers and a broken nose. They were accidents no matter what Nathan claimed, but they were still unsettling.

Even last October when they'd gone up to Maine for a weekend and been forced to share a tent hadn't ended well for Nathan. How the poor bastard ended up being shoved out of the pup tent into the rain, he still didn't know. Not that he had cared at the time since he'd been happily snuggled up with a very warm Joe.

He carefully crawled into bed with Joe and pulled her into his arms. She immediately relaxed back into his arms and let out a content little sigh.

"How long do you think they'll keep her on light duty for?" Nathan whispered.

Eric sighed heavily. "Normally they'd probably keep her on light duty for a week, but knowing how stubborn she is, she'll probably manage to get back to work in a few days."

"I still can't believe a mental patient attacked a cop and went for his gun. You're both lucky that he didn't get it free," Nathan pointed out. Eric's arms tightened around Joe. They had been lucky, but it had been close, very close. When he spoke to Nathan earlier on the phone he left off the little fact that the patient had managed to switch the safety off just seconds before Joe's little stunt.

Joe's little groan had him loosening his hold and pressing a kiss to the top of her head. He had to figure a way to get Joe the hell off the truck before something bad happened.

"Nathan?"

"Yeah?"

"Are you still looking for a secretary?" he asked, glad that it was too dark for his brother to see the calculating expression on his face.

Nathan sighed heavily. "Yeah, business is really taking off and I could use a hand in the office to free up some of my time. Why? Do you know someone?" he asked, sounding eager.

Eric couldn't help but smile. This was going to be too easy. He knew how much Nathan's internet company meant to him. He'd built it from the ground up when he was barely sixteen years old. It was his baby, his pride and joy and he knew the man was nervous about letting anyone near it.

This was perfect. Joe needed a new job and Nathan needed someone he trusted. He mentally congratulated himself on his fast work. This was going to be easier than he thought.

"Joe," he simply said.

"Joe, what? Is she awake?" Nathan asked. Eric heard the telltale sound of the sleeping bag zipper being pulled down and wasn't too surprised to find Nathan standing next to the bed, peering down at Joe nervously. The man clearly wanted to make sure Joe was okay and what better way to do that then to give her a safe job?

Too fucking easy.

"She's fine."

"Oh," was Nathan's obviously confused response.

"I meant you should hire Joe."

There was a heavy pause before Nathan snorted his reply. "No way. No fucking way in hell. Not happening."

"What the hell do you mean 'no way'?" Eric demanded, shifting Joe out his arms so that he could sit up and properly glare at his brother.

Nathan simply turned his back on him and returned to the safety of his sleeping bag. "Just what I said. There's no way in hell that I'm hiring Joe. Besides, she has a job already. A good job I might add."

"Why the hell wouldn't you hire Joe?" Eric demanded, unable to stop himself from feeling insulted on her behalf. "She's a good worker, never late, and she works her ass off."

"She's also stubborn, pushy, and would laugh her ass off the first time I asked her to do something," Nathan pointed out.

Eric opened his mouth to argue, but then closed it, realizing that he was right. Nathan would probably fire Joe's ass within the first hour. Joe was a great EMT and never argued or copped an attitude with one of their supervisors, but she'd have a hard time taking orders from a pushover like Nathan.

"Besides," Nathan continued, "it's not like she'll be on light duty forever and I need someone for the long term."

This is where it was going to get a little tricky. Thankfully Joe was still lightly snoring so he didn't have to worry about her overhearing the conversation and kicking his ass.

Yet.

"After tonight, I was thinking it might be better if Joe found something else to do."

"You decided?" Eric could almost picture Nathan cocking an eyebrow with that tone.

"Yes, but it's not only about tonight. This field is too dangerous for a woman like Joe," he ignored Nathan's snort of disbelief, "she needs a decent paying job, something that won't interfere with her having a life."

"She seems to like her life just fine."

"She deserves better."

After a moment Nathan sighed warily. "I don't think Joe would be happy doing anything else, but after seeing what that bastard did to her tonight I have to admit that I wouldn't mind seeing her in a safer position, too."

"Then you'll help me convince her to find something else to do?" Eric asked, trying not to sound too eager. He needed his brother on board with his plan. Tag teaming Joe might be his only hope. Of course if he got his mother on board......

"Yeah, I'll help," Nathan said, not sounding too happy about it. "But when she finds out, and we both know that she will, don't be surprised when I sell your ass down the river."

"Duly noted," Eric said happily as he lay back down and pulled Joe back into his arms. As long as she was off the ambulance and safe she could kick his ass and he'd take it with a smile.

* * * *

Joe continued to glare at the empty spot in her closet where her uniforms should be. She had absolutely no doubt who took them and why. It was probably the same reason why her car keys were gone.

After throwing one last glare at her closet she stomped over to her nightstand, ignoring the bottle of pain medication, and snatched up her cell phone and dialed the number of the first bastard she was going to kill.

"You take your pills?" was the first thing she heard when the phone connected.

"You. Bastard," she bit out.

"Did you take your pills?" he demanded again in a bored tone.

"I don't know who you think you are, but you get your ass back over here with my uniforms or so help me I will-"

"I'm sorry, but I can't have this conversation with you until you take your pills," Eric announced, cutting her off.

"Why you little-"

"Take your pills."

"No," she snapped, even though her head was killing her.

"If you want to talk then you'll take them," he said calmly.

Glaring at absolutely nothing, Joe did her best to reign in her temper. After a minute she said, "Fine. I took them. Are you happy?"

Eric sighed heavily. "I would be if you actually took them."

"Fine!" she snapped, grabbing the small bottle of pills, knowing she wouldn't get anywhere until she took them. She quickly popped two into her mouth and swallowed them with the water someone left by her bed. "Now are you happy?" she asked as soon as she swallowed them.

"Extremely," Eric said, sounding smug. The bastard.

"Now bring back my car keys and uniforms," she bit out between clenched teeth.

"Sorry, no can do. You're not supposed to drive while you have those pills in your system. So, I guess you'll just have to stay home and rest like a good little girl."

"Eric,-" she started only to be cut off.

"Besides, I can't really talk right now. I'm kind of busy here with work and all, but before I forget I was supposed to tell you that mom is really upset with you and hurt that you wouldn't let us call her last night."

"W-what?" she choked out. "Who the hell told mom?" she demanded, wondering which one of them had broken their pact to keep Alice in the dark about injuries and hangovers. It had to be Nathan, she thought, inwardly cursing. Eric knew better. Besides he would never screw her over like this.

"I did of course. You know it's really not nice to keep mom in the dark. Now, if you don't mind I really do have to get back to work," he said cheerfully.

"Please tell me you're kidding," she said, panicking.

"Nope," he said, making the word pop.

Just as a few choice words popped into her head she heard her front door open. She swallowed hard. "Eric, please tell me that's you coming into the house right now."

"Sweetheart?" Alice called, ruining all Joe's hopes that Eric had lied. "I made Jello!"

"I hate you," she mumbled into the phone before hanging up, but not before she heard Eric laugh. The rat bastard.

Chapter 12

"Did they arrest him?" Greg asked Teddy as the two of them leaned against one of the box ambulances.

Teddy shrugged as he pulled out a cigarette. "They probably will."

Eric shifted the empty oxygen tank to his left hand so he could reach out and flick the cigarette out of Teddy's mouth. "No smoking in the garage, dickhead," he said, gesturing to the oxygen refill station to their right.

With a sigh, Teddy put his pack away, but made no move to help Eric as he prepared truck fifteen for service. That didn't surprise him since the prick was lazy. He only exerted himself when he had to, and he made damn sure that he didn't have to most days. Normally that was bad enough, but today they had Greg third riding with them because the damn kid still needed to complete his training time. He really wished Bill had managed to get someone else to fill in for Joe today. He hated having this jerk influencing any of the newbies. The last thing any of them needed was another Teddy.

"Has anyone showed you how to fill the tanks?" he asked Greg.

"Yeah, I learned that a few days ago," Greg said in a bored tone.

"Good," Eric said, thrusting the empty tank in his arms. "Then go fill this up."

Greg looked like he was going to argue, but thankfully kept his mouth shut. He was not in the mood to deal with any bullshit today.

"What will happen to him?" Greg asked, picking the conversation back up as he did what he was asked.

"He'll probably be sent for an evaluation and have his medication tweaked until they find a dosage that works. Then he'll probably be sent to a new residential program," Eric said, walking over to the supply shelves to grab a box of synthetic gloves, size extra large. He was just about to grab a box of mediums out of habit when he remembered that Joe wasn't working with him.

"He won't get arrested for hurting Joe?"

"No," Eric said. "He's a mental patient. He's pretty much covered while he's receiving help."

"That's fucked up," Greg said.

"That's the job," Eric said, grabbing a box of pens and a fresh pack of run sheets.

"What about the residential home? Will they get into trouble?"

Eric chuckled without humor. "A slap on the hand."

"Joe could sue the program," Teddy suggested, mostly to start shit.

"She can sue?" Greg asked, sounding too damn eager for Eric's peace of mind.

"She could, but she won't," Eric said firmly. That was too much drama, time, and bullshit for Joe.

He finished checking out the ambulance and gestured for Teddy to get his ass in the truck when the other man headed for the door, no doubt he thought he was planting his lazy ass on the couch and staying there until they had a call. Normally he wouldn't care so much, but he had a lot of shit to do today

"Let's go," Eric said, grabbing the oxygen tank from Greg and secured the tank into its hold and attached the valves.

"We don't have a call," Teddy pointed out when Eric jumped out of the back of the ambulance. "Until then I'm sitting down," he said, absently running his fingers over his taped nose.

"I want to go check on Joe," Eric said, gesturing for Greg to climb in the back. After a short hesitation he grabbed his backpack and climbed inside.

Eric walked around to the driver's side.

"Check on her?" Teddy repeated, sounding confused. "Oh, come on!" he said seconds later. "You just talked to her!"

"Are you done with your hissy fit, cupcake?" Eric said, pausing by the driver's side door. "Cause if you are I'd like to go check up on Joe before we get a call."

Teddy waved him off. "Then go. Afterwards come and pick me up," Teddy said, heading for the door.

"Get in the truck," Eric snapped, tired of this bullshit. He wasn't about to receive a write up because he left his crew member behind. If they received an emergency call it would be his ass in the sling for not having his partner. He'd have to refuse the call and that's a game he wouldn't play.

"Or what? You'll write me up?" Teddy snorted.

"In a heartbeat," Eric said with absolutely no hesitation as he climbed into the driver's side. He pulled on his seatbelt and started the vehicle, ignoring the little rant the prick was having. He wasn't too surprised when a minute later Teddy climbed into the passenger seat and slammed the door shut.

"You're a fucking asshole, Eric," Teddy bit out angrily.

"Uh huh," Eric said absently as he reached for the mike. "Echo seventeen to dispatch," he said.

"Go ahead Echo seventeen," dispatch said.

"We're on the air," he said, ignoring Teddy's murderous glare.

"One minute, Echo seventeen."

Eric slowly drove out of the garage as he waited for dispatch to tell them they were clear. Even though he'd left her less than two hours ago he was anxious to get back to her and make sure that she was okay. Thankfully his mother had a free day, not that she wouldn't have dropped everything to take care of Joe otherwise he would have banged out of his shift to take care of her.

He didn't want to be here today working with this prick, but he knew if he missed work that would just piss Joe off more and only make her more determined to get back to work. She was too damn stubborn sometimes. He was not looking forward to the bullshit he was going to have to go through to get her off the truck permanently, but as long as she was safe and happy it would be worth it.

"Echo seventeen?"

"Echo seventeen," Eric said, knowing that tone. They were about to get a call. As long as it was short and sweet he didn't care. His eyes darted to the dashboard clock. It was barely half past nine in the morning. He hoped they didn't get screwed all day. Not that he had a problem with working, he didn't. He hated to sit around and normally loved to stay busy, but he was hoping for a chance to swing by Joe's and bring her something for lunch, knowing his mother wouldn't allow her to eat anything more than Jell-O and broth all day.

"Echo seventeen, I need you to respond to Sunflower Nursing Home on 34 Chestnut Avenue for an unwitnessed fall."

"Echo seventeen, responding to Sunflower Nursing home for an unwitnessed fall," he said into the mike.

"Son of a bitch," Teddy snapped, pulling out a run sheet as Eric flipped the emergency lights on.

"No one saw the patient fall?" Greg asked from the back of the ambulance, thankfully sounding a lot less nervous than he had last week.

Teddy snorted out a chuckle. "They're all unwitnessed," he said, filling in their information on the run sheet.

"What does that mean?"

"It means," Eric started only to pause as he slammed on the brakes as some dumb fuck sped through the intersection almost slamming into them as they tried to race through before they lost the green light.

He chuckled when he spotted a police car waiting in the opposite lane throw its emergency lights on and go after the prick. Eric paused in the middle of the intersection, allowing the police officer to take the turn and go after the jerk. With a wave of appreciation to the officer, Eric proceeded through the intersection.

"Holy shit!" Greg gasped. "Weren't they supposed to stop?"

"Yup," Eric said, switching the sounds of the sirens in demand for the cars in front of him to move out of the way. "You'll find that most people have enough common sense to move out of the way or stop at intersections so we can go, but there are others-"

"Assholes," Teddy added, and for once they were in complete agreement about something.

"-who will refuse to move out of the way, or will rush through the intersection whether or not they had the green, and my personal favorite are the assholes who ride our tail when we're responding."

"Those are the ones who usually get creamed," Teddy pointed out.

"Seriously?" Greg asked.

"It usually happens when they try and follow an ambulance through an intersection," Eric explained, pulling into the long driveway of Sunflower Home.

"That sucks," Greg mumbled distractedly.

"Echo seventeen on scene," Eric said into the mike as he pulled to a stop at the front entrance.

He shut the ambulance down and pulled the keys out. Some crews left the trucks running or the keys in the ignition and he would be the first one to admit that he used to make that mistake. A mental patient stealing a running ambulance right outside an emergency room a few years ago helped him break that habit quickly.

Everyone had laughed at the crew even as they cringed, thinking that could have easily been any of them. The patient didn't damage the ambulance, but she did have a hell of a ride. Three hours later the police found the ambulance parked behind an abandoned building with the crew's lunch smeared all over the inside of ambulance. Thankfully no one had been hurt, but it could have easily gone the other way.

"What did you mean about all the falls being unwitnessed?" Greg asked when Eric opened the doors to the back of the ambulance.

"It usually means that whoever witnessed the fall or caused the injuries doesn't want to get written up so they usually report it as an unwitnessed fall," Eric explained as he jumped into the back of the ambulance and loaded the stretcher with the long backboard and the trauma bag.

"And they get away with that?" Greg asked in disgust.

"Yup," Teddy said, grabbing a handful of gloves to stuff in his pocket.

"Are we going to report them?" Greg asked.

"Can't report them unless you have clear proof or you witnessed the incident," Eric explained, hoping to calm the kid down. He knew how he felt. Sometimes it was frustrating to work in this field and see the things that they saw on a daily basis, but he knew that running to the state and reporting every little thing could actually cause more problems than they'd solve.

"So they get away with it?"

"No," Eric said, shaking his head and wishing Joe was here. She usually answered these questions and did a hell of lot better job at it than he was doing. "You have to remember that not every injury is abuse, especially when you're dealing with the elderly population. A lot of the calls you get that claim the patient fell and no one was around will be true. A lot of patients, young and old are bullheaded and hate asking for help or get sick of waiting for help and try to do things on their own that they know they shouldn't. So don't go jumping the gun and assuming abuse."

"But you said-"

"I know what I said," Eric cut him off. "The only thing that you can do is to write down every detail of the call and that includes the scene and what the staff says. Don't ever voice your opinion on a run sheet. That's the fastest way to find yourself either fired or facing a lawsuit. Stick to the facts. It will not only cover your ass, but provide your patient with evidence if needed."

"I hate to admit this, but he's right," Teddy said, helping Eric pull the stretcher out of the ambulance. "If you go around writing up staff members you're going to find your job a lot harder to do when the staff snubs you."

"Just mind your own business and cover your ass and you should be fine," Eric said in what he hoped was a reassuring tone, but judging by the nervous expression on the man's face he'd failed.

Actually, upon closer inspection he noticed the man looked a little under the weather.

"You're not going to puke are you?" he asked even as he shifted himself and the stretcher away. Teddy must have noticed the look on their third rider's face because he jumped the hell out of the way.

"No, I'm not-*oh shit*!" Greg said, covering his mouth and making a mad dash towards the bushes.

Eric and Teddy shared an exasperated look before they headed for the front door. He made a mental note to make the kid carry breath mints from now on.

Chapter 13

"What do you think you're doing, young lady?"

Pasting a smile on her face, Joe turned around and tried not to wince under the maternal glare that was being sent her way. She seriously wondered when that look would lose its effect on her. Probably never, she thought with an inward groan.

"I was just looking for something to read," she lied, hoping Alice would go back to whatever she was doing so Joe could find the backup set of car keys she had lying around somewhere in her office/guest room.

She'd already searched through her small desk, the pullout couch, and her bookshelves to no avail. The damn things had to be here. She definitely remembered tossing them in here when she had them made up last year.

"If you were looking for something to read than why are you dressed?" Alice demanded, arching a brow, silently challenging Joe to lie to her.

"I was cold?"

"It's eighty degrees in here, sweetheart," Alice pointed out the same time that she stepped to the side and gestured for Joe to get her butt back to bed. It was a small gesture, but one she recognized nonetheless.

There was no point in arguing, Joe decided grumpily. She'd already tried that for the past five hours and failed miserably, considering Alice had simply ignored her and shoved green jell-o down her throat for "sustenance" as Alice liked to put it. She'd made damn sure that jell-o stayed down, knowing the next step in Alice Parish's home care treatment was beef broth.

She couldn't even stress how much she hated beef broth.

"Where are you going?" Alice asked when Joe veered to the left instead of heading for her bedroom.

"I'm going to get a cold drink," and think of a way to get back at Eric for this. They were supposed to be partners and best friends. After all the shit they'd gone through and the times she covered for him she couldn't believe he did this to her. Granted, he probably knew without Mom here she'd find a way to get to the fire station.

Damn him.

"I can get it for you, sweetheart. You should be resting," Alice offered. "I can make up some broth if you think you can handle it."

Joe couldn't help it, she cringed. "No, that's okay, mom. Thanks."

Her stomach growled viciously, reminding her that she hadn't eaten anything since yesterday morning and she sure as hell wasn't counting the nasty green goop Alice practically shoved down her throat as food.

"You want more jell-o? I made a big bowl."

No, she wanted the delicious steak that Eric owed her, but probably wasn't going to have anytime soon thanks to her babysitting detail.

"No thanks, mom," she said, grabbing an ice cold Coke and heading back to her room. "I think I'm just going to lie down and take a nap," she said, knowing that she didn't have a choice in the matter.

"That sounds like a good idea," Alice said, following her anyway as if she didn't trust her, which would actually hurt if she hadn't been caught trying to climb out of the bathroom window two hours ago.

"Do you need anything?" Alice asked as she pulled back the covers and fluffed the pillows.

She needed to get to work, but Alice wouldn't be happy to hear that so Joe forced a smile and said, "No, I'm going to take my pill and get a little more sleep."

"Okay," Alice said, smiling pleasantly as she picked up the pill bottle and held it out to Joe, expectantly. Again with the trust, Joe thought with an inward sigh as she took the bottle and downed a pill.

"You don't have to stick around, mom. I'm most likely going to sleep well into the night now," Joe said, hoping Alice would take pity on her and leave. It was bad enough to be stuck in the house, she didn't really enjoy being fussed over on top of that. If she was going to be stuck here then she'd rather do it in peace and quiet so she could contemplate all the ways she was going to get back at Eric.

"Well, I do have a few things I have to do, but I promised Eric that I'd wait around until he got home," she said, looking at her watch. "I guess he got held over."

Joe nodded absently as she pulled off her sneakers. "It happens, but he'll probably be here soon," she said, not knowing if that was the truth or not and not really caring. For all she knew it could be hours before he got here and she had the pleasure of kicking his ass out.

"I'll stick around for another half hour, but then I have to go before the grocery store closes," Alice sighed.

Joe frowned as she sat down on the bed to pull her sneakers off. "Berkley's doesn't close until ten," she pointed out.

Alice waved her hand impatiently through the air. "I can't go there anymore."

"Why not?"

"Camie," she said as if that would explain everything. Sadly enough it did. She looked at her watch again, looking anxious.

"Mom, you can go. Don't worry about it. If anything happens I'll call one of the guys."

She looked like she was about to agree, but reluctantly shook her head. "No, I'll wait around a little while longer. If worse comes to worse I'll go to Berkley's and deal with those rather disturbing glares."

Knowing there was no point arguing, Joe sighed heavily and headed for the bathroom, grabbing Eric's favorite tee shirt, an old faded...well, she really wasn't sure what the hell it was, but she knew that it was Eric favorite. Ten minutes later she was curled up in bed and drifting off, wishing it was Eric's arms around her instead of his old tee shirt.

* * * *

"Shh, go back to sleep," Eric said softly sometime later as he curled his large warm body around hers.

"Get out," she mumbled even as she snuggled against him.

When he chuckled she buried her face in her pillow and decided to ignore him.

"How are you feeling?" he asked quietly, gently running his fingers through her hair.

"Like kicking your ass," she muttered into the pillow. "I can't believe you called mom on me."

"You didn't leave me with much of a choice on the matter, now did you?"

"Bastard."

"Get some sleep," he said, pressing a kiss against the top of her head.

"I'm going to work tomorrow," she informed him, inwardly daring him to argue, because if he did she was going to kick his-

"I know," he said, surprising her.

"You know?" she repeated slowly, not sure if this was a trap of some kind.

"Mmmhmm, I know you're too stubborn to listen to the doctor. I already talked to Bill and he figured as much, which will actually work out because we have Greg again."

That got her attention.

She rolled over, shoving Eric away so that she could face him. "Why the hell is he still third riding?" The man should already be assigned to a more senior partner to finish his probation period, especially since they were only required to do five ride alongs and he must have done at least a dozen by now.

"He's nervous as hell. Every time he comes close to a patient he loses his lunch and if it's an emergency he loses it when the ambulance comes to a stop. No one's even let him get behind the wheel, afraid that he'll black out and crash," Eric said, lazily scratching his bare chest as he lay back on the bed.

"If it's that bad then maybe he should consider doing something else," she suggested, feeling bad for the man, but not bad enough to suggest someone that would endanger patients should work on one of the ambulances.

"Bill wants you to take another crack at him and see if you can help. If he doesn't improve within a week he's going to have to let him go," Eric said, fighting back a yawn.

She sighed heavily as she flopped back down on the bed and laid her head on Eric's shoulder and wrapped her arm around his waist. As she tried to figure out a way to help Greg deal with his nerves she snuggled closer to Eric. He pressed a kiss to the top of her head as he wrapped an arm around her and pulled her closer.

"I'm not sure if a week's enough time to help him," she said as she absently traced circles over Eric's chest and stomach, loving the way the light dusting of hair felt against her fingers.

"No, it's not. Normally I'd offer to grab a few extra shifts, but with you injured," she rolled her eyes at that, "and the Fireman Muster games this weekend we won't have a chance. I'm hoping Bill will give us until next Friday before he makes his decision."

As bad as she felt for Greg her mind had moved onto another pressing matter. She couldn't believe she almost forgot about it, especially since she was competing again for the first time in four years. "We're going to kick ass this year," she said, knowing it was true.

For years they competed together in the ambulance portion of the Muster, a competition between neighboring fire departments to put their skills to the test, they always won. The last four years she got stuck behind the scenes helping out, but she was sick of that and told Bill he could find someone else to deal with the venders because she was going to kick some ass instead.

Eric gently ran his fingers through her hair, careful of her cut. "Are you sure you're up to it?" he asked softly.

She snorted her disbelief. "Hell yeah, I'm up to it. We are so going to kick some Blackford ass this year!"

"They kicked our asses last year and the year before," Eric pointed out.

"That's because I wasn't competing," she reminded him.

"There is that," he admitted, pressing a kiss to the top of her head. "Get some sleep, Joe. Tomorrow's our twenty-four hour shift and I have a feeling we're going to need every minute of rest that we can get."

Frowning, she tilted her head to look at him. "Why do you say that?

He sighed heavily as he pressed a kiss to her forehead. "Because we have Greg for the entire shift," he announced, making her groan and bury her face against his chest.

"I'm demanding a raise," she muttered against his chest.

"Damn straight."

* * * *

"Wow, you look like you got your ass handed to you by a psych patient," Jeff said brightly as he held the side door open for her.

Joe shook her head as she walked past the man. "No, this is what Eric did to me when I talked back," she said with a shrug.

"She needs to learn her place," Eric informed Jeff with a straight face.

"They all do," Jeff agreed quickly, earning a playful glare from Joe.

He followed Joe to their bunkroom, wondering how exactly he should tell her. He'd considered making a run for it while she was in the shower this morning and leaving her a note, or send a test message, but he knew that would just piss her off more. Maybe he should just tell her.

It was probably for the best that he just tell her and get it off his chest where they had a modicum of privacy for the fight that would no doubt follow. No doubt she'd be pissed at him, but he could make her understand and he would. This was only temporary anyway, well hopefully it would be.

Actually, he hoped to have her the hell out of this line of work and somewhere safe soon. He was still hoping against hope that Nathan would change his mind and let Joe come work for him, but if that failed, and it probably would, he would find something else for Joe. If worse came to worse he could, and probably would anyway to help out, move in with Joe and take over her bills while she figured out what she wanted to do for the rest of her life.

If she wanted to go back to school that was more than fine with him. He'd take care of her, pay off her regular bills and take as much overtime as he could get to help pay for college. Hell, if she just wanted to relax for a few months he'd be more than fine with that. As long as she didn't have to worry about her any longer he'd be more than fine with whatever she wanted to do.

He closed the door behind them as Joe began the tedious job of making her bed. She sent him a questioning look, but thankfully didn't say anything as she tucked the top sheet in. After a minute he realized there was no point in putting it off any longer. She'd find out soon enough and really it was better that they handle this in private.

Praying she wouldn't kick him in the balls, he said, "You're on light duty."

She paused mid-tuck. "What did you just say?" she demanded without looking back.

"I said you're on light duty," he repeated, trying not to wince when she abruptly stood up and glared up at him. "For the entire shift. You're not allowed to lift or drive," he quickly explained, mentally kicking himself for not wearing a cup.

"If I'm not allowed to lift or drive then what the hell am I supposed to do?" she asked evenly as she walked over to him, crossing her arms over her chest as she waited for his answer.

"Rest?" he suggested seconds before she slammed her foot down on top of his. When he leaned down to check his poor abused foot she shoved him out of the way and stormed out of the room, probably to track down Bill and give him a piece of her mind. He just hoped the man didn't sell his ass down the river and inform the grouch that it had been his idea to keep her on light duty.

Of course the man would rat his ass out. His only hope was that Joe didn't turn her anger on his balls.

Chapter 14

"Are you still in a pissy mood?" Eric asked as he sat next to her on the couch and threw his arm around her shoulder.

In answer, she rammed her elbow into his side. "Shit!" he gasped as he bent over and sucked in a breath.

If she wasn't stuck on light duty she might feel bad about it, but she was. Some people might enjoy light duty, but she was not one of them. Neither was Eric. It was boring, incredibly boring and now she was stuck on it for at least this shift, a twenty-four hour shift, she'd like to point out.

The only thing she was allowed to do for the next twenty-four hours was sit around, walk with Eric and Greg to get patients. She wasn't allowed to drive, help with the stretcher, move a patient, or even fill out paperwork, because apparently that would be too strenuous, she thought dryly. Hell, if they ended up with a heavy patient she wouldn't be allowed to help them. They'd have to call for a lift assist, another ambulance or an available supervisor would be asked to come help lift the patient, while she stood around feeling useless.

She liked staying busy during her shifts, especially during her twenty-four hour shift. It made the time pass by quickly. As much as she loved her job, and she did, it could get a little boring when there was nothing to do and it appeared that she had nothing to do for twenty-four hours.

"Such a baby," Eric said, sighing heavily as he stood up, grabbed her hand and yanked her to her feet so that he could steal her place on the couch and yanked her back down onto his lap. "There. That's much better," he mused as he settled back into the corner of the couch and got comfortable.

Most of the guys were used to their odd relationship and didn't care enough to tear their eyes away from the game. Greg on the other hand wasn't and every few minutes sent them a questioning look that she decided to ignore. She was pissed and in no mood for any bullshit today. She swore if he asked her out again she was going to stomp on his foot, too. The only thing she wanted to do was sulk all day.

Of course she also wanted to get the bastard, who was absently running his fingers over her arm, back for yet another betrayal. She couldn't believe he'd sold her out to mom, but this worse, much worse. This was twenty-four hours of boredom and he knew damn well that she did not do well with downtime. He knew that and it pissed her off like nothing else that he'd gone behind her back and did this to her. He was her best friend and was supposed to have her back, not screw her over.

With a muttered groan she climbed off his lap, barely resisting the urge to ram her elbow into his stomach. She ignored his questioning look and walked away.

"Uh oh, looks like someone's in trouble," one of guys said, but she ignored him and the snickers and snorts of laughter that followed and walked outside.

With nothing else to do she walked over to the picnic table on the side yard and sat down on the table. Barely an hour into her shift and she was already feeling useless. She thought about washing the ambulance, but Eric already did that and when she tried to help he actually had the nerve to shoo her away.

True to his stubborn word he hadn't allowed her to do anything. She hadn't been allowed to grab more run slips, check the ambulance out, get more supplies, or make the stretcher. Standing around watching them work had been boring and kind of embarrassing.

She could do this job and they both knew it. A simple little head injury wasn't going to interfere with her job and he knew it, but he was being so damn stubborn and she didn't know why. Being overprotective of her wasn't exactly something new, but he'd never gone this far with it before. The only thing she could think of was that the other night had thrown him through a loop and he felt responsible for her injury, which was really stupid.

Getting injured was a hazard of the job and he knew that. Well, he used to know that. Now he was just hell bent on pissing her the hell off.

"Are you mad at me?" he asked with a little pout that she refused to find cute so she pointedly looked away from him.

"Yes."

"You know you shouldn't even be at work right now," he said as he sat down next to her.

"I'm fine," she gritted out and she was. Her head didn't hurt as much, she could see straight and she was no longer wobbling when she walked. In her book that more than constituted fine.

"It's just for a little while," he said, sighing as he reached over and took her hand into both of his.

She yanked her hand away as she turned to glare at him. "What do you mean by 'for a little while'?"

His eyebrows arched slightly in confusion. "Bill didn't tell you?"

"No."

"Oh, well," he cleared his throat, "you're on light duty until the stitches come out," he said, giving her a reassuring smile that pissed her off.

"You......bastard," she bit out evenly.

He went to put his arm around her shoulders, but she shrugged him off. "I don't want you to be upset about not participating in the muster this year. There's always next year," he explained.

"What the hell do you mean I'm not participating?" she demanded, coming to her feet to better glare at him.

He noticeably winced as he looked past her. "You didn't tell her?"

"I thought you had," she heard Bill mutter like a coward.

She turned her glare on her boss. "I'm on light duty for a week? Really?"

He shot a nervous look at Eric before nodding. "I'm afraid so. You suffered a head injury and we don't want you to strain yourself. I'd rather you stayed home on medical, but-"

"Fine," she said, cutting him off.

"What?" Bill asked, frowning.

"Fine, I'm on medical. I'm going home. I'll be back in a week after I get cleared medically," she said, heading inside to grab her things and fighting the urge to stomp her foot like a child.

There was no way she was going to come in for a week and put up with this bullshit. One twenty-four hour shift of twiddling her thumbs was bad enough. There was no way she was going to do that for an entire week. Since she would be getting paid no matter what she did, she decided that she'd rather take the week to get some work done at her house and run some much needed errands.

"Joe?" Eric said, but she didn't stop. She walked past the guys, who were either too focused on the game or recognized a woman on a war path and left her the hell alone.

She walked to the bunkroom, grabbed her belongings, not bothering to fold them, and stormed out of the bunkroom and back through the break area and stormed past Bill, Eric, and Greg. For a moment she almost felt bad about Greg, but she knew she really wouldn't be much help if she couldn't help him by showing him how to perform his job.

It would probably stress the hell out of him to be forced to interact with the patients. To be honest, if he couldn't suck it up and try over the next week then he didn't belong in this field. He seemed like a nice enough guy, but she wasn't exactly a miracle worker.

"I'll see you in a week," she said to Bill and hopefully Greg. She'd like to see him pull through, but it fell on his shoulders now.

She heard someone sigh behind her and didn't need to look back to know that Eric was there. "I'll swing by and check on you if I get a chance."

"Don't bother," she said, unlocking her door.

"Fine. I know you're mad. I'll see you in the morning," he said softly.

She shook her head as she climbed into her car. "Don't bother."

* * * *

"You can't still be mad at me."

Joe continued scrapping the garage as she ignored the man who wouldn't take a damn hint and go away. She'd been doing this for two hours, hoping that the hard work and the sun would exhaust her and dull some of her anger, but so far it hadn't. She was still super pissed about getting screwed over.

"I brought you a Milky Way milk shake," Nathan said, sounding hopeful and damn him for knowing her weakness.

With an annoyed little sigh she stopped scraping the cracked white paint off the garage door and turned around. She took the large fast food cup from Nathan and took a long sip and couldn't help but let out a little moan as the delicious mixture of chocolate, caramel and vanilla hit her tongue.

"So, you forgive me?" Nathan asked, rolling back on his heels as he sent her a puppy dog look that had her rolling her eyes as she continued to drink the delicious beverage.

After taking one last healthy sip she sighed heavily and handed him the scraper. With a frown he took it, sending her a questioning look.

"Fine. I forgive you," she said, gesturing regally towards the garage, "now you may help me."

Chuckling, he stepped forward and began to work. "You're so generous, Joe."

"I know," she said, nodding in agreement as she turned her attention back to the delicious beverage that required her focus.

"You want to tell me what he did to piss you off this much?" Nathan asked, reaching back and swiping her drink. Before she could launch an attack to retrieve her drink back he took a long sip and was handing it back to her.

She decided not to hurt him since he was helping her and of course since she'd be sending him out later to get her another one. Not that he knew that, but he would. Nathan was such a pushover when it came to her and Alice. He could never seem to do enough for them and she normally wouldn't take advantage of his giving nature, but this was a Milky Way shake, the king of shakes. Besides, he had no one but himself to blame for getting her addicted to the damn things in the first place.

When they were in high school he got a part time job at a burger joint so that he could earn some money to buy a computer. She would have loved to work with him, but she'd already taken a job with Eric at a lumber yard. Every day she stopped by on her way home and he'd make her a Milky Way milkshake before walking her home.

"Well?"

"Well, what?" she asked, enjoying the last sip of her drink. Yeah, he was definitely going to have to go out and get her another one.

"What did he do?"

"Who?" she asked, playing stupid since she didn't feel like talking about the big jerk that screwed her over. She dropped the empty cup in one of the trash cans she'd pulled away from the garage, grabbed another scrapper, and went back to work.

"You know who."

"If you're speaking of your brother then you should know that he's dead to me," she said with a sniff as she focused on her work.

"Uh huh," he said like he didn't quite believe her.

"What the hell's that supposed to mean?" she demanded, perhaps scraping a little more forcefully than what was needed.

"Exactly what it sounded like," he said, pausing in his work to use his tee shirt to wipe sweat off his face.

"Meaning........," she prompted, feeling her annoyance with the man renew. If he kept this up she was going to tell him to leave.......

Right after he got her another shake.

"You've never been able to stay mad at him for more than a few hours, a day at the most. By tomorrow night you'll forgive him for trying to get you to quit and find another job and the two of you will be back to.....to....to.....oh....shit." Nathan's words trailed off when he looked up and met her glare.

"What the hell are you talking about, Nathan?" she demanded, gripping the scrapper in her hand tightly as she ran his words through her head again.

"Um, what are you talking about?" Nathan asked, trying to backtrack as he dropped the scrapper and stepped back.

"He's trying to get me to quit?" she asked, stepping in front of him and blocking his exit. "Why?"

"You'd really have to ask Eric about that," he said, shifting nervously.

"I'm asking you," she said, tossing the scrapper away so that she could cross her arms over her chest to intensify the effect of the glare.

"I-I don't think I should say," he said, licking his lips as he moved to step around her only to find his exit cut off.

"You can."

"I can't."

"I'll cry," she threatened, knowing she just might have to do the unthinkable and shed a few tears to make the big softie confess.

He narrowed his eyes on her. "You wouldn't."

Oh, but she would. Her bottom lip wasn't quivering ten seconds before Nathan broke down and confessed. An hour later she was sitting on the hood of her car, sipping a new milkshake and contemplating manslaughter.

Chapter 15

He couldn't remember the last time he'd been this relieved that a shift was over, but he was. When dispatch dismissed him after holding him over for five hours he damn near kissed the ground in thanks.

Wincing when the muscles in his right shoulder protested in agony, he grabbed the two bags of takeout and shut his truck door. Thanks to Greg he'd fucked up his shoulder when the little bastard lied about being able to lift a hundred and fifty pounds.

Then again it was possible that he'd been telling the truth and the patient simply startled the hell out of him when he started seizing on their stretcher. If it hadn't been for Brian, the paramedic that filled in for Joe, the stretcher would have tipped over, but thankfully the man jumped in and grabbed the stretcher and righted it just in the nick of time. It hadn't saved his shoulder though. It hurt like hell, but nothing some ice and rest wouldn't fix.

He had the next two days off and planned on spending them with Joe. He had a game plan to not only make her forgive him, but one that would get the ball rolling on her starting to think about employment, *safe employment*, elsewhere. It would take time and a whole hell of a lot of charm, but he was pretty damn sure that he'd have her thinking it was a great idea before they started in on dessert. He just had to find the right moment to approach the subject.

"So, you want me to quit working on the ambulance, huh?" Joe asked casually as she stepped out of her house and leaned a hip against the small porch railing.

Apparently there was no time like the present.

"Do you think we can go inside and discuss this while we eat?" he asked, raising the bags of takeout.

"Sure," she said, shrugging and surprising the hell out of him.

He'd expected a fight, but he wasn't going to complain. He was too tired and hungry at the moment to question it. Without another word he followed her inside and placed the bags of food on the table.

"I'll be right back," he said around a yawn as he walked down the long hallway towards her bedroom. He could have used the guest bathroom, but he preferred hers.

On the way to her bathroom he grabbed a pair of his grey boxer briefs out of her bureau. He stripped out of his clothes and jumped in the shower, wishing he could take a nice long leisurely shower to work the strain out of his muscles, but he was starving and wanted to take advantage of Joe's receptive mood while he could.

Five minutes later he walked into Joe's kitchen, feeling slightly better. He just wanted to eat and get this conversation out of the way so that they could focus on her future. Joe was just starting to fill their plates when he walked past her on his way to the refrigerator.

He grabbed an ice pack for his shoulder and thought about grabbing a couple of beers, but he didn't want her to drink in case she took a painkiller. So instead he grabbed a couple of Cokes. He placed one by her plate and sat down across from her at the small round table.

Other than a murmured "Thank you" she didn't say much to him as they ate for which he was immensely relieved. He was so damn hungry. They had back to back calls all night and the only thing he'd eaten was a stale packet of peanuts he managed to wrestle from a vending machine.

"You want to tell me why you want to get rid of me?" Joe asked when he finished his third helping.

"I'm not trying to get rid of you, Joe," he said, feeling exhaustion threaten to knock him on his ass.

"That's what it sounded like to me," she said, leaning back in chair as she crossed her arms over her chest. "From what I hear you tried to unload me on Nathan." Her tone was friendly, but the look she was giving him was anything but.

Shit.

"This isn't the way I planned on doing this, but I've been thinking that maybe it was time for you to move on and do something else with the rest of your life," he explained. When she only sat there glaring at him he decided that perhaps he needed to explain the situation a little better before she decided to go for his balls.

"Well," he said, clearing his throat and feeling a little uncomfortable under her glare, "you know you couldn't do this forever." She cocked a brow at that little announcement so he added, "Could you really see yourself doing this job when you were fifty?"

"Yes," she said with absolutely no hesitation and made his job of convincing her to do something else more difficult. He decided to get rid of the bullshit pleasantries and get to the point.

"There's no way you'll be able to lift a grown man when you're fifty, Joe, and if you think so then you're crazy. Hell, you'll probably have problems doing it when you're forty. Besides that, Joe, you shouldn't have to do a job like this where you have to put your neck on the line and never really able to have a life because you never know if you're going to get out on time or have to pick up a shift," he said, noting the way her eyes narrowed dangerously on him.

"I have a life," she shot back defensively.

"Oh, really?" he asked, cocking a brow. "When's the last time you had a date?"

"I don't know," she said, shrugging it off like it was nothing, "it doesn't mean anything."

"Uh huh, and when's the last time you got laid?" he asked, silently daring her to lie to him. He knew it had been at least a year and a half for her.

"It's none of your business!" she snapped as she visibly tensed in her seat.

"Yeah, that's what I thought, Joe," he said, pushing his plate away. "You don't date. You don't have much of a life outside of work. Hell, I can't remember the last time you turned down overtime. You're thirty, Joe, and if you keep this job you're going to be forty and lonely and wondering how the hell life passed you by. You need to find something else that's safe and will allow you to have a life. I was thinking that I could help with-"

"What about you?" she suddenly demanded, interrupting him and sounding pissed.

"What about me?"

"You don't have a life. You don't date and I doubt you've gotten laid in the last year," she announced and he had to grind his teeth as he forced away the memory of why he hadn't gotten laid in too damn long to be normal. "Are you going to be looking for another line of work?"

He frowned. "No, why the hell would I?"

"Exactly," she said, placing her hands flat on the table and standing up. She leaned forward. "So it's okay for you to still be doing a job you love at forty, but not for me?" she demanded.

He got to his feet and leaned forward, closing the space between them until their noses were only a few inches apart. "Damn straight."

"Why exactly is that?"

"Honestly?" he asked, not really sure if she wanted to hear the truth.

"Of course," she said tightly and if it had been any other woman he wouldn't have laid into her, but this was Joe and he wanted her safe and if that meant pissing her off then so be it.

"While you think that you're one of the guys, Joe, you're not," he said, ignoring the flash of hurt in her eyes. "You're a woman and while that comes in handy when we have a patient that needs a reassuring word or two and a little handholding it's also a huge problem. You're smaller and weaker and when the shit hits the fan it means that not only does your partner have to handle whatever's going down, but he also has to make sure that you're safe and out of the way. It's a huge fucking liability that no one needs and it's only going to get worse as you get older and you know it."

For a moment she didn't say anything as she looked at him and he thought that maybe he needed to push the point a little more, but thankfully she seemed to understand. "I see. So, it's distracting to work with me," she summed it up.

"Yes."

She shrugged as she stepped away. "Then I guess I don't have any choice but to call up Bill and have him reassign me to another shift since I'm such a distraction for you."

Everything in him went still as her words hit home. She was going to work with someone else? Not fucking happening. As long as she was working on the truck, and if he had his way it wouldn't be much longer, she was going to work with him. He didn't trust some other asshole to keep an eye on her and keep her safe.

That was *his* job.

"No," he said evenly.

"No, what?" she demanded.

"You're not switching off of our shift."

"That's not your decision, Eric. In fact, I believe you just made it painfully clear that it's a problem to work with me. Well, I found a solution so you should be happy that I'm going to be out of your hair soon," she bit out angrily as she moved to walk passed him.

He stepped in front of her. "You're not fucking switching off our shift, Joe. As long as you're determined to be pigheaded about this you're going to work with me so that I can keep you safe."

She shoved him back. "Who the hell do you think you are?" she demanded, stepping forward to shove him back again. "You're not my boss or my keeper! If I want to switch my shift then I'll switch my damn shift! And if I want to keep working on the truck until I'm old and gray then that's my goddamn business!"

"Bullshit!" he snapped, grabbing her hands when she went to push him again and shoved them behind her back. The movement forced her to arch into him until her breasts were plastered against his bare chest and she was forced to glare up at him. "Anything that concerns you is my business."

"No, it's not!" she said, struggling against his hold. "I can take care of myself!"

"You don't have to!"

"Yes, I do!" she yelled.

"Why?" he demanded, yanking her back against him when she managed to put some distance between them.

"Because I don't have anyone, you asshole! Now let me go!"

He glared down at her. "That's bullshit, Joe."

"No, it's not" she snapped, renewing her struggles, but he didn't let her gain so much as an inch this time.

"You have me, Joe! You've always had me," he bit out evenly. How the hell could she say that or even think that?

She'd always had him. Always. They'd been inseparable since they were eight years old and that hadn't changed, wouldn't change. She was just too damn stubborn to realize that she wasn't alone in this world, but she was hung up on that bitch that abandoned her and refused to see that she'd done her a favor. She was the most important person in his life and he thought that he was the same for her. It killed him to know that she thought she was alone. She wasn't. Not as long as he was around.

"No, I-"

Whatever she was about to say was cut off when he did the one thing he'd longed to do since the dare he'd accepted when they were fourteen, he kissed her. For a moment she stood there, tense, but he didn't let that stop him from enjoying her lips. They were so warm and soft and he couldn't seem to get enough.

He knew he'd fucked up, but he couldn't help himself. She felt so good in his arms and when she moved her lips slowly against his she felt perfect. It was so damn good, but he wanted more.

With a groan he released her hands and wrapped his arms around her, pulling her impossibly closer as he tilted his head and traced the seam of her lips with the tip of his tongue. When she opened up to him he didn't hesitate. He slid his tongue inside of her mouth and couldn't help but feel like he was coming home.

She suckled his tongue into her mouth as her arms wrapped around his neck. In seconds the kiss went from cautious to out of control and desperate. He couldn't get enough of her and if the way she was fisting his hair was any indication then she felt the same way. They stumbled back until his back met the wall.

Without breaking the kiss he turned them around until she was against the wall. He removed his arms from around her and slid his hands over her back to her sides and up. He ran his hands over her breasts, earning a needy little growl from Joe as her hard nipples teased his hands through her shirt. She felt so good, a thousand times better than he ever imagined she would.

After a moment he needed more. He released her breasts and reached down, cupping her behind her knees and pulled her legs up. She didn't hesitate in wrapping her legs around his waist and he sure as hell didn't waste any time in shifting until his erection was pressed against her center.

Even through multiple layers that separated them he could feel her heat. He couldn't remember ever wanting a woman more than he wanted her at that moment. He ground himself against her as he swallowed her moan of pleasure.

She ran her hands over his back and ass, encouraging him on and he knew by the sounds of her breathing and the way she dug her nails into his back that she was close and god help him, but so was he. It wouldn't be enough. Not nearly enough, he thought as he pulled her away from the wall and placed her on the edge of the kitchen table. He needed to be inside of her.

He reached for her pants button when he heard her front door open. They both went completely still.

"Joe? Look, I can't stand you being mad at me so I brought you another milkshake."

The moment he pulled away from her, reality crashed in over them like a bucket of cold water and they both realized they'd just fucked up.

Chapter 16

"Are you going to share that with me?" Nathan asked, pouting.

"No," she said, sighing as she took a big bite out of her fried dough. She didn't really want it, but she needed something to do in order to distract herself from the colossal mess she'd made out of her life.

"Cheap," Nathan mumbled, throwing her a little pout that had her rolling her eyes.

"You can have some of mine, Nathan," Caitlyn said, smiling sweetly up at Nathan.

"Thank you," Nathan said, looking a little uncomfortable as he accepted a bite of her fried dough. Caitlyn must have noticed it too, because her smile slipped a notch.

She just barely stopped herself from slapping him upside his head. What the hell was wrong with him? Caitlyn was smart, funny, sweet and kind and he was pushing her away. He did this so often that she knew the signs by heart now.

Right now he was distancing himself from Caitlyn and in a week she'd be gone from the picture. In another month or two he'd find another woman that was just as perfect for him and he'd be happy until whatever stupid notion he allowed to take over his common sense had him pushing that one away too. She wanted to scream at him and slap some sense into him, but she honestly didn't know where to start.

"I-I'm going to go get a drink. Does anyone else want one?" Caitlyn asked, shifting uncomfortably.

"No, thank you," Joe said, throwing Caitlyn what she hoped was a warm smile.

"I'm all set," Nathan said absently as he watched the teams of firefighters run a relay race with rolled up hoses.

"Okay," Caitlyn said softly as she turned and walked away.

"Do we need to send you to therapy?" she asked when Caitlyn was out of hearing distance.

He frowned down at her. "No. Why?"

She rolled her eyes as she gestured towards Caitlyn's retreating back. Nathan followed her gesture and sighed.

"It's just not working out," he said with a shrug.

"Then tell her that instead of dragging this out. It's not fair to her."

"I will," was all he said and she had to ball her hands into fists to stop herself from choking some sense into him. What the hell was wrong with him that he couldn't even see what was right in front of him? How the hell could he push someone who was obviously perfect for him away like that?

The man needed his ass kicked. That's really all there was to it.

"What's going on with you two?" Nathan asked, gesturing towards the row of ambulances lined up for the EMS competition. She spotted Eric leaning against the ambulance, shirtless of course, talking to an equally shirtless Dave, the EMT that took her spot, but the sight of Dave didn't send her heart racing, make her palms sweat or confuse the hell out of her.

After their momentary lapse in sanity he hadn't said one single word to her. He simply stepped away from her and went to her bedroom to get dressed, leaving her sitting on the table, confused, aching and furious. Of course the milkshake Nathan brought her had helped calm her down. It really was too bad they weren't selling them here because she could really use one right about now.

By the time Eric reappeared he was dressed and wouldn't make eye contact with her for which she'd been immensely grateful. She'd never been more embarrassed in her life than in that moment. He kissed her and what had she done? She'd turned into Super Ho and practically swallowed his tongue and rubbed against him.

She still couldn't believe it happened and if there was any doubt in her mind then the way her nipples tightened and tingled every time she thought of him was proof enough. It didn't help that she couldn't stop thinking about him and what almost happened. It didn't matter that she'd always been attracted to him. He was her best friend and she didn't want to lose that.

When he kissed her she should have put a stop to it and pulled away and laughed it off like she did when they were fourteen. But had she done that? Oh no, not her. She practically swallowed his tongue and was seconds away from begging him to screw her on the kitchen table before Nathan thankfully came by.

Now they weren't talking. They'd never gone a day without talking, but not one word from him over the past three days. Then again she wasn't exactly reaching out and trying to connect with him either. For the past of couple of days she'd been screening all her calls and avoiding all his usual haunts. If Nathan and Caitlyn hadn't showed up and bugged the hell out of her until she gave in and let them drag her here to the Fireman's Muster she'd still be avoiding him.

"You're not still mad at him, are you?" Nathan asked, thankfully drawing her attention back to him before Eric saw that she was watching him. The last thing she needed was for Eric to think that she thought that kiss meant something when it clearly didn't.

Not at all.

She barely even thought about it or how good it felt to be in his arms. It was the furthest thing from her mind. Of course she also wasn't curious about what would have happened if Nathan hadn't showed up or wondered if it would have been good. She didn't, because that would be counterproductive when she was trying to forget it ever happened and figure out a way to act like it never happened.

"Everything's fine, Nathan," she said with a shrug.

"Really? Is that why he won't even look this way and you haven't gone over there to kick his ass for getting you kicked out of the competition?" he asked, throwing his arm around her shoulders and gave her a gentle pull until she was walking with him towards the food vendors.

"It's just a simple misunderstanding. It's nothing," she explained as they stepped in line, hoping he'd let it go. Thankfully by some miracle he did.

"I'm starving. What are you buying me?" he demanded as he gestured towards the two man team working the grills.

"Nothing. You kidnapped me. That means you feed me."

"I guess I'm not up to date on my kidnapping etiquette."

"Guess not," she said, feeling her lips twitch in amusement. "You'll have to work on that."

"I guess so."

"Hey, Joe!" a familiar voice suddenly yelled.

She looked past Nathan to see Johnny, an EMT from the 505, waving to get her attention. "We need a patient. You interested?"

Was she? Yes, yes she was. The fact that she'd be helping the competition beat Eric didn't hurt. She was still pretty pissed about being kicked out of the Muster and after all this weirdness was behind them she fully planned on kicking his ass for screwing her over like this.

"I'll take a rain check on that double rack of ribs," she said, pulling away from Nathan to go help kick Eric's ass.

"Wait. When did I promise to buy you a double rack?" Nathan asked, sounding adorably confused.

"About ten seconds before you promised to buy me a double fudge brownie sundae," she said, throwing him a wink.

"Gold digger!"

* * * *

"What the hell is she doing?" Dave asked as he gestured behind him.

Eric looked back and had to bite back a curse or two as he watched Johnny Powers sweep Joe off her feet and place her on his stretcher. His eyes narrowed to slits when the bastard ran his fingers through her hair as he moved it out of her face.

What the hell was she doing?

Was she really that pissed at him that she was willing to help his competition? Or was it something else, he wondered. Everyone knew that Johnny had the hots for Joe. Although whenever anyone told her that she'd just laugh it off. She thought Johnny was just a buddy and being friendly. She was so fucking naive sometimes.

"That reminds me. We're going to need a patient too. Should I go get my sister?" Dave asked, moving to go do just that.

"Nah, I got it covered," he said, tossing the straps back on the stretcher.

He ran his fingers through his hair, questioning his motives even as he weaved his way through the other teams getting their equipment together.

"Maybe after this we can go get a drink," Johnny asked, sounding eager.

Joe opened her mouth, probably to say yes since the damn woman no doubt thought it was just the guys hanging out together. He really had no idea why the hell she couldn't figure out that she was pretty much the only one that saw her as one of the guys. All the other guys as far as he knew looked her at her as a hot piece of ass and she was too damn oblivious to see that, which was pretty fucked up since she wasn't like this with guys from outside of work.

"She's busy," he said, cutting her off before she could inadvertently lead the poor bastard on as he shoved past Johnny and scooped her up. He ignored her sputtered protests as he carried her back towards his ambulance.

"Where the hell are you going with my patient?" Johnny called after them.

"She's mine, dipshit," he yelled over his shoulder, wishing like hell that he didn't like the sound of that.

He dumped her ass on his stretcher and before she could make a run for it he clipped her in. Of course she moved to unclip the safety restraints, but he simply readjusted them so that the belt at her waist covered her forearms and tightened it so that she couldn't move. He did the same with her legs of course.

"Comfy?" he asked brightly as she glared up at him with all sorts of promises of pain and misery in his future. As long as she didn't go for his balls she could have her little revenge.

"What is wrong with you?" she demanded. "Let me go!"

"Sorry, can't," he said with a bored shrug. "The patients are expected to be on the stretcher at the start of the competition."

"I'm not your patient!" she snapped.

"Of course you are," he said, leaning against the open back door of the ambulance, forcing her to tilt her head back to glare at him.

"No, I'm not," she said, struggling against the restraints.

"If you're not my patient then what are you doing on my stretcher?" he demanded, cocking a brow.

"Because you're an ass?" she suggested, struggling and getting her left arm free.

"Is everything okay?" Dave asked as he walked towards them, carrying a couple of bottles of water.

"No!" Joe of course said, making Dave frown and look a little uncomfortable.

"Ignore her. It's just her time of the month," Eric explained with a careless shrug.

"*You betraying bastard*!" Joe hissed out and he knew the second that the competition ended that she was going for that nut shot, which of course meant that he was going to have to leave her strapped to a backboard to protect his boys.

* * * *

"Flip the backboard!" the announcer ordered over the bullhorn.

Joe took a deep breath, but it didn't quite prepare her for being turned over until she was facing the ground. She wished she could turn her head to glare at the bastard but thanks to the neck collar, tape and the fact that she was secured from head to toe on a long hard plastic backboard she couldn't move an inch.

As one of the refs checked each restraint she was forced to ground her teeth as she seethed with anger. She couldn't believe the nerve. First he screws her over at work and then he screws with her head and body and then ignores her only to piss her off by manhandling her. She couldn't wait for this damn contest to end. The second, the very second he let her out, she was going to beat the shit out of him and then tell him off.

When she was flipped back over and placed on a stretcher, anticipation coursed through her veins. He thought she was weak? She'd show him. She'd also show him that he couldn't push her around or screw with her head. He might be her best friend, but that didn't mean that she had to put up with archaic bullshit.

He would learn......oh, would he learn........

"What the hell are you doing?" she demanded when she suddenly found herself being placed in the back of the ambulance.

"Enjoy the ride," Eric said before the backdoors slammed shut and the roar of the ambulance vibrated all around her.

He wouldn't dare.........

He did.

Chapter 17

"Where's Joe?" Nathan asked as he pulled out a chair and sat down while scanning the bar.

"She's out enjoying a joy ride," Eric said, feeling his lips twitch. He idly wondered how she was enjoying her scenic drive down Old Man Mason's road, a ten mile stretch of country road that hadn't seen so much as a tar patch job in twenty years. It was one of those obscure roads that everyone forgot about, except for the kids who liked to race on the potholed, cracked mess for a challenge.

Nathan threw him a curious look, but shrugged it off as his continued to look around the bar.

"Where's Caitlyn?" Eric asked, looking around the bar for the cute little brunette.

"We broke up."

He really shouldn't be surprised by this point, but he really was. He'd only met the woman a handful of times, but she seemed sweet and perfect for his brother. Then again he hadn't met any of Nathan's girlfriends that he didn't think was perfect for him.

"Why?" he asked, taking a sip of his beer while his brother continued to scan the bar.

"It was just time," he said with a shrug, never ceasing in his perusal of the busy bar.

"You're a fucking idiot." Had he said that out loud? Based on his brother's sudden glare he would have to go with a yes on that one.

"What?" Nathan demanded, turning his attention on him.

He could apologize, but this bullshit had gone on for far too long.

"You heard me. You're a fucking idiot. You had a great girl, another great girl I might add who from what I could see adored you and was perfect for you and what do you do? You toss her aside on a whim. What the hell is your problem?"

"Stay out of it," Nathan bit out tightly.

"Sorry. Not going to happen. I want to know what the hell your problem is. You keep meeting these great women that seem to make you happy, but for some fucked up reason you keep letting them go. I don't understand what the hell your problem is."

"Look who's talking," Nathan spat out.

"What the hell are you talking about?" Eric demanded.

"Joe," Nathan said, making Eric turn quickly in his seat to look for her. "Yeah, that's what I thought," Nathan said coldly, drawing his attention, but not before he scanned the bar once again for her.

"What are you talking about?" he asked distractedly as he turned to see if she was standing next to the jukebox since that's the first thing she always did before ordering a beer was to see if there were any new songs added to the playlist.

"That you have a lot of balls to talk."

"Meaning?" Eric asked, taking a sip of his beer as he kept his eyes leveled on his brother, not entirely sure he liked where this was going.

"You think I don't know?" Nathan demanded with a harsh laugh. "Everyone fucking knows."

"Then maybe you should clue me in," he said, placing his beer down on the small table.

"You're in love with Joe," Nathan said with a smug smile that had Eric chuckling.

"That's bullshit and you know it," Eric said, taking another sip of beer with a casualness that he didn't feel.

"Is that why you watch her like a hawk and warn off any man dumb enough to get within touching distance of her?"

"I protect her, the same as you," Eric said, slamming his beer down on the small table hard enough to make the small wooden bowl filled with empty peanut shells bounce.

Nathan snorted at that. "I protect her because she's my sister. You protect her because you don't want anyone else touching her."

"You're full of shit and you know it," Eric said, hating like hell that they were even talking about this. It was something he didn't want to think about never mind discuss.

For years he'd done his damndest to ignore the way Joe made him feel, like he would go out of his mind if he didn't touch her and now that he had it was a constant battle not to go after her and pull her right back into his arms. She was his best friend, the only person he could go to for absolutely anything or nothing. He loved being with her and just talking to her over the phone eased his soul and that's exactly why he shouldn't be feeling this way.

If they ever took it to the next step he knew it wouldn't be long before it ended badly. They both sucked at relationships. None of his previous girlfriends could hold his attention longer than it took to get them into bed and that usually didn't take long at all. After sex being with them felt like a chore, one he despised.

The same could be said for Joe. None of the guys that she dated could hold her attention for very long. For the most part they seemed to irritate the living hell out of her. She didn't do long term relationships, a month for her was too much. Hell, two weeks was too long for him and that's exactly why he knew this would never work.

She was forbidden fruit and the moment he had her he knew he'd tire of her too. Then they'd be left with an awkward situation that even their relationship wouldn't be able to recover from. Then what? Did he continue with her, pretending that he still wanted her because of their friendship? For her he would try, but he knew he'd come to resent their relationship and push her away like he'd done with so many women before her.

Then what? If they managed to go back to being friends there would always be an awkwardness between them. They might continue being friends, but their relationship would never be what it once was and he'd miss that. He'd miss their easy conversations, her companionship, her smiles, the way she busted his balls, but most of all he'd miss her. She might be the woman that he lusted after twenty-four seven, but she was also his best friend, his world and no amount of sex was worth risking that.

"So, it wouldn't bother you if she was in the arms of another man right now?" Nathan asked, sounding amused.

Yes. "No," he gritted out.

"Good," Nathan said, nodding. "Then it probably shouldn't bother you that Dave and Johnny have their hands all over her right now."

"What?" The word practically exploded from his mouth as he surged to his feet, sending his chair flying back in the process. He turned around ready to kill someone only to come to an abrupt halt when his eyes landed on the trio near the door. He felt his brows clear his hairline and he doubted that he was the only one at the moment.

"Just let me go!" Joe demanded as she fought against the two large men struggling to hold her back. "I promise I'll only kill him a little bit!"

He felt his lips twitch as he watched as Joe managed to drag the men a few feet towards him.

"You said that you only wanted a drink!" Johnny said accusingly as he doubled his efforts to pull the little spitfire back.

"I do. Killing makes me thirsty," she explained tightly as her eyes landed on him and narrowed dangerously.

Any other man would probably realize that he was in deep shit and haul his ass out the back door, but that wasn't his style. This was the reason why he was going to make damn sure that he never touched her again. He loved her, loved the way she drove him crazy and he *really* loved pissing her off.

"How was the ride, Joe?" he asked, walking over to her and enjoying the way she tried to lunge at him.

"It was great. Nothing like a smooth ride through the country. Why don't you come closer so that I can thank you properly?" she suggested sweetly even as she stomped on Dave's foot, forcing the poor bastard to let her go.

She didn't waste any time in reaching up and going for Johnny's nipple. The look on the poor besotted bastard's face was priceless. He took one look at the hand nearing his nipple and practically dove away from her, leaving Eric with absolutely no doubt that she'd done it before. Probably as soon as she got loose from the backboard.

Joe wasted no time in going for him and probably would have gone for his throat if Nathan hadn't suddenly appeared between them and caught her around the waist with a bored sigh and threw her over his shoulder, wrecking all of Eric's fun.

"Let me go, Nathan!" Joe demanded, grabbing the back of Nathan's pants to push herself up so that she could scowl his way.

"Are you going to behave if I do?"

"Yes!" she lied and everyone knew it. She was eager to kick his ass and as much as he'd enjoy a good laugh it probably was for the best if he didn't have a reason to put his hands on her right now.

"Will it make you feel better if I take you out to dinner?" Nathan offered even as he headed for the door.

Joe glared at him for a moment as she thought it over. "Can I have dessert?"

"When the hell did you turn into such a little gold digger?" Nathan demanded, earning a rather cute little eye roll from Joe.

"Don't turn your back on her, Nathan!" he called after them, "or she'll add an appetizer!"

"Betraying bastard!"

* * * *

"Are you still mad at me?" he asked as he stepped into the bunkroom and tossed his sleeping bag and backpack on the empty bunk.

She didn't look at him while she jammed the pillow into the pillowcase with more force than he thought was necessary.

"Why would I be mad at you?" she asked mockingly.

He could easily think of five things for her to be pissed at him for. There was getting her pulled out of the Muster competition, getting her ass on light duty, their little fight last week, sending her on a bumpy little joy ride, but the thing that probably pissed her off the most was when he convinced Bill not to allow Joe to switch to a different shift. As long as she was safe, and he made damn sure that she was, he really didn't care if she was pissed at him.

In fact it would probably be for the best if she didn't talk to him for a week or two. That should be more than enough time for them to forget their moment of stupidity and get over it. There was no doubt in his mind that in a month or two they'd be laughing their asses off about what almost happened. That moment couldn't come fast enough for him.

They hadn't spent any time together or spoken in a week and he missed her. He felt so damn lost without her. Being without her was hell and he'd do whatever it took to get them back to where they needed to be, where he needed them to be. He needed to talk to her, touch her and hold her.

For the past week he hadn't been allowed to do any of those things. This past week had been the first time since they were kids that they'd ever really spent any time apart and he'd hated it. Every day the ache in his chest intensified until he didn't think he'd survive another moment without her.

He'd tried calling her, but he only got her voicemail. The few times he swung by to see her hadn't gone well either. After the third time she slammed the door shut in his face he'd gotten a little desperate and bought one of those milkshakes that she was addicted to only to have the little brat snatch it out of his hand before slamming the door shut in his face.

Obviously she needed time and he'd give it to her if it meant that things would go back to the way things used to be. Of course the fact that she couldn't get away from him and was stuck working with him for at least forty hours a week probably had something to do with his calm acceptance of the cold shoulder she was giving him, but whatever. He got to spend time with her and that's all that mattered.

She tossed her bag on the freshly made bed, grabbed a book and threw him a killing glare as she walked past him. He should probably give her some space, he mused, but then again she'd had a week without him. He followed after her, knowing that she'd probably kick his ass, but what the hell, it would be worth it just to see her smile.

Chapter 18

"Let me up," she whispered tightly as she struggled to get up, but the big jerk simply tightened his arm around her waist and held her on his lap.

"Hold you tighter?" he asked, sounding put out. "Fine. I suppose I could do that."

Not laughing was one of the hardest things she'd done in a while, but somehow she managed it. She was mad at him, pissed actually and she couldn't believe that he had the nerve to act like nothing was wrong, but this was Eric and they both knew that she couldn't stay mad at him for long no matter how hard she tried.

After what the jerk did she really should stay good and mad at him for a long time, but she just couldn't. She hated the fact that she'd pretty much forgiven him. He cared about her even if he was going about it in a dumb ass way. Instead of talking to her he'd gone the high handed route, but that was Eric and he wasn't going to change and to be honest she didn't want him to.

That didn't mean he got to control her life. He didn't. He may think that he had a say in her life, but he didn't. As much as she appreciated him, Nathan and Alice, she was still very much on her own. She loved them more than anything, but she wasn't their responsibility and sure as hell didn't want them to see her as the burden they got stuck with.

Eric might want to take care of her, but she didn't want to be his responsibility. That was the reason why they'd never moved in together even when they were first starting out in life and sharing an apartment would have made sense. It was the same reason why she worked two mind numbingly boring jobs to pay for EMT training even though Alice and Nathan both offered to pay for it and why she refused to let anyone co-sign with her when she bought her house even though she probably would have gotten a better mortgage if Alice had signed.

Her mother might have been comfortable with leaving everyone else to take care of her responsibility, but she never would be. She liked taking care of herself. She loved knowing that she would never have to depend on another person again for anything as long as she lived.

It was because she could take care of herself that she would never have to worry about coming home only to find her things thrown out because someone didn't pay the bills. She would never have to worry about going hungry or being cold in the winter. She paid her bills, bought her food, had no debt besides her mortgage and had money in the bank for an emergency and paramedic school and last week that had been more than enough to allow her to sleep at night.

Now she was worried. She wasn't sure if it was because of the close call she had or what Eric said, but he had a valid point. Not that she would ever tell him. That would only encourage him and his bossy ways, but she now realized that she needed a backup in case something ever happened that prevented her from working as an EMT.

Her savings were decent and could probably hold her over for eight months, but that wasn't good enough. She never wanted to struggle to pay the bills and she sure as hell didn't want to be put in the situation where she had to take a handout, especially from Alice, Nathan, or Eric, her family. If it ever came to that she would split town, because she just couldn't become someone's charity case.

Over the past couple of days she'd done a lot of thinking and decided that she'd use some of her savings to get more training. She was going to keep her focus on emergency medical services, but she was going to make sure that if anything ever prevented her from working on the ambulance then she'd have a career to fall back on.

"I wasn't done reading that page," Eric grumbled.

"You can read it after I'm done," she explained even as she turned the page back so the big baby could read it.

He snorted. "I don't read romance novels."

She snuggled closer to him, laying her head back on his shoulder so that he could see the book. "Um, you're reading a romance novel now."

"No, I'm not."

"Then what do you call it?"

"Killing time," he said with a shrug.

"Uh huh, you could just as easily kill time by watching the game with the guys," she said, nodding towards the flat screen that had everyone else's attention.

"Why would I do that when we're getting to the sex scene? Would you turn the page already?" he demanded impatiently.

"Sex?" one of the guys repeated and just like that she had ten guys standing behind her as they shoved each other out of the way to get a better look.

This was why she never got to read during her downtime, she thought as she got to her feet, trying not laugh as the guys groaned in disapproval. She rolled her eyes when she caught them pouting. "Here," she said, sighing as she tossed the book to Jim, a firefighter in his thirties. "Just toss it on my bunk when you're done."

"Why the hell did you do that? We were just getting to the good part!" Eric bitched, moving to grab the book back only to find the men gathered tightly around the book.

"Are you coming or not?" she asked, not bothering to look back as she made her way to the ambulance bay.

"Where are we going?" Eric asked as he quickly caught up with her.

"You're buying me breakfast," she informed him.

"No, I'm not," he said, opening the garage door for her.

She turned to glare up at him. "I don't know how the two of you got so damn cheap, but you are buying me breakfast and that's final."

"Yeah, good luck with that, Sweetheart," Eric said, throwing his arm over her shoulders and she couldn't help but let out a little sigh of relief. Whatever insanity had taken over last week was clearly over. They didn't talk about it, but then again they really didn't need to.

They'd been friends for over twenty years and at this point some things didn't need to be said. That little incident in her kitchen had been a mistake, one that made her ache, but a mistake nonetheless and they both rather put it behind them and forget about it. It was just one of those things that was better left alone.

* * * *

"Thanks for dinner," Joe said, smiling contently as she nibbled on a ketchup drenched fry.

"You're not welcome," he grumbled, wondering how the hell she got him to pay for breakfast, lunch, an ice cream, and dinner.

Oh, that's right, he thought dryly, she stole his wallet and refused to give it back. Since he caught the little gold digger eying the Hungry Man's Breakfast menu at Rick's Dinner earlier when they grabbed lunch and heard her mentioning something about trying the supreme breakfast tomorrow morning he knew he was going to have to steal his wallet back while she slept.

Normally he wouldn't mind buying her whatever she needed. Of course he busted her chops, but this was his Joe and he made damn sure that she was taken care of, but today everything she did was pissing him right the hell off.

She'd obviously forgiven him since she was talking to him, smiling and even joking around like nothing happened and that had him seeing red. Any other woman would have brought up that disaster in the kitchen at least a hundred times by now. At the very least she should have wanted to ask how he felt about it, but had she?

Hell no, not Joe. She acted like it was over and done with. Did she really want to pretend that she hadn't sucked on his tongue and that he hadn't ground the hardest damn erection he'd ever had against her? Well, he didn't.

He knew he was being an idiot, but he couldn't help it. His pride was taking a beating on this one. Was he really that forgettable? The thought really pissed him off, well, pissed him off more. It irritated the hell out of him that the woman he'd been drooling after for years thought he was that forgettable. Every time she came near him he had to curl his hands into fists to stop from grabbing her and showing her how unforgettable he really was.

"I think we should talk about what happened," he said before he realized what the hell he was doing, but once the words were out of his mouth he decided that they were damn well going to have this little talk.

She shrugged it off as she finished off her last fry. "The nurse was an idiot," she simply said, referring to an earlier call they had where a nurse decided to light up a cigarette next to their patient while they were stuck outside of a nursing home waiting to be buzzed in. They'd both gotten into it with the nurse and were expecting a call from Bill, but he wasn't worried.

"That's not what I was talking about. I think we should talk about what happened last week," he explained and when she frowned in adorable confusion he added, "in your kitchen."

"Well, I gave that some thought," she said, collecting their trash and opened the ambulance door and walked off, leaving him frustrated. Any other woman and he would have thought that she was just trying to create a little drama by waiting to finish that thought, but Joe liked the ambulance tidied up immediately after a meal so that the empty containers didn't stink up the ambulance.

"And?" he prompted when she climbed back into the ambulance and pulled her hair back into a lazy ponytail.

"And I made a few calls and I'm going up to New Hampshire Friday for three days of training through one of the schools to get a few certifications," she explained.

Since that wasn't what he was talking about and the last goddamn thing on his mind at the moment it took him a few minutes to figure out what the hell she just said.

"You're going for certification?" She nodded. "For what?"

"Dispatch and teaching First Aid and CPR."

He frowned, surprised that she'd listened to him and was actually going with it. Well, that had been easy. Maybe a little too easy, he realized as he narrowed his eyes on her.

"Are you taking a job in dispatch?" he asked, already deciding that would probably be the perfect job for and most importantly it would get her the hell out of a truck where she didn't belong.

The stubborn woman shook her head. "No, I want the certification. I talked to Bill and after I go through on the job training they're going to hire me for dispatch as per diem to cover shifts and keep my skills up."

"Then you plan on teaching First Aid and CPR fulltime?" he asked, wondering how the hell she expected to make enough money to support herself doing that, but if that's what she wanted he'd make damn sure that it happened.

Again she shook her head. "No, I talked to Bill and he said after I passed he'd give me the part time job if I wanted it. I think I'm going to take him up on it."

"Wait," he said, trying to clear his head. "Then what the hell are you planning to do for a living?"

She looked over and frowned. "What I'm doing now."

He stared at her for a moment, wondering if she was kidding. Judging by the way she met his glare head on he figured that she was dead serious. That was a problem for him, because he needed her the hell off the truck as soon as possible.

"Why the hell would you keep working on the truck when dispatchers get paid more?" he demanded, trying to keep his tone even.

"Because I love what I do," she said with a shrug. "But you had a good point the other day so I decided to look into a few things and this way I'll have something to fall back on."

She was kidding. She had to be.

"You don't need something to fall back on, Joe, because I would always take care of you!" he snapped, feeling his patience fray. "What you need to do is find a safer job so that I don't have to worry about you every fucking minute of the day!"

"We've been over this, Eric. That's not your job," she said tightly as she buckled her seatbelt with clipped motions.

"The hell it isn't," he said, snatching the microphone, realizing they needed to put a little distance between them or they were likely going to kill each other, or at the very least he was going to spank some sense into her ass.

"Dispatch, this is Echo seventeen, are we clear to return to base?" he asked, ignoring the glare Joe was sending his way.

"*Echo seventeen, you're clear*," dispatch answered.

He threw the ambulance into drive and headed back to base. The entire time neither spoke or so much as looked at the other. By the time they reached the fire house his chest was tight and he felt sick.

How the hell did they get back to this point? He didn't want her mad at him. He wanted her safe and happy and he kept pissing her off, but then again she was pissing him right the hell off so it was okay.

"Asshole," she muttered as she climbed out of the ambulance and slammed the door shut before she stormed inside, leaving him sitting there feeling like the biggest asshole on earth and wonder why the hell it hurt so damn much when she was unhappy?

Chapter 19

"Jerk," she muttered as she pulled her boots off and threw them at the cement wall. It made her feel marginally better, but not by much. Hunting down Eric so that she could put him in a headlock would make her feel a hell of a lot better, she decided even as she pulled off her uniform shirt, leaving her in a tight baby blue tank top.

She climbed into bed only to climb back out seconds later when she decided it was too damn hot and she was too damn aggravated to try and sleep in her pants. Tonight she just wanted to sleep through the rest of her shift, go home and take her anger out on cleaning her attic.

Twenty seconds after the light was shut off and she was curled up in bed and she felt like crying. She hated fighting with Eric, absolutely hated it. There was a reason why she was so quick to forgive him, because staying mad at him hurt like hell.

She still remembered the time they were ten and she'd worked all day cleaning out Mrs. Pembroke's garage. At the end of the day she was dirty, tired, sweaty and five dollars richer. Excited that she finally had enough money for a new bike, well new to her anyway, she ran all the way home.

Of course she hid her money in her shoe before she walked into the apartment she'd shared with her mother and her mother's boyfriend of that week. After double checking that the coast was clear she dug the rest of her money out of an empty Comet can she'd cut the bottom off and had hidden among the cleaning supplies, knowing it was the last place her mother would ever think to look.

Once she had all of her money she raced out of the house and ran all the way to the church's thrift shop where she'd seen a used pink bike with a slight touch of rust early that morning. When she spotted the bike still outside the thrift store she ran inside and bought it without a second's hesitation.

She'd been so excited to have her own bike. She didn't care that the tires were flat and the chain was rusted, the bike was hers. After deciding that Eric and Nathan just had to see her bike she pushed it to their house, placed the bike against the garage and ran inside the house. She didn't stop searching until she found one of them. Without a word she dragged Nathan away from his video game and back outside only to come to an abrupt halt when she didn't see her bike.

The horrible sound of metal being bent drew her attention to the garbage truck in front of the house and Eric walking towards them. Her eyes darted from Eric to the truck, back to Eric before she launched herself at him. Ten minutes later Alice had them each by the ear and demanded to know what happened. When she told her what Eric did his expression became pained.

Even at ten he thought it was his job to take care of her and it just about killed him to know that he'd done something to hurt her. After he explained that he thought it was garbage his father had left against the garage for him to bring to the curb she forgave him. She was still upset about the bike, but she just couldn't stay mad him, knowing how upset he was over the whole thing.

Of course Eric made it up to her. Three months later he banged on her apartment door, interrupting her peanut butter sandwich dinner to drag her downstairs to show her the new bike he'd bought her. He'd saved up his allowance, done extra chores around the house and even worked for the neighbors to save up the money to buy her a bike. It had been the sweetest and most thoughtful thing anyone ever did for her.

It was things like that that made it so damn hard to be mad at him. He screwed up, a lot, but he always made it up to her. She knew he never meant to hurt her even when he was being a pigheaded jerk like now. He wanted her safe and she was.

She was careful at work, followed her training and never took stupid chances, but that incident more than a week ago made him nervous and now after twelve years on the job together he was letting his fear cause problems in their relationship. They worked great together and she knew that all he needed was a little time before he realized that. Until then she'd have to resign herself with him being an asshole.

When the door opened she tensed, waiting for the fight to continue. She didn't want to fight with him. She hated fighting with him. All she wanted to do was go back to the way things were before he said those things that hurt her and before he kissed her, robbing her of her sanity and made her wonder about things that she had no business even thinking about.

"Joe?" he said softly.

Instead of answering him she closed her eyes and pretended to be asleep. It was cowardly, she knew that, but she wasn't sure how much more she could take. She was glad that he didn't insist on coming with her this week like he normally would have done. They both needed some time apart to think about a few things. If things didn't change by the time she got back, meaning they weren't able to go back to the way things were between them before they'd both messed up then she was going to ask for a transfer to another station.

She laid there and listened as he pulled his boots off. She thought about asking him to leave so that she could get some sleep and avoid another argument, but instead she just laid there soaking up his presence. When she felt the bed dip and he curled his body around her seconds later, she felt like crying. She hated fighting with him, hated not being able to go to him with her problems, and hated feeling like a part of her was dying.

"I am so sorry, Joe," he whispered, gently pushing her hair away from her face and neck. "I know I keep fucking up," he said, pressing a kiss to her neck, "and that by all rights you should bitch slap me, but I can't stand the idea of you getting hurt."

His hand found its way to her panty clad hip and gave her a gentle squeeze. "It kills me to think of what could have happened that night, Joe," he explained softly as he pressed another kiss to her neck. "Do you have any idea how lost I would be without you?"

"You're my entire world, Joe," he said, pressing another kiss to her neck, this time lingering. "I don't know what I'd do without," he said against her skin.

Nibbling her lip, she turned onto her back and reached up with her right hand to cup his jaw, loving the way the stubble felt against her hand. "And what the hell do you think I'd do without you?" she demanded.

His large warm hand landed on her stomach, gently caressing her skin. "Everything would be okay. Nathan would watch out for you and take care of you, Joe," he said soothingly as he pressed a warm kiss to her forehead.

"I don't need anyone to look out for me!" she snapped, sick of this constant babying. When exactly did she become a weak needy woman in his eyes? It was really insulting. She was anything but weak and he damn well knew it.

He sighed heavily even as his hand continued to caress her stomach through her thin shirt. "Yes, you do."

"What the hell is it going to take for you to realize that I can take care of myself?" she demanded, trying not to sound hurt, but probably failed miserably. She didn't want to appear weak and needy in his eyes. She wanted.......

Hell, she didn't even know what she wanted, but she knew she didn't want that. She didn't want him hanging around because he thought that she needed a keeper.

"If I thought having a boyfriend in my life would get you to back off I'd run out and get one," she said, not noticing the way his hand suddenly stilled on her stomach, "but we both know that wouldn't help since you become a complete jerk whenever I'm dating someone."

"What are you talking about?" he asked tightly and she wished she could see his expression. This little news flash really couldn't be a shock. Everyone knew that when she dated someone Eric developed a raging case of PMS.

"What am I talking about? Are you serious?" she asked, feeling a little muscle begin to tick in his jaw when he nodded firmly.

"How many of my ex-boyfriends have you beaten up?" she asked, arching an eyebrow, almost daring him to lie about it.

"I have no idea what you're talking about," he grumbled, shifting to move away from her, but she wasn't having that. She turned into him, pressing her hands to his bare chest and threw a leg over his hip as she moved up, giving him no choice but to lie on his back as she straddled his waist.

She really couldn't help the smug little smile that played at her lips since she'd just proved that she was more than physically capable of taking care of herself. He would just have to suck it-

"Hey!" she cried out in surprise as she suddenly found herself pushed onto her back with him situated between her legs and her arms held down firmly by her head.

After a brief struggle that didn't improve her situation she gave up with a sigh. "Just know that I could kick your ass at any moment, Eric. You're lucky I'm tired."

His amused chuckle was kind of insulting even if she did find it soothing. "I know. I'm counting my blessings right now," he said, pressing a kiss to the tip of her nose as he settled himself more comfortably between her legs.

"Well?" she demanded, curious to see if he'd admit to being an overbearing jerk when she dated.

"Well, what?"

"You're not going to admit that you don't trust me to take care of myself and that you sure as hell don't trust any of the men I bring into my life," she said, wondering if he was going to play it off like he usually did when she called him on it.

"You date assholes and losers," he said, shocking her. Not that she didn't realize that her taste in men sucked, but he usually just shrugged it off like it was nothing. He'd never acted like he didn't like the guys she dated even when she knew for a fact that he didn't like them. He always treated her boyfriends like they were his long lost friends, but as soon as it was over he gave her ex the cold shoulder. She also knew that he'd given more than one of them a reason or two to visit the ER.

"Then why the hell do you act like you like them?"

"It makes it easier to keep an eye on you," he explained as he pressed a quick kiss to her forehead. "It's the same reason why you pretend to like the annoying women I date, Joe. You don't want to be pushed off to the side," he said softly as he entwined their fingers together.

"They really are annoying," she agreed on a sigh.

"I want you safe, Joe."

"I am safe," she said, biting back a groan. What the hell was it going to take for him to see that?

"I hate being away from you and I know if I keep pushing this that you're going to pull away from me so for now I'm going to drop it, but I'm really hoping that you discover that you like dispatching more than working on the truck," he said, pressing a gentle kiss to her lips that shocked her, but what shocked her even more was her reaction to the simple chaste kiss.

When he moved away from her, cursing softly, she leaned up and brushed her lips against his, unable to help herself. She knew that she shouldn't be doing this, but she couldn't help herself. Years of holding back, pretending that she didn't want him, need him, shattered with that first kiss last week and any hope of holding back what she felt for this man was gone.

This was probably going to wreck their relationship, but at the moment she didn't care. She needed to hold him, to touch him, and be with him more than she needed her next breath.

It wasn't fair that the one man she craved was the one she shouldn't be touching. He was her best friend, the person she counted on, needed, and loved more than anyone on this earth and she was going to lose him over this.

His mouth crashed down on hers, forcing her head back onto the pillow as he devoured her mouth. When his tongue slid into her mouth and tangled with hers she moaned. He released her hands as he kneeled between her legs, putting space between their chests. She cupped the back of his neck to keep his mouth right where she wanted it, afraid that he was going to put a stop to this madness.

He reached between them and grabbed the hem of her shirt and yanked it up hard along with her sports bra until both of her breasts were bared. She let out a groan of pleasure when he cupped one of her breasts and gave it a gentle squeeze. When he ground his erection against her, she suckled his tongue.

She wrapped her arms around him, loving the combination of warm skin and solid muscle. Her hands slid down his back and beneath the waist of his pants and onto smooth muscle that flexed erotically with each shallow thrust.

"We shouldn't be doing this," Eric said, panting as he moved his mouth to her neck the same time he reached between them to pull her damp panties to the side. He brushed his fingers teasingly over her slit.

"Yes, we should," she said breathlessly as he slid a finger deep inside of her.

"Yeah, we should," he said tightly the next second as he struggled to undo his belt. When he couldn't get the belt off with one hand he unzipped his pants. The sound of his zipper being pulled opened was one of the most erotic sounds she'd ever heard.

"We can't let this wreck what we have," he said, sounding desperate as he removed his finger and replaced it with the large blunt head of his erection.

"It changes nothing," she said, sliding her hands up his back to fist them in his hair and pull his mouth back to hers.

He slammed into her.

She squeezed her eyes shut as she sucked in a sharp breath. Never in her life had she ever felt this full. She'd known that he was large, but this was incredible. He stretched her almost to the point of pain, but she wanted more.

As he moved she cupped the back of her knees and pulled her legs up and to the sides, opening herself up more for him. This time when he slid back inside of her he was buried to the root. He let out a growl of appreciation as he slowly swirled his hips in a way that had her whimpering and pleading against his mouth.

"Shhhh," he said quietly against her lips, reminding her that they were not alone. They were surrounded by other bunkrooms and the break room was right down the hall.

He pulled away to kiss his way to her ear. "Do you like that, Joe?" he asked, deepening his movements.

Beyond words now, she nodded as she licked her lips and moved her hips against his, desperate for more. If they got a call right now she was pretty sure she would die.

"You have no idea how many times I've imagined doing this to you," he whispered against her ear, his warm breath fanning her sensitive skin and sending a shiver through her body that caused her nipples to tighten impossibly further.

"Have you ever thought about me fucking you, Joe?"

"Yes!" she hissed quietly, not wanting to draw attention to what they were doing. She had thought about him, from her first time to the last time. It was Eric's face she pictured when she made love to a man. He made her feel safe and loved and she needed that.

"If there wasn't a very real possibility that we'd be interrupted I'd show you all those things I've imagined doing to you over the years," he promised hotly before returning to her mouth.

She wrapped her arms around him as he quickened his thrusts, but when the bed made the telltale sounds that would give them away he slowed his pace once again. The kiss on the other hand was out of control. He didn't hold back and neither did she. She couldn't get enough of him. She loved the way he teased and dueled with her tongue.

It wasn't long before he was swallowing her screams and biting back his own. She felt him harden impossibly further before she felt him come inside of her. It was the first time she'd ever felt a man come inside of her and she couldn't believe how good it felt. She was even more surprised when it set her off into another orgasm.

"Shit," Eric groaned as he continued to thrust inside of her until she stopped squeezing him and her legs dropped back onto the bed while they both desperately tried to catch their breath.

"What the hell are we going to do now?" Eric muttered against the nape of her neck. She wrapped her arms around his sweat slicked back, wishing she had the answer.

Chapter 20

He'd never been more relieved to receive a call from dispatch in the middle of the night as he was right then.

They'd fucked up.

Why after all these years did he finally give into his body's demands and taken her? He knew the trouble he was courting by doing it. She was his best friend, the only woman besides his mother that he ever loved and he'd just fucked up big time.

Every time he toyed with the idea of fucking her he always thought that he'd work her out of his system. It was just leftover hormones from when he was a kid and first noticed her, he'd always told himself, but he'd been wrong. If anything having her just made it worse.

He wanted her, now, tomorrow and always. The way his body felt let him know it was going to be a long time before he tired of her. That was a problem because he didn't know if could give her up. He needed her in his life and as great as the sex was, and there was no question in his mind that it was the best sex he'd ever had, he'd gladly give up the chance to touch her again if it meant that she wouldn't leave him.

His chest tightened just thinking about it. He needed her in his life, always. Their friendship came first and he wasn't sure if they'd survive taking the next step, but thankfully dispatch was giving them a chance to step back and focus on something else for the moment. It also gave him a chance to cool down and figure out if he could do this.

What if he fucked up and hurt her? He'd never cheat on her, hit her or say an unkind word to her, but he did have the ability to piss her right the hell off. With sex involved that might complicate things and she would no longer feel that she was able to come to him for everything. He sure as hell didn't want her confiding in some other guy.

"MVA," Joe said as she hung the phone back up. She ripped the piece of paper she wrote the details of the call on off her small notebook and went to stuff it in her pants pocket only to remember that she wasn't wearing pants. He loved that beautiful blush that crept up her face as she turned to quickly get dressed.

His Joe was shy after sex? He would never have guessed, he thought with a chuckle. He had to wonder what else he didn't know about her. The idea that there were still things to discover about her intrigued him. Even after twenty-years she was still a mystery to him.

He finished tucking in his shirt and headed for the door, pausing only long enough to grab the scrap of paper with the details of the call out of her hand and to give her a quick kiss that seemed to leave her momentarily stunned. She looked so cute standing there looking all confused, but they had a job to do.

"We'll talk later, okay?"

She looked up at him. "All I care about is that this doesn't change anything, Eric. I don't want to lose you."

He gently cupped her cheek, brushing her swollen lips with his thumb. "You'll never lose me, Joe. No matter what we decide to do about this." He pressed a quick kiss to her lips before he took her hand and gave it a small tug in the direction of the door.

* * * *

"It's gotta be some kind of record," Joe said, fighting back a yawn as Eric pulled the ambulance into the small line of ambulances and a Fire department SUV to fill the gas tank up. He threw the ambulance in park as they waited for their turn at the gas pumps.

It had been a long, weird night and she was more than ready for it to be over. The only thing she wasn't ready for was the "talk" they would have to have. She knew they had to talk about what happened between them, but she just wasn't sure what to say.

The sex had been great, fantastic, and surprisingly she didn't regret it, which was kind of stupid since it could very well be the beginning of the end of their friendship. What were they supposed to do now?

They had sex one time and she didn't exactly equate that with a declaration of love. She knew he loved her and would never hurt, at least not on purpose. This was Eric she was talking about here. There was no arguing that he was the best friend she'd ever had and she would never hurt him or say anything unkind about him, but she couldn't lie.

Eric was a lousy boyfriend.

He treated all the women he dated as annoyances, barely gave them any consideration and had a short attention span. On more than one occasion she had to remind him what his date's name was and jump the hell out of the way when one of them grabbed whatever was nearby and chucked it at him. It never took much for him to get bored and move on.

She'd rather have Eric as a best friend than a boyfriend any day of the week. The best friend she could have for the rest of her life, that is if they got over this little bump in their relationship, but Eric as a boyfriend? He'd be hauling ass in less than a week.

Part of her thought that he'd treat her differently, but that would only make her an idiot. The two of them had been stepping around falling into bed for years and it happened. Dwelling on it would only cause her heartache that she didn't need or want. She loved him, couldn't live without him, but knew that if she had any hopes in keeping him she had to bite back her feelings and laugh this whole thing off when they had their little "talk" later.

"Why don't you head out? I've got this," Eric said, surprising the hell out of her.

Not once in twelve years had he ever offered to put the truck away on his own. Of course she'd never asked, but that's because they enjoyed working together. It didn't hurt that working together to put the truck away meant they could both leave quicker.

She opened her mouth to say no, but then thought better of it. He obviously didn't want to have this talk and neither did she. Common sense said that they should have it soon before it became awkward, but if he was willing to be a coward about it then so was she.

"Are you sure?" she asked, her hand hesitating over the door handle.

"Yeah, go ahead," he said, not bothering to look up from his clipboard.

She climbed out, feeling unsure for the first time since they met. When he still didn't look at her or say anything about what they'd done she shrugged it off and shut the door.

The next thirty minutes were a blur as she hauled ass to grab her bedding, punch out, and drive off. The entire time she was afraid that he was going to change his mind and want to have the talk that she was so not ready to have. By the time she pulled into her driveway she was a mass of nerves. It didn't get any better once she walked into her house.

Every few minutes she'd look up from what she was doing, half expecting Eric to come sauntering in. When he didn't show up an hour later she was both relieved and disappointed. She was glad that they weren't going to have the talk just yet, but she was disappointed because she wanted to see him, be with him.

She was such an idiot, she decided as she headed to her room. She quickly undressed and forced herself to take a long hot shower when all she wanted to do was wait by the phone like some love sick teenage girl. This was bad, this was very bad. If she was going to convince Eric that she could get over what happened between them then she couldn't go around acting like this.

He was her best friend and that's all. That much was clear when she was done with her shower, dressed and hitting her fridge for a drink before she went to bed. She knew that if he wanted to be here that he would already be here, but clearly he'd realized they'd made a mistake.

Fine, she thought, grabbing a bottle of water from the fridge before heading to her room. If that's what he wanted then that was more than fine with her. She could pretend that he hadn't given her the best sex of her life or that she was dying to touch him again. She was a big girl. She could handle a little rejection. She closed the blinds, darkening the room and flopped down on the bed more than ready to put this day behind her.

She was going to kick his ass, she decided three hours later when she couldn't fall asleep or get him out of her mind. If he didn't want anything to do with her then he could have damn well said so instead of giving her the cold shoulder and treating her like every other woman in his life. She'd been his best friend for over twenty years and deserved a hell of a lot more consideration than he was giving her at the moment.

Furious, she grabbed her keys and headed for the front door as she thought up all the ways she was going to make him pay for this bullshit. After she was done with him he was going to wish-

"Where the hell are you going?" Eric demanded when she practically ripped open the front door, startling her, but not enough to distract her from her purpose.

"To kick your ass," she snapped.

That slow sexy grin of his did not affect her. It didn't. She also didn't care that he looked as exhausted as she felt or that she was happy to see him. Nothing mattered except that he'd discarded her and spent the entire remainder of their shift acting like nothing happened. That pissed her off. Then he added insult to injury by brushing her off so that he wouldn't have to deal with her.

Well, now he was going to do deal with her because she was so ready to kick his-

Her thoughts sort of drifted off when he grabbed the back of her neck and leaned down and kissed every last coherent thought out of her head. She was barely aware of him guiding her back into the house or when he shut her door and locked it. All of her attention at the moment was on his mouth and the way he was kissing her breathless.

When he finally stopped kissing her, and she wanted to kick his ass for that alone, her mind began to clear and she remembered that she was angry with him. Who the hell did he think he was treating her like that? she wondered as she pushed him away.

"I take it you're mad at me," he noted with a sigh.

"You could say that," she snapped, crossing her arms beneath her breasts as she glared at him and waited for the typical Eric response to any form of female drama. When he didn't give her some lame ass excuse like giving her time to calm down and a promise to call later she was a bit surprised.

"Look," he said, running both of his hands down his face in frustration, "I know I shouldn't be here and that I should be giving you some time to sort through things, but I couldn't stay away."

Her eyes narrowed on him. "You were giving me time?" she asked, not even bothering to hide disbelief in her tone.

"Well, that and I got held over for two hours after you left," he said, sounding miserable as sat down on the arm of her couch.

"Why did you get held over?" she asked, inwardly wincing when she realized that he must have covered for her. Although it wasn't a rule at their station, if dispatch was looking for them and there was only one of them there putting away the truck they could get pissed.

"I had to do a favor for Bill."

"What favor?" she asked, leaning back against the wall to put some space between them. It was a little disconcerting that she couldn't think rationally with him in the room. All she could think about was running her fingers through his hair and over his body.

What in the hell was wrong with her?

She should still be focused on kicking his ass, but she couldn't stay mad at him. It was a weakness that she really needed to work on, but later.

"He asked me to go over all of the equipment with Greg," he said around a yawn.

"Greg?" she asked, surprised that he was still around. He rode the truck daily for what must have been two weeks and not one of those shifts counted towards his training time.

He gave her a firm nod that told her he wasn't too happy about the situation. "It seems he has an uncle on the City Council who called in a favor. He's claiming that Greg was just a little nervous and would like Bill to give him another chance so guess who's getting a third rider for the next two weeks," he said dryly.

"Us," she said, biting back a groan.

"Mmmhmm," he said absently as he ran his eyes over her. "And the best part of course is that somehow the little bastard is even cockier."

This time she didn't bother biting back her groan. She knew the man was going to be trying to save face by acting like it was no big deal, but that was going to make their jobs a hell of a lot harder. It also meant that he was probably going to ignore whatever they tried to show him. It should be a fun two weeks, she thought dryly.

"You were coming to kick my ass?" he asked, drawing her attention back to *their* problem.

"Maybe," she said, shrugging it off like it was nothing.

"In only my old t-shirt and panties?" he asked, running hungry eyes over her.

She felt a blush burn its way up her neck when she realized that she had been seconds away from storming outside like this to go kick his ass, but not because she was wearing a t-shirt and panties, but because she was only wearing a t-shirt.

Something in her expression must have given her away because that sexy bad boy grin that she loved so much suddenly graced his face. He crooked a finger in her direction. "Come here."

She just barely stopped herself from doing just that. With a snort she shook her head. "I'm not your bitch. You come here," she snapped, stubbornly crossing her arms over her chest even tighter, mostly to hide her nerves.

This was such a bad idea. Was she really thinking about tackling him, bringing him down to the ground, ripping his clothes off and licking his body from head to toe before she had her dirty little way with him?

Yes, yes she was.

Before she could rethink her plan or add a few things here and there to prolong her enjoyment, he was pushing off the arm of the couch and was standing in front of her. He placed his forearm against the wall by her head as he leaned in.

"Are you wearing panties, Joe?" he asked in a seductively dark whisper that had her licking her lips.

"Shouldn't we talk about this?" she asked, avoiding his question.

"About your panties?" he asked teasingly as he gently laid his other hand on her hip.

"No," she said, trying not to smile, "about what we're doing here. We need to talk, Eric."

"Okay," he said, slowly nodding his agreement as he leaned down to press a kiss to the tip of her nose. "Well, first I'm going to see if you're wearing any underwear. Then I'd thought we start living out every fantasy I've ever had about you, starting of course with the ones I had in high school. Then I thought we'd make up a few together," he said, pressing a line of kisses to her mouth before he brushed his lips teasingly against hers.

Her hands tightened around his shoulders in response to the very carnal visuals that were now running through her head. When she put her hands on his shoulders she had no idea, but she wasn't willing to let him go out of fear that her trembling legs would give out.

"That's not what I meant," she said weakly even as she tilted her head to the side to give him better access to her neck as he licked and kissed his way down.

"You don't want to live out a few fantasies?" he asked against her neck as his hand slid from her hip, down her thigh until it went past the edge of her t-shirt and them moved up under the t-shirt. His warm hand moved up her bare skin until it was once again resting on her bare hip.

Yes, she really did. In fact she had about a hundred fantasies that she would love to live out with him. "We'll talk afterwards?" she asked, gasping when his hand moved to her bottom.

Chapter 21

They really should be talking, but he knew that talking could lead to the decision that they should never do this again so he was going to be an asshole and get his fill before that. He didn't know what she wanted or what he could give her and was in no rush to end this. He wanted her too badly to do the right thing right now.

When she'd left this morning he'd been determined to do the right thing by her. Letting her walk away was one of the hardest things he'd ever done in his life. If Bill hadn't bugged the hell out of him until he gave in and helped him out with the annoying cocky bastard he probably would have done something stupid like go after Joe and promise her things they both knew he couldn't deliver.

During the time he spent trying to teach Greg how to use the equipment he thought about her. He loved her, they both knew that and he never wanted to hurt her, but he would. He didn't know how to be what she needed because he never cared enough to try that for any other woman. He'd love to be the man that could take care of her and be there for her, but he had some serious doubts about his own abilities.

After he'd finally had enough of putting up with Greg's bullshit he went home, showered, and tried not to think of her, but it had been a losing battle from the beginning. He gave in not too long ago because he promised himself that they'd have tonight and tomorrow before she had to go to New Hampshire and then they'd see where things took them from there. He knew it would probably lead to nothing, but he couldn't help but give himself a little hope that he could be more to her.

"*Hell*," he groaned when his fingers brushed against her slit.

She was wet, soaking wet and the knowledge that a few simple touches had turned her on almost as much as him nearly sent him to his knees. A second later the thought of her soaking wet did send him to his knees.

When she spread her legs without a word and he had to suppress a groan. He had a feeling that she'd be demanding in bed and he couldn't be happier about that fact. He pushed up her t-shirt and kissed the skin he exposed. He followed the smooth strong thigh that smelled of vanilla up until he came to his new favorite sweet spot and pressed a kiss against the puffy moist lips.

Joe's moan caught his attention and when he looked up she grabbed the hem of her t-shirt and pulled it up and off, letting it drop to the ground next to them. He'd seen her naked dozens of times, but seeing her leaning against the wall with her legs spread and ready for him almost had him losing it.

He frantically grabbed onto his self-control and forced himself to relax. Last night, or rather this morning he'd fucked her hard and fast and didn't get a chance to enjoy the body that had starred in every fantasy he'd ever had. Today he would not make that mistake.

Keeping his eyes locked on her face he leaned in and ran the tip of his tongue through her wet folds. He did it again when she licked her lips and closed her eyes in pleasure. When her flavor hit his tongue he groaned and licked her again, desperate for another taste.

She tasted so good, better than he ever imagined she would and he wanted more. He ignored the demand his dick made to be freed and reached up and gently spread her folds open with his fingers.

Beautiful, absolutely beautiful, he thought as he leaned in to lick her from core to clit. When she fisted her hands in his hair he did it again this time flicking the tip of his tongue over her clit before pulling it between his lips and suckling gently.

"Eric," she moaned.

He gave her clit one last pull before sitting back and slid a finger inside of her, slowly. For a moment he was content to watch his finger slide in and out of her, but the need to taste her again became too strong to ignore. He kept his finger inside of her as he kissed, licked and suckled her clit.

All too soon he felt her body tighten around his finger. One minute the sounds of his groans and her panting and soft moans could be heard in the room and the next she was screaming his name and holding his mouth tightly to her core. He felt her body slump against the wall and before her legs gave out he had her in his arms and was carrying her to her room.

"What now?" she asked, panting and desperately trying to catch her breath as he laid her carefully on top of her bed.

"Now," he said, reaching back and grabbing a fistful of his shirt, "we move onto the next fantasy."

* * * *

"Not yet," Eric grumbled against her mouth as his hand caught hers heading south, again.

His next fantasy turned out to be a bit of a surprise. After he stripped his clothes off and climbed under the sheet to join her, he kissed her. That was it. His hands didn't wander and every time one of hers tried to he stopped her and just kept on kissing her.

They'd been kissing for at least a half an hour and it didn't appear as though he was going to grow bored anytime soon. Actually, he seemed to be really enjoying himself. At least the incredibly hard erection poking her and the way he moaned against her mouth let her know that he liked what they were doing. Truth be told she loved it as well. She loved the way he held her in his arms, ran his hands over her back soothingly while he slowly devoured her mouth.

Unfortunately it turned her on a little too much and left her aching. If he didn't do something soon she was going to kill him that's all there was to it. When several minutes passed and he still didn't do anything she decided it was time to take the reins. She moved her hands up his chest as she moved to sit up, giving him no choice but to lie on his back or break the kiss.

When he laid back she didn't hesitate. She threw her leg over his waist and straddled him. He didn't seem to register the move until she ground herself against his hard length. Then he let out a pained groan and tried to roll her back onto her side, but she wasn't having that.

She rolled her hips forward before pushing back. When she felt the silky head of his erection press at her entrance she didn't hesitate in pushing back until he was sliding inside of her. He felt so damn good. He wasn't her first lover, but he was undoubtedly the best.

He was also the first man she'd ever had unprotected sex with and god help her but she never wanted anything to come between them. She wasn't worried about catching something from him. They both got tested every six months whether or not they'd been with someone and she knew it had been a long time for him. She also wasn't worried about getting pregnant. She'd been on birth control since she was sixteen out of fear that she'd screw up like her mother.

"I wasn't done," he complained even as he rolled his hips to fill her.

"Yes, you were," she said breathlessly as she gave him one last kiss before sitting up.

Never in her life had she felt fuller. She swore she could feel the tip of his penis inside of her. It felt good, better than good and she wanted more. Slowly, she moved up and dropped back down on him, earning a groan from him. She did it again, this time more slowly. He felt so good sliding inside of her. She met his eyes and nearly moaned when he licked his lips hungrily.

Sex had never been this good before. Her body never tingled in pleasure like this before and she'd never felt so close to losing control like this. Her body felt so good with him inside of her. She ran her fingers through her hair as she slowly rode him, letting the hair drop all around and noted the way he watched her.

She loved the way he looked at her, the way he made her feel and wanted more. She wanted him to hold her while they made love, needed it more than anything. He must have felt the same way. Before she could cover him with her body he was sitting up and wrapping his arms around her.

For a moment she thought he was simply doing it to take over like a few guys had done in the past, but when he made no move to take over she knew he'd done it just to hold her. The realization almost made her cry, but she held it back as she wrapped her arms around his neck and kissed him as she slowly rode him.

"I love you, Joe," he said against her lips.

"I love you too, Eric," she said, seconds before he swallowed her screams.

* * * *

"This is a fantasy for you?" she asked, unable to hide her disbelief.

"Oh yeah," Eric said, pulling her closer.

"Seriously?"

"Mmmhmmm," he said, pressing a kiss to the back of her neck.

"Yes, now be quiet the good part is coming."

She sighed heavily as she settled back against Eric's chest and settled in to watch the horrible action flick that only a guy could appreciate. She wasn't exactly sure how spooning on her couch and watching a movie that was threatening to put her to sleep counted as a fantasy. They'd done this a thousand times already.

Okay, granted they'd never done this naked with only a throw blanket covering them from the waist down and Eric's hand cupping her breast, but still. When he told her he wanted to live out his fantasies she was thinking a strip tease, licking whip cream off each other and a hundred other things she'd thought of over the years.

When his lips touched her neck she tilted her head to the side to give him better access. His hand tightened around her breast as he teasingly traced her hard aching nipple with his thumb. She was just about to roll over onto her back so that she could kiss him when she felt the head of his erection slide against her bottom.

"You have no idea how many times I've imagined doing this to you while I held you in my arms," he explained as he slowly pushed inside of her.

"You imagined doing this?" she asked, trying not to moan as he slid all the way home.

"Constantly."

* * * *

"Oh, *god*," Eric groaned as his orgasm ripped through him. His hands tightened on her hips, holding her in place as he suffered through her body throbbing around his sensitive shaft.

When she dropped face first on the mattress he wasn't far behind. He rolled onto his side and pulled her into his arms. His eyes shot to the alarm clock and he couldn't help but wince. It was after three in the morning and she had to drive up to New Hampshire for her classes in a few hours.

He opened his mouth to tell her he'd drive her, but then stopped himself. He couldn't go with her. She would be gone for three days and they needed that time to figure out what the hell they'd done and what they wanted. Even if she was willing to risk what they had he wasn't sure that he was.

There was no question in his mind that he loved and absolutely adored this woman, but he knew that he was a fuckup when it came to relationships and he couldn't stomach the idea that she would be yet another woman that he'd hurt. He knew ending this after the day and night they spent was risky, but it was still the preferable choice to setting her up for an even bigger disappointment.

He wanted to try for her, but he was scared shitless. What if he fucked up and she never spoke to him again? Worse, what if they went for the long term and he fucked up only to have her draw away from him. He would never survive losing her. It didn't matter that having her in his arms would put him out of his misery, he just couldn't risk having her leave him.

Joe groaned as she buried her face in her pillow. "I have to get up in a few hours."

"Get some sleep," he said, pressing a kiss to the back of her head.

"Only if you manage to keep that damn thing leashed," she said and he didn't need to ask what she was talking about.

Even though he'd just made love to her for the.........Well, he wasn't sure how many times they'd made love. All he knew was that his body wanted more even though the damn thing should have fallen off by now. As discretely as he could he pulled his hips back, wincing when the damn thing just had to go and caress Joe's backside as he moved away.

Joe let out a long suffering sigh before turning in his arms and hooking her leg over his hip. "Fine. You may have your dirty little way with me," she said, sounding put out.

"You're very generous," he said, gripping her hip as he slid home.

She nodded solemnly as she arched her back to take him deeper. "Very generous."

Chapter 22

"I'll see you Sunday night, Joe. We'll talk then," Eric said as she did her best to hide her stunned reaction to the news he'd laid at her feet only moments before.

He wasn't coming with her. For the first time since she could remember, she was doing something completely on her own and he wasn't bugging the hell out of her to tag along. It actually made her a little nervous, not to do something on her own, she was fine with that, but that he didn't insist on coming with her.

Just to test the waters she mentioned that the hotel and school were on a large lake known for its insanely large bass and trout. He didn't even bat an eye as he wished her a safe drive. At first she thought he was dying. Eric never passed up an opportunity to fish, never. Then she realized that he was giving her space so that they could both think over a few things. Of course him explaining that probably saved him from being bitch slapped for pissing her off.

"I think we both need time to figure out what we want and where we should go from here," he explained as he took a step back, already putting distance between them, she noted. "A few days and nights apart will do us both some good."

She didn't need to ask to know that he hoped she would change her mind on this. He didn't want to go forward with this, but he was giving her a chance to make that decision. Last night had been a way to work things out of his system, nothing more. He didn't want to risk losing them by going forward. She understood that even as she inwardly cursed him for being a coward.

What happened between them scared the hell out of her too, but she was willing to take a chance. After waking up in his arms this morning and making love again how could she not? She loved him and she knew that he loved her, but he didn't know how to make this work and she sure as hell wasn't going to push him into it.

If he didn't love her enough to risk everything then she didn't want him. She wanted a man who loved her and would do anything for her, not someone too scared to do anything about it. She'd keep him in her life, because she knew that she couldn't live without him, but she'd move on. One day she'd find a man who thought she was worth the risk.

Maybe she should have a little fling over the weekend and work him out of her system. Even as the idea floated through her mind her body screamed in protest. It didn't want anyone but Eric touching her and that was going to be a problem considering the fact that he seemed to be done with her.

"Have a nice weekend, Eric," she said, not even bothering to get a hug from the man. She climbed into her car and drove off without a look back. If he wanted her he was going to have to make the first move because she was done.

* * * *

"Are you going to keep checking your phone or watch the game?" Nathan asked as he grabbed another beer.

Eric didn't bother answering the man as he sent him a glare. He put his phone back on top of the pizza box where he could keep an eye on it and grab it if it rang. Then of course he snatched the beer out of Nathan's hand and took a nice long sip just to aggravate the man for pissing him off.

Nathan let out a snort of disgust as he grabbed another beer. "I don't know how Joe puts up with you."

He didn't know either and that was part of the problem. He loved her so damn much and he didn't have shit to offer her. Well, that wasn't true he could be her best friend, but he wanted more, a hell of a lot more, but couldn't allow himself to go for it.

The last twenty-four hours was going to have to be enough to last the rest of his life because he knew he couldn't touch her again. After this weekend Joe would know that too. He knew she realized that he was pulling away and he hoped like hell she thought about the reasons behind it.

They were great together, could talk about anything and everything or nothing at all and he didn't want to lose that. They'd lose everything if they tried to make this work, because sooner or later he'd fuck up big time and she'd stop talking to him the way she did and soon they'd realize they'd made a mistake, but by then it would be too late.

"Why the hell are you here?" Nathan demanded, thankfully drawing him out of his rather depressing thoughts.

"I live here," he said, frowning and wondering if maybe his brother had had one too many beers already.

"I didn't mean here," Nathan said, chuckling. "I meant, why are you here while Joe is in New Hampshire?"

"Because I'm not taking a class," he answered quickly, hoping is brother would just let it go.

He should have known better.

"So? That usually wouldn't stop you. Why didn't you go with her? Is she still pissed at you?"

Eric did his best not to cringe at the question. Was she *still* pissed at him? No. But he'd be willing to bet that by the end of the weekend he wouldn't be her favorite person. It was hard to miss the hurt expression on her face when he told her that he wouldn't be going with her or calling her. The accusing glare that quickly followed had turned his stomach.

She probably thought he'd used her and she'd be right. He knew he couldn't have a lifetime with her so he greedily took a night with her. When she got back she'd be pissed, but he knew she'd get over it and in time they'd go back to the way things were and last night would just be another fond memory, he told himself even as he crushed the can in his hand.

"Everything's fine," he said, tossing the crushed can into the small wastebasket by the couch.

"If you say so," Nathan said with a shrug.

"I do."

"Then you'll be happy to know that Joe just responded to that text message you made me send her."

"What did she say?" he asked, trying to sound casual.

Nathan sent him an amused look as he said, "That she arrived safely. Hasn't checked into her hotel yet because she had to go straight to the school. She said it's boring and that she hates you."

"What?" he demanded, reaching out and snagging Nathan's phone away from him. He found her message and scrolled down. "She didn't say that," he said, turning an accusing glare on his brother.

Nathan shrugged, taking back his phone. "It was insinuated."

"Bastard," he muttered, turning his attention back to the game. He had absolutely no idea who was playing or winning for that matter. All he could think about was Joe.

Last night she'd surpassed every one of his fantasies, well the fantasies they had time to play out. There were still thousands of fantasies that they hadn't had time for and never would. Besides the fact that he wouldn't allow himself to touch her again there was also the little issue of work.

He may have dropped the subject, for now, but he was still trying to figure out an approach that would get her the hell off the truck. Right now he was laying all his hopes that she'd enjoy the dispatcher class enough to go fulltime with it. If not he was going to have to figure out another way to get her off the truck. Maybe she'd meet some guy and get married and start having babies, he thought.

The idea of another man touching her turned his stomach and made him want to hit something. He didn't want anyone else touching her or giving her children, but one day that would happen. It would be the worst day of his life, but if she was happy that's all that mattered. He could pretend to be happy for her and act like he didn't want to kill the bastard.

As long as Joe was happy and safe he could do anything.

"You want to talk about it?" Nathan asked.

"Nope."

"It would probably help to talk about it," Nathan mused.

Eric turned his glare on his brother. "Oh? Really? Then I guess you'd like to get a few things off your chest."

The scowl Nathan sent his way was answer enough. He mumbled something before turning his attention back to the game. Good. He didn't want to talk about Joe anymore than Nathan wanted to talk about Caitlyn. As long as Nathan kept his ass close by so that he could manipulate the bastard into sending text messages to Joe for him then he didn't care if his brother was sulking or pissed. He had his own shit to deal with and didn't-

"She's not Joe," Nathan said softly, grabbing his attention in a big way.

"What?" he asked, frowning at his brother.

"I ended things with Caitlyn because she's not Joe," Nathan admitted.

"Oh, I see," Eric said slowly as his brain struggled to comprehend what Nathan said and when it did he found himself on top of Nathan and beating the shit out of him.

"Stop!" Nathan snapped, but he couldn't. He knew Nathan would be the better man for Joe and that he should just step back and wish him well, but jealousy was a bitch and currently had him beating the hell out of his brother.

The fight quickly turned into a wrestling match with Eric trying to get a few more shots at his brother while Nathan did his best to shove Eric off and get away.

"What the hell is your problem?" Nathan demanded as he shot an elbow to Eric's gut to get him off.

"You want Joe," Eric said, moving to throttle the bastard.

Nathan's horrified look gave him pause. "I don't want Joe!" he snapped, sounding disgusted and looking close to vomiting at the very idea.

"What the hell is wrong with Joe?" he demanded, pissed at that look of revulsion on Nathan's face.

"She's my sister, asshole! Now get the hell off of me!" Nathan said, shoving him away so that he could get to his feet.

Eric got to his own feet, noticing the blood dripping from his nose for the first time. Well, it looked as though Nathan got in a few shots. Thankfully the man hadn't broken his nose, but it still stung like a bitch.

"What the hell is your problem?" Nathan demanded as he wiped blood off his lip with the back of his hand.

"What's yours?" Eric demanded right back.

"You are!" Nathan snapped, looking ready to leap at him.

"What did I do?"

"Joe!" Nathan shot back, shoving a frustrated hand through his hair as he started pacing Eric's small living room.

"What about her?" Eric asked, wondering if Nathan knew what happened between the two of them.

"You're a fucking idiot," Nathan practically snarled.

"You want to explain that?" Eric bit out tightly as he took an aggressive step towards his brother. Between the bullshit at work, what happened with Joe and having to push her away for her own good he was in no mood for any more bullshit.

"You have a woman who is beyond perfect for you, loves you, and who would walk on glass for you and you don't even see it," Nathan spat out.

"I don't know what you're talking about," Eric lied, wishing like hell they weren't having this conversation.

"Bullshit!" Nathan snapped, getting into his face. "You love her. I know you do and she loves you. I've seen the way you look at her. I know that the two of you have a connection that anyone would kill for," he said before muttering, "I would kill to have a woman who made me feel the way Joe makes you feel."

"How exactly do you think you think she makes me feel?" Eric asked, wondering how the hell they ended up here. He didn't want to have this conversation and was more than willing to go back to trading punches to avoid it.

"Whole," Nathan said, hitting the nail on the head and damn near making him stumble.

That's exactly how she made him feel. When she was around he felt complete, happy and at peace and when she wasn't around he felt lost. He hated being away from her and hated knowing that it was something that he would have to get used to it.

"I want what you're refusing to see," Nathan explained. "I want a woman that makes me feel complete, makes me happy and someone I couldn't imagine living without."

"We're just friends," Eric said lamely as he tried to ignore the ache in his chest. He missed her, wanted her and he was too fucking scared to go for it.

"Bullshit! She's everything to you and you damn well know it. While I would kill to have my own Joe you're throwing yours aside like it's nothing. What the hell are you going to do when she finds someone else? You don't think that will kill you to watch her with another man, knowing it could have been you?"

"Yes!" he roared. "It will fucking kill me to watch her with another man. Are you fucking happy?" he demanded, ignoring the look of pity on his brother's face as he scrubbed his hands down his face. "I'm not good enough for her. I wouldn't have the first clue about how to treat her."

"What the hell are you talking about? No one would ever treat her better and we both know it."

Eric let out a humorless laugh at that. "Really? What exactly are you basing this on? I sure as hell hope it's not based on how I treated all my old girlfriends because we both know that's exactly how it will be with Joe. I'll grow bored and it will be over and I'll lose her."

"You're avoiding being with her because of your past?" Nathan asked, looking at a loss for words when Eric nodded firmly. Nathan shook his head in disbelief. "You really are a fucking idiot."

Chapter 23

That bastard, Joe thought as she forced herself not to check her phone. She refused to be that woman. There was no way in hell that she was going to wait around for a text message or a phone call from a guy, even if that guy was Eric.

He'd made it more than clear that he had no intentions of calling her this weekend so she wasn't going to worry. She was going to force herself to stay awake during the mind numbingly boring slide show presentation. Then she was going to her hotel room, changing, hitting a bar and getting a drink and having some fun. Then tomorrow and the next day she would come back to this beige classroom that smelled like alcohol wipes and doing this all over again.

She really wished Eric was here. Normally they took all of their refresher courses and continuing education courses, the requirements that OEMS required every EMT to do to keep their EMT ticket active, together. He would keep her entertained while they sat through things like this, but he wasn't here and wouldn't be here tomorrow or the next day.

There was no doubt in her mind that she'd be doing a lot more things in the future without him. He didn't want to be with her and after what they did last night she had no doubt that he was going to start pulling away more and more. She idly wondered while she stared blankly at the graphs blown up on the screen if his reasons for not pursuing this were the same as hers.

He wasn't the best boyfriend and he had to know that by now. He wouldn't want to hurt her. She knew he loved her, but he didn't realize that he was hurting her by doing this. There really was no point in lying and saying that she wasn't afraid that he was going to end up hurting her, but after last night she was willing to take that chance.

Eric wasn't.

She wanted him, but she wasn't going to beg him. He needed to want to give them a chance. If he wasn't.........

Well, he might just get his wish after all. She knew herself well enough to know that it would become hard enough working with him day in and day out, but that didn't mean she wanted to watch as other women threw themselves at him, or worse when he started dating them. When it became too much she'd either switch out to a different station or work in dispatch full time where she wouldn't have to see him.

Of course she'd still see him at family gatherings and that was fine with her. She wasn't willing to give up Nathan or Alice for anything. They were her family and she loved them. For them she'd pretend she was happy when he was around. She'd do the same for him. She'd never stop loving him, but if it made his life easier then she'd move on.

Oh, he still had an ass kicking coming and she fully planned on giving it to him, but she knew she wouldn't be able to stay mad at him even for breaking her heart. He'd move on and so would she.

"If you want the results of your test you can call the office Tuesday," Brian, the instructor from hell, said, catching her attention.

It was over? Finally, she thought as she got to her feet and grabbed the notebook she'd filled up with doodles. That reminded her that she'd have to swing by a store and pick up two more if she had any hopes of staying mildly entertained during the next two days. Of course if Eric was here she'd just draw on his arm to keep herself entertained, but he wasn't so she'd just have to learn to deal.

She headed for the door and quickened her pace when she spotted Alex, a brand spanking new EMT that decided to take the class, following her. Normally she was patient with new EMTs, well she tried to be anyway, and she understood it was an exciting job and that some of them got a little wrapped up in it, but she really didn't think she could take another minute with him.

During her breaks when she just wanted to relax and enjoy the fresh air he'd talked and wouldn't stop talking until Brian announced that the break was over. She could have probably handled a chatter box, but this guy decided that he had to share every single detail of every single call he'd ever been on. He'd been an EMT for all of six months and was sure that he'd seen it all.

She had to laugh at that. She'd been on the job for twelve years and knew damn well that she hadn't seen everything. No two days were alike and that's what she loved about the job. She could probably do this job for a hundred years and still see new things that surprised and shocked her. Alex didn't see it that way. He told her that he was already growing bored with the job and was looking into becoming a paramedic or a fireman.

When she made the mistake of encouraging him, mostly to end the conversation, he listed all the reasons why he should be a fireman. Her only escape had been the woman's room, but it was a short lived escape. He waited for her outside the restroom and jumped right back into his little spiel as though he'd never stopped. He did the same thing during their lunch break, making it impossible for her to get a bite to eat.

Now she was hungry, cranky and in no mood for another minute of listening to another "Whacker" story. She just wanted to go to her hotel room, shower, change and go out for the night. Of course with her luck she'd run into him wherever she went.

When he called her name she pretended that she didn't hear him and jumped into her car. Thank god she'd come straight here otherwise she would have had to walk the quarter mile back to the hotel room and he'd catch up with her. She really hoped he wasn't staying at the same hotel that she was.

Two minutes later she was groaning when she spotted his beat up green pickup truck pulling into the hotel parking lot right behind her. Would this day never end? she wondered. She shut down the engine, grabbed her bag and made a mad dash for the hotel lobby, hoping it would be a quick check-in so that she could escape to her room. Then again the way her luck was going he'd probably end up being her neighbor. She sent up a silent prayer that that wasn't the case as she opened the hotel lobby door and nearly tripped over her own feet.

Nathan and Eric were sitting in dainty chairs that looked really uncomfortable as they were forced to watch some daytime talk show. She ran her eyes quickly over their faces and noted a few bruises and cuts and wondered about that, but just as quickly pushed her curiosity aside.

"Hey, Joe! Wait up," Alex called, drawing Nathan and Eric's attention.

Nathan looked relieved to see her and Eric looked pissed as his eyes shifted from her to the guy trying to get her attention. She was just about to ask them why they were there when Nathan walked over and put his arm around her and gave her a gentle tug in the direction of the hotel clerk.

"Let's check in, shall we?" Nathan asked cheerfully. When she tried to look back at Eric he gave her another gentle tug in the direction of the hotel clerk.

"What's going on?" she asked as she pulled out her license and the credit card she used to hold the room.

"Nothing much," Nathan said, shrugging. "We thought we'd come up and see how the fish were biting."

"Okay," she said slowly, sneaking a peek to find Eric leaning against the wall near the elevators as he glared at something behind her. Frowning, she looked back to find Alex standing behind her and looking eager to continue where they left off.

Silently groaning, she signed her slip, bit her lip when Nathan asked for two key passes to her room and once again wondered when this nightmare would end. She didn't think Eric would bring Nathan up here if he wanted to be with her, which meant he brought Nathan up here for moral support.....for her.

That kind of pissed her off since she'd already figured things out for herself. She didn't need him coming up here and wrecking her already boring weekend with this drama. He didn't want her? That was fine with her. He could tell her and then go on his merry way and she'd work him out of her system starting tonight.

"Let me carry that for you, Joe," Alex said smoothly as he picked up her bag and gestured towards the elevator. He either didn't notice that Nathan was standing next to her or was cocky enough to have already dismissed Nathan, probably the latter.

"No need. I've got it," Eric said coldly as he grabbed the bag away from Alex.

"Who the hell are you?" Alex demanded, crossing his large arms over his chest as he tried to glare up at Eric.

"Her boyfriend, asshole, so move along," Eric said, shocking the hell out of her.

Alex turned accusing eyes on her. "You didn't say anything about a boyfriend."

She opened her mouth to inform the man that he'd never asked. Hell, he never let her get a word in edgewise. Not that she would have claimed Eric was her boyfriend when he'd made it more than obvious that there would never be anything more between them. But before she could say anything Nathan smoothly stepped in.

"She doesn't talk about him because she's ashamed of him."

Joe couldn't help but nod in agreement. "It's true. I am."

Eric snorted at that as he gave her hand a gentle tug towards the elevator. She couldn't help but feel a little awkward when Nathan and a pouting Alex joined them and Eric still didn't let her hand go. She dared a glance at Nathan to see how he was taking all of this only to catch the man grinning hugely.

She didn't know what was going on, but right then she didn't care. As soon as she got into her room she was taking a hot soothing bath and then she was going out. Whatever brought Eric and Nathan up here could damn well wait until tomorrow, she decided as the elevator doors slid open and Alex practically stomped off.

Biting back a few choice words, she pulled her hand away from Eric, grabbed her bag and followed the signs to her room, hoping the guys got the hint and left her alone. So when they followed her into her room she couldn't exactly say she was really all that surprised.

"Get out," she said, not bothering to look at them as she tossed her bag on one of the double beds and began to dig out the things she'd need for a bath.

"No can do," Nathan said, walking past her to drop down on the other bed.

She turned her glare on Eric who was glaring right back at her like she'd somehow pissed him off. She wasn't the one who gave him the brush off after the most incredible night of her life. No, that was all him. Did he really think that she'd be happy to have him come all the way up here to give her the bad news? Was she receiving special treatment because of their friendship? Knowing him, probably.

"You didn't have to come up here to do this. I got the hint this morning," she stressed, hoping he'd get the hint and get out of here. She really didn't want to talk about this in front of Nathan if she could help it.

"Yeah, I saw," he said tightly. "Who was the asshole?"

When she could only frown he added, "The asshole sniffing around you downstairs."

"Just a whacker from class," she said, sighing. "Now that you know that, both of you can get the hell out of my room."

Eric stubbornly shook his head. "Sorry, like Nathan said we can't do that."

"And why's that?" she asked, grabbing her things and headed for the bathroom, hoping they would be gone by the time she was done.

"Because there are no other hotel rooms available. Looks like we're sharing."

* * * *

"You know, you were right," Nathan mused as he lounged back on the bed. "You really suck at this."

Eric flipped him off before following Joe into the bathroom. When she tried slamming the door in his face he shoved it open enough so that he could step inside. Then he shut and locked the door behind him.

"Get out," Joe said, sounding pissed when she sure as hell didn't have the right to.

The entire ride up here he'd been a nervous wreck, but an excited nervous wreck. He couldn't wait to see her and tell her that he wanted to give this a shot and of course Nathan tagged along to watch the whole thing. Nosey bastard, but he was glad that the man came along. At least having him around would give him an ally, something he sorely needed at the moment.

"No, you and I need to talk," he said, expecting her to yell at him or throw something at him like most of his ex-girlfriends would have done, but instead she gestured for him to get on with it.

"I got the message loud and clear this morning, Eric. There really was no need for you to come all the way up here," she said, turning her back on him to start a bath.

"I'm sorry about that," Eric said, at a loss for words to make up for hurting her.

"It's fine," she said, shrugging it off the same way she began to shrug out of her clothes.

It was a bit distracting and he wished she wouldn't do it, but he kept his mouth shut about it. The last thing he needed was to really piss her off. He needed to fix this and quickly.

"I love you, Joe," he told her, wishing like hell that he knew what to say to convince her to give him a chance.

She sighed as she settled into the bubble filled bathtub. "I know," she said softly. "I love you too, Eric, which is why I'm not going to push you into anything that you don't want. I'd rather be your friend than lose you," she said, sounding miserable.

"And I'd rather have you, Joe. I'm in love with you and I want to be with you, Joe," he said, praying that she gave him a chance. He'd already fucked up so badly and didn't know what he'd do if she told him to fuck off.

He went to the tub and got on his knees and barely resisted the urge to take her in his arms. "I know I don't have the best track record for dating, but you have to know that I would never treat you that way."

"How can you be so sure?" she murmured, drawing her knees up and hugging them to her chest.

"Because they weren't you, Joe. I didn't want them the way that I want you and I sure as hell didn't love them. I love you, Joe, and I want to be with you," he said, unable to resist the urge to skim his fingers over her delicate jaw.

When she didn't say anything for a minute he shifted nervously, racking his brain for a way to get out of his hole he'd dug himself into. Just when he decided to go ask Nathan since the man knew what the hell he was doing when it came to dating, Joe let out a long drawn out sigh.

"I'm willing to give this a chance, but you should probably know that if you treat me like crap then I'll have no choice but to kick your ass."

He nodded solemnly even as his lips tipped up into a smile. "That's a fair warning."

"I thought so," she agreed even as she reached for him. Not that she had to since he was already moving to pull her into his arms. He leaned in to kiss her when the banging on the door started.

"I'm hungry!" Nathan bitched.

"So? Go get something and leave us the hell alone!" Eric snapped, moving in to kiss Joe's sweet lips.

"You promised to buy me a steak dinner if I came up here with you," Nathan pointed out.

"I lied!"

He ignored the gasp of shocked outrage and closed the distance between them and nearly groaned at the taste of her.

"You lying bastard!"

"You know you're buying me a steak dinner, don't you?" Joe whispered against his lips.

He couldn't help but chuckle against her lips. "I knew you were a little gold digger."

Chapter 24

"I want to go home and go to bed," Joe said, knowing she was whining, but couldn't help it. After an eight hour class and a two hour drive she wanted nothing more than to go home and go to bed.

Okay, so maybe that wasn't the only reason she was tired. Since Eric gave her the shock of a lifetime on Friday they'd been inseparable once again. That is when she wasn't stuck in class. They went for walks, talked, went out to eat, went dancing, and cuddled and whispered most of the night while Nathan snored a few feet away. They hadn't had a chance to make love since they decided to give this relationship a chance and she fully planned on rectifying that just as soon as she found a way to get out of this and get some sleep.

"Can't," Eric said, reaching back and grabbing her hand when she tried to make her escape. "Mom called a family dinner."

"But I'm not hungry. I'm tired. Can't she call a family nap instead?" she asked, sounding hopeful.

Eric simply chuckled as he threw his arm around her and herded her towards the door. She waited for Nathan to open the front door before she tried to pull away again, but Eric simply tightened his hold around her and pulled her into the house.

She loved Alice, she really did, but she was so damn tired. She hadn't slept much during their twenty-four hour shift on Wednesday and got even less sleep during the next night when they came together and even less during the weekend. It was a struggle just to stay awake at the moment. All she wanted to do was sleep.

"This is too perfect," Nathan said, chuckling softly as he stepped into the kitchen in front of them.

Biting back a yawn, Joe followed him into the kitchen wondering what was so amusing when she saw it, or rather her. Sitting at the table chatting with Alice was a twenty-something bleach blond woman wearing an eye catching blouse that sadly didn't have much cleavage to fill it out and a calculating expression that landed on Eric.

Why hadn't she realized this was why Alice called a family dinner? Because she'd been too exhausted to think straight. Well, it looked like Alice was making another attempt to fix Eric up and she suddenly found herself very much awake and ready to be entertained. Was it wrong to start a relationship by screwing him over?

She didn't think so.

Just because they were free to be with each other and didn't have to hold anything back shouldn't mean that they couldn't have a little fun and judging by the look the woman was sending Eric she was going to have a lot of fun.

"Amber, this is my son Nathan and my Joe," she said, gesturing towards her and she didn't miss the look of dismissal the woman gave her before it shifted right back to Eric, "and my son Eric that I was telling you about."

Joe didn't even bother hiding her grin as she ducked out from beneath Eric's arm and avoided his mad grab. "It's nice to meet you, Amber," she said sweetly as she sent Eric an evil little grin and eyebrow wiggle.

"Very nice to meet you, Amber," Nathan seconded, sending her a wink.

This really was going to be so much fun, she decided as she took a seat next to Alice and gave the older woman a kiss on the cheek. She wasn't too surprised when Eric tried to yank Nathan out of the way so that he could sit next to her, but Nathan was fast. He had his butt in the seat next to hers and his arm draped over the back of her chair in seconds.

Eric glared at Nathan as he reluctantly sat down in the only other chair available, the one right next to Amber. As soon as Eric sat down she shifted her chair closer to him.

"What's for dinner, mom?" Nathan asked.

"I thought we'd order in. What are you in the mood for?" she asked brightly as she watched Amber and Eric with a pleased little smile.

"I could go for Chinese," Joe said, deciding that now that she got her second wind she was hungry.

"Pizza," Nathan said, giving a strand of her hair a playful tug.

She noticed that Amber squished her face up in disgust. Alice must have noticed it as well. "What would you like, Amber? Chinese or pizza?"

"Neither actually. There's too many carbs and fat. But I know a great tofu place," she added with a smile that clearly stated that she always got her way and this time would be no different.

As much as she'd love to screw over the guys, she was not a tofu kind of girl. The one time she tried tofu she ended up slapping a hand over her mouth as she made a run for the bathroom. The matching grimaces on the guys' faces told her exactly what they thought on the matter. Even Alice had a hard time biting back a grimace.

"What about the Chinese buffet on Harrison Street? That has a tofu and sushi bar," Eric said, already getting to his feet. Nathan sighed with obvious relief as he got to his.

"That sounds great," Alice said, latching onto the choice that would save them all from eating things that scared them.

The only one that didn't get up was Amber. She crossed her arms over her chest, looking putout as she explained, "But it's not organic."

"Hmmm," Alice said, looking thoughtful and making Eric look nervous and for good reason. The woman was up to something and they all knew it. The only question at the moment was how hard was this going to make Nathan and her laugh.

"Why don't you take Amber to the restaurant that she feels more comfortable with and Nathan, Joe, and I will grab something to eat and meet you at the movies," Alice suggested.

"Movie?" she said at the same time as Nathan and Eric.

"Since when are we seeing a movie?" Eric demanded, shifting away from Amber as she sent a smug smile his way. Seriously, where did Alice find these women? Even though it entertained her, it was a bit creepy.

"I think it would be a nice chance to spend some time together," Alice said in that motherly tone that none of them dared argue. It didn't matter that they all saw each other at least twice a week, Alice wanted to go the movies then they were going to the movies.

"That sounds like fun," she said brightly, sending Eric another evil little smile that was met with a scowl.

"Fine, but Nathan should bring Amber since he loves tofu," Eric explained as he reached out and grabbed Nathan by the arm and yanked him out of his way. In seconds he was by her side with his arm around her. The glare Amber sent her way was a little concerning, but she shrugged it off mostly because the woman was providing her with free entertainment.

"No, I don't. I love Chinese," Nathan grumbled.

"Don't be silly, Eric. You take Amber out and we'll meet at Emerald Cinemas at nine," Alice said, grabbing her purse off the kitchen counter and heading towards the living room door as if everything was settled, but she knew Eric wasn't about to let this go. Even if they weren't seeing each other now she knew he'd do anything and everything to get out of this.

"Mom, I have something I have to tell you," Eric said, giving her shoulder a squeeze.

"Oh? What is it?" Alice asked, pausing by the door.

"I can't take your friend out because Joe and I have decided to start seeing each other," he explained. "So, as you can see it would be a little awkward taking another woman out and ditching my girlfriend," he pointed out with a helpless shrug.

Amber's glare on her intensified as Alice narrowed her eyes on them.

"Joe?" was all Alice had to say.

She could confirm Eric's story and get the woman who looked close to clawing her eyes out the hell away from her or she could have a little more fun. In the end she knew what she had to do. She loved him and knew how much he hated these little setups of Alice's.

"I have no idea what he's talking about," she said, shaking her head in wonder as she stepped away from him.

Nathan grinned hugely as he reached out and took her hand. Eric's shocked gasp of course pleased her.

"You betraying bitch!" he hissed, making a mad grab for her hand.

"Honestly, Eric. You'll do and say anything to get out of trying something new. It won't kill you to give tofu another try. I'm sure the rash you developed last time was just a fluke," Alice said, starting to head for the door once again.

"This isn't over!" Eric called after them.

* * * *

"What the hell are you doing here?" Nathan asked as he loaded his plate with chicken fingers.

"Contemplating manslaughter," Eric said, snagging the plate away from his brother and moving down the line to add beef teriyaki and pork fried rice. With a resigned sigh Nathan grabbed another plate.

"Where's your date?" Nathan asked, chuckling.

"You mean your date? She's sitting at the table waiting for you," Eric said, nodding towards the woman who looked seconds away from throwing a tantrum.

Nathan frowned. "What the hell are you talking about?"

Eric shrugged even as his eyes sought out the little traitor loading her plate up three tables down. "After I explained that I was unavailable, but that you were looking for someone like her, she decided to give you a chance," Eric said, slapping his brother on the back before moving on to his next prey.

"You better be kidding," Nathan bit out. "You are kidding, right? Eric?" he said, sounding nervous. Good. The bastard should be nervous. That woman was a nightmare.

The second his brother pulled out of the driveway with their mother and Joe she started in on him, telling him she didn't appreciate his attitude one bit. He just barely stopped himself from sending her packing when he decided to unload the woman on Nathan to let the bastard see how it felt to be set up with a psycho.

When she started in about Joe he set her straight on that subject. He told her that he was in love with her and the damn woman was just nervous about letting his mother know since she wouldn't want to get Alice's hopes up. Not that she could. She was his and that's all there was to it.

"He said what?" he heard his mother suddenly demand.

His eyes shot over to the table where he left Amber pouting and he tried not to wince as his mother turned a glare on him. It was just so wrong that one look from his mother could still make him cringe.

"Uh oh, looks like someone's in trouble," Joe said in a mock whisper as she walked past him.

With a glare that admittedly dropped to her ass several times he followed after her, snatching the soda out of Nathan's hand on the way. He waited for Joe to sit down and then sat down right next to her and thankfully well away from the two women glaring in his direction.

He pointedly ignored them as he put his arm along the back of Joe's chair and ate. Occasionally he looked up to send a smug smile in his brother's direction as the harpy his mother tried setting him up with chatted his ear off about fashion and diets. Every time the poor bastard went to eat something she went into a lecture about animal cruelty that Eric easily ignored. When Nathan filled his plate up with vegetables, probably to get her to shut the hell up, she lectured him about oils and choosing organic foods.

Joe happily ignored the woman's pointed comments in her direction and enjoyed her meal. When she finally shoved her plate away, a clear sign from Joe that she was done, he took her hand into his and was surprised when she didn't pull away. Then again they'd always been close so this wouldn't be a big deal to his mother. Even though he could appreciate the fact that she was still his Joe and clearly enjoyed screwing him over for a good laugh, he fully planned on getting her back.

"Aren't you getting dessert?" he asked, reaching over to smooth a loose strand of her honey blond hair behind her ear.

"Now why would I do that when you're going to buy me something at the movies?" she asked, sending him an impish smile.

Nathan snorted at that and muttered something that sounded suspiciously like "gold digger," but he ignored it, mostly because he agreed with his brother. What was it with women these days? Any other woman and he would have laughed and wished her luck with that, but this was his Joe. So he might just treat her to a soda, small of course.

But he wanted a kiss first and he wanted it now. He stood up, giving her hand a small tug that had her standing up. "We'll meet you outside," he told his family as he stepped away from the table, dropping enough money on the table to cover his and Joe's share plus a tip, and headed for the door before his mother could stop him.

"Why exactly are you in a rush to leave the restaurant?" Joe asked once they reached his car.

"For this of course," he said, pulling her into his arms so that he could kiss her.

Over the past couple of days they'd snuck a few kisses, but it had been damn difficult to kiss her the way he wanted with Nathan always under foot. He had no proof, but he was pretty sure the bastard was doing it on purpose to screw with him. More than once over the past couple of days he thought he'd die if didn't touch her and now that she was in his arms he didn't want to let her go.

"Come home with me," he murmured against her lips.

"What about the movie?" she asked, tightening her arms around his neck.

"We can watch a movie at my place," he suggested, loving the idea of living that particular fantasy out again.

"Do I get to pick the movie?" she asked in between nibbling on his lips.

"Yes," he said, knowing that he had absolutely no plans on watching the movie.

"He's just really shy," he heard Nathan explain. "But I know he's interested."

"Yes, he is-*Eric Parish, what are you doing*?" his mother demanded in a bit of a hysterical screech.

He pressed one last kiss to Joe's lips before pulling back, noting the beautiful blush that painted her cheeks.

"Kissing my girlfriend. What does it look like?" he asked, turning to face his mother while he took Joe's hand into his.

He couldn't help but be amused as he watched the play of emotions float over his mother's features. She went from shocked, to horrified when her eyes landed on Amber and then turned pleased, very pleased.

His mother grinned hugely as she faced Amber. "Did I mention that Nathan is single?"

Chapter 25

"We have to go," she said, but didn't pull away from him as he reached between them and undid her pants. She said even less as he shoved her pants and panties down around her knees. After one last kiss that left her panting he turned her around and urged her to her knees.

When she felt him kneel behind her she reached back and grabbed him by the back of his head and yanked him down for another kiss. While his tongue slid across hers she felt him grind his uniform pant covered erection against her bare bottom. She ground herself back against it, loving the way he felt and she knew that she'd never get enough of him.

He pulled back only to release himself and she cried out in relief when he ran the tip of the velvet head over her bottom. Just when she didn't think she could take any more teasing he gripped her hip and pushed between her legs until he came in contact with her core. She felt herself drip with excitement and knew that he felt it too when he let out a sexy little growl that had her arching her hips and pushing back until she felt the large head slide inside her.

As he released himself so that he could push further inside her he reached around and slid his hand beneath her shirt and over her stomach until he could snake a hand beneath her sports bra and cup a breast. She leaned back against him as he slowly slid all the way inside of her. They released moans of pleasure when he was fully inside of her.

His mouth never left hers as he took her on a slow deep ride. She loved the way he touched her, made her feel and set her body on fire and knew that she would never want another man. She loved him and no longer doubted his ability to stay with her and see this thing through. She'd been worried when he told her that he wanted to give them a chance. With his history she would have been a fool not to worry, but she loved him and couldn't deny him a chance to try.

It was the best decision of her life. She had the man that she loved and had never been happier, but thanks to the way her mother brought her up that made her nervous. This was almost too good to be true and she was afraid that it wouldn't last. She'd been raised to believe that good things didn't happen to people like her and it was hard to accept that right now her life was perfect.

"Are you okay?" Eric asked, pulling away to look down at her, but thankfully he never stopped his slow thrusts in her because she was pretty sure she'd kill him if he did.

"Yeah," she said huskily as she wrapped her arm around his neck and pulled him down for another kiss.

It wasn't too long before she needed more. Keeping one arm wrapped around his neck she reached down between her legs and traced her fingers over her open wet slit and over his shaft as it slid inside of her. She carefully ran her nails over his exposed shaft and nearly came when he let out a loud growl of approval.

"Don't stop," he whispered against her lips as his hold on her breast tightened. He pinched her hard nipple between his fingers and gently twisted it, sending a shocking surge of pleasure throughout her body.

For the next few minutes she ran her fingers from his shaft to her clit as he continued to take her slowly. When she managed to reach between them and run her wet hand over his balls he slammed into her so she did it again and again until he let out a ragged curse and pushed her down onto the floor where he followed. He wrapped an arm around her waist and with his other hand he grabbed a fistful of her hair and gave it a tug until she tilted her head back for his kiss.

His thrusts became hard and punishing, leaving her barely able to breathe as pleasure like nothing she'd ever known before coiled between her legs. When his hand slid down her stomach to dive between her legs she screamed and didn't stop screaming until she felt his cock harden impossibly further inside her. He groaned long and loud in her ear as she felt him release inside of her.

Minutes later as she struggled to catch her breath he slid out of her and got to his feet. When she could only lay there watching him, he let out a long suffering sigh and reached down and pulled her up onto her feet.

"You might want to get ready. We're going to be late for work," he said, giving her bare bottom a little pat and squeeze before he headed for the door, whistling, she noted.

"I was ready twenty minutes ago," she pointed out, even as she struggled to pull up her panties.

"Uh huh, sure you were," he said, tucking himself back in and zipping up and just like that he was ready for work and she needed to head back to the bathroom to get ready again. Sometimes it really sucked to be a woman, she decided as she stumbled thanks to the pants around her ankles.

* * * *

"Is it true?" Jeff asked the second Eric stepped into the station.

"Is what true?" he asked, noticing that every conversation had stopped and all eyes were on him.

"About you and Joe? Mark's sister claims that she saw the two of you making out at the movies Sunday night," Jeff said, looking a little too interested for his comfort.

After ditching his mother and brother at a chick flick they'd gone to see an action flick and the moment the lights went out his mouth was on hers until some kid with too much acne and a flashlight asked them to leave. Before he could bitch the kid out Joe was dragging him out of the theatre and to his car and demanding that he move his ass. He would have argued with her, but she chose the moment he started driving to reach between his legs and caress his aching erection.

"Yeah, so?" he asked, wondering what the big deal was.

Jeff grinned hugely at that little announcement. He turned to the group of men playing pool. "Pay up," he said, holding his hand out as several men slapped money in his hand.

"I didn't think Joe was that desperate," one of the men grumbled.

"I'm not," Joe said, walking past him. "I lost a bet," she said with a helpless shrug that earned a laugh from the men and admiration from him. He didn't think he could love a woman more than he loved her.

"Is our third rider here yet?" he asked as he stepped behind Joe to punch in.

That quickly ended whatever amusement the men felt. "Yeah, the cocky little bastard is out in the garage hanging out with Teddy," Jeff said.

"Bill really fucked up when he had him do a third ride with that asshole," another man grumbled.

"Did he ride along this weekend?" Joe asked as she walked over to the open kitchen to grab a bottle of water.

"Uh huh," Dan, a firefighter of fifteen years said. "Teddy volunteered to work with him and guess what? The little shit got his first write up for talking shit to a nurse."

"And he's still here?" Eric asked, shocked that he hadn't been given his walking papers then and there. The man wasn't union and Bill usually didn't put up with that type of bullshit.

"Bill tried to give him the boot, but his uncle called in another favor. They're hoping the two of you will get the little shit to mellow the fuck out," Bret, an EMT, said as he walked into the room. "Personally I'd love to bitch slap the little bastard, but Bill already asked me not to do that."

He shared a look with Joe and knew that she was considering killing Bill for forcing them to put up with him. Two weeks they had to put up with him, he thought with a groan as he took Joe's water from her and took a sip before returning it to her. With one look at her face he knew they were both on the same page.

As long as Greg did what he was told, watched his mouth and didn't pull any bullshit they'd deal with him, but the second the little shit stepped out of line he'd yank him back and if that didn't work he'd drop his ass back at the station. He didn't give a flying fuck if the city council had a problem with that. As a trainer that was his right. It was also his right to refuse to sign him off, which he'd already done and wouldn't hesitate to do again. He didn't give a damn who the kid's uncle was. If he wasn't fit to work on a truck then he needed to find another job.

He was fine with giving the kid a second chance. Working on an ambulance was a stressful job and he knew there was nothing out there to prepare a person for what to expect. Greg was a nervous wreck and he could work around that. What he couldn't deal with was too much attitude, which the man apparently had in spades.

Every time Greg fucked up he got even cockier to hide his nerves and now that he thought his job was protected by his uncle it was only going to get worse. It was the same problem everyone had with Teddy. He didn't belong on a rig, but his training officer, from another station he'd like to add, had let him slide by and signed him off. They'd paired him with a senior EMT who was more than happy to run the show and by the time everyone realized what an asshole he was it was too late. He'd made it past his probationary period and made it into the union.

That wouldn't be happening with Greg. If the man couldn't get his act together and accept some help with learning this job then he'd be out of here. Let his uncle push him off onto another station because he sure as hell wasn't going to sign the kid off and have some patient's death on his conscience.

Without a word, Joe grabbed a shift checklist and headed for the garage. He followed after her, chuckling as the guys' smart ass remarks followed. They walked over to the pegboard and found the slot for ambulance seventeen's keys empty. Hoping the crew from last night simply left the keys in the truck they walked over to the van style ambulances and found Greg and Teddy leaning against the ambulance, trading bullshit stories about women they'd fucked.

He cleared his throat and thankfully they got the message. They sent Joe a look before changing the conversation. Teddy was a pig, but he knew better than treat any of the females that worked at the station like shit. Every man here would be all over him if he made any of them uncomfortable, well on purpose anyway. The guy seemed to make everyone uncomfortable.

Joe tried to open the driver's side door, but it was locked. When she groaned in annoyance after peaking through the window he knew the keys weren't locked inside. Great. They were going to be down a truck until whoever worked the truck last night hauled their ass back here with the keys or Bill came in and unlocked the backups.

"Guess we have to call dispatch to see if they can track down a set of keys for us," Joe said resignedly, shifting her backpack over her shoulder.

Greg shook his head as he held up the keys for the ambulance. "There's no need. I got them right here."

"Did you check the truck out?" Joe asked, holding her hand out for the keys, but Greg either didn't see her or ignored her as he put them back in his pocket.

"That's the crew's job to do at night. It's a waste of time to check it out in the beginning of the shift," he said with a shrug, moving to turn his back on Joe.

"It's part of the job, Greg. We need to check the truck out before we go into service. Hand me the keys, *please*," she said tightly and he knew she was just barely reigning in her temper.

He simply shook his head. "The truck's all set," he said dismissively.

Before Joe could take another calming breath he was in the little bastard's face. "She's your training officer. When she asks you to do something you better fucking do it. I don't give a flying fuck who your uncle is. If you don't pass our standards you will not be working in this station. Understand?" he asked as he held his hand out for the keys.

Grounding his jaw, Greg reached into his pocket and handed the keys over. He shot a look to Teddy who of course kept his mouth shut. If he thought that Teddy was going to put himself out for him he was mistaken.

He tossed Joe the keys as he gestured to the ambulance. "Get in there and start checking out the truck."

With a glare in his direction Greg moved his ass and he knew he was going to have to double check everything afterwards. The man hadn't been here a month and he was already adopting Teddy's work ethic. As Joe walked past him she muttered a few unkind words about his ego, but he let it go since he knew she was just pissed off that he had to handle the prick for her.

By the time he bought her breakfast, and apparently since it was his fault that she couldn't grab a bite to eat before they left for work this morning he was treating, she'd forgive him. He supposed since he loved her that he could spoil her a little. O'Malley's bakery ran a two for one deal on coffee rolls every Tuesday so he supposed he'd get her one.

"Is it true what I heard about you and Joe?" Teddy asked.

"Depends on what you heard," he said, climbing in the back of the ambulance and double checking the oxygen levels.

"I heard lots of things, but I was referring to you finally manning up and going for it."

"We're together. Is there a problem with that?" he asked in a bored tone.

"Nah, I'm just shocked that Joe became that desperate that's all," Teddy said, sounding amused and he had to wonder how many times today he was going to hear that.

"I'm not desperate!" Joe yelled from the front of the truck. The admission pleased him until she added, "I was drunk."

"I'm not buying you breakfast for that, smart ass!"

"You really are a cheap bastard," he thought he heard her say, but decided to ignore it and the bastard laughing at him.

Chapter 26

"Let me get that for you, Joe," Greg said, reaching past her to pay the cashier when Eric stepped in front of him, forcing the man back and making Joe wish that she banged out today.

Their shift only began two hours ago but already she wanted to bitch slap them both. Not a good sign when she still had fourteen more hours to go before her shift ended. She really wasn't sure she'd be able to tolerate this little pissing contest for that long.

In Eric's defense, Greg really did seem to be going out of his way to piss him off. It was pretty obvious to her at least that Greg hadn't appreciated being put in his place and was trying to use her to piss Eric off. Every five minutes he seemed to be hitting on her, but only when Eric was around. The only thing it was accomplishing was giving her a headache.

She really didn't need this. All she wanted to do was work. If he wanted to be trained then she'd do that too, but his attitude clearly stated that he wasn't here to learn. He was too damn cocky to realize that he didn't have what it took to do this job and instead of admitting that and asking for help he was too busy pretending that he knew what he was doing.

Eric handed over the money for their order and grabbed the bakery bag and cardboard tray with their drinks and gestured towards the door. "Get your food and meet us in the truck," he said, not bothering to look Greg's way as they headed towards the door.

She held the door open for Eric and caught a glimpse of Greg glaring at Eric's back. Yup, this was just getting better and better. After twelve years she really should be used to this testosterone charged environment and for the most part she was. She just wasn't in the mood for it today.

"Are you okay?" Eric asked as they climbed into the ambulance and shut his door.

"Yeah, I'm fine," she said, forcing a smile as she accepted her hot chocolate and chocolate frosted coffee roll from him. She took a sip of her hot chocolate before placing it in the cup holder above the control unit located between their seats. She shifted until her back was against the door and used the steering wheel to rest her elbow as she nibbled on her coffee roll.

"I think Nathan's still pissed at me," Eric said, sounding pleased.

"Can you blame him?" she asked, inwardly wincing on Nathan's behalf.

After Amber stormed off Sunday evening Eric decided to make his brother's life a living hell by taking Alice aside and explaining that Nathan felt left out and would really like her to help him find someone special, but he was too embarrassed to ask. Unfortunately for Nathan, Alice jumped on board with that plan and if she wasn't afraid to draw Alice's attention to their relationship and any type of future she would have said something.

Maybe......

The whole thing did promise to be rather entertaining and she did love a good laugh at family dinners so maybe she'd just sit back and enjoy it for a while. She had a feeling that Nathan wouldn't be able to sidestep his mother's efforts as easily as Eric had. He was a pushover so he'd probably end up taking at least a few of them out to please his mother. Of course she'd have to tag along and she'd bet every last cent she had that Eric would be more than happy to join them.

"You know that Teddy tried signing Greg out of third riding this weekend?" Eric asked, drawing her attention.

She frowned at that little announcement. "He can't sign him out. He's not a trainer," she said, wondering what the hell was wrong with Teddy. Even he should realize that Greg didn't belong on a truck.

"Bill already chewed him a new one," Eric said, opening his bakery bag and grabbing his coffee roll.

"Why the hell would Teddy do something so stupid? There's no way he did it to get Greg as a partner. If he worked with Greg he'd have to do all the work and there's no way in hell Teddy would willingly screw himself over."

"I think he was hoping that Greg's uncle would put a good word in for him to get him the supervisor job over at the 603," he said with a shrug as if he hadn't just said something truly frightening.

Teddy as a supervisor? She prayed that never happened. Bill wouldn't allow that and thankfully the city council didn't have a say when it came to promotions. She knew that Teddy wanted a supervisor position to get the hell off the truck and sooner or later he'd realize that that wouldn't happen as long as he worked for the city.

A private ambulance company was a different story all together. She'd heard horror stories about assholes being promoted who didn't deserve it. As much as she hated to admit this she'd seen incompetent supervisors from private ambulance companies show up at the scene of an accident and screw everything up.

As much as she loved her job she wasn't sure she could ever go the private route. From what she'd seen there was too much drama and backstabbing. A few years ago when overtime became tight Eric looked into working part time for a mom and pop ambulance company. The guy had been an asshole with a chip on his shoulder against Bill and spent the majority of the time trying to convince Eric that Bill was an asshole who had no business being a supervisor. Halfway through the interview Eric got up and walked out. It wasn't too hard to find out that the man used to work for the city and had been fired for stealing equipment.

"Never going to happen," she said, shaking her head as she popped another bite of coffee roll into her mouth. She looked towards the coffee shop and saw Greg leaning against the counter, talking up one of the servers through the large storefront window.

Eric cleared his throat and she couldn't help but look over at him. He looked suddenly nervous as he toyed with his coffee roll. "What do you want to do tonight?" he asked, throwing her a nervous glance.

"What I do every Tuesday night after our shift," she said slowly, wondering what the hell was going on with him. He was never like this around her. Then again the dynamics of their relationship had changed so maybe she should give him a little slack, she thought as he shifted uncomfortably in his seat.

"And, ah," he cleared his throat, looking uncomfortable, "what are your plans tomorrow?"

"Unless I get overtime I thought I'd clean up the house and relax a little. Why?"

He cleared his throat again. "I was thinking that maybe we could-"

"*Echo seventeen*?" dispatch chimed in over the radio, cutting off whatever he was about to say.

Shooting Eric a sideways glance she grabbed the mike. "Echo seventeen."

"*Echo seventeen, I need you to take a priority three call at Hillsmith nursing home for an unknown medical.*"

"Priority three at Hillsmith nursing home, received," she said, returning the mike to the dashboard. She placed her half-eaten coffee roll in the bag and handed it to Eric, who looked surprisingly relieved. She was curious about that, but it would have to wait until later.

She started the ambulance and gave the horn a little push to get Greg's attention. He held up a hand, indicating that she should wait while he finished up his conversation with the cashier. Shaking her head in disbelief, she threw the ambulance in reverse and headed for the road.

"Not in the mood for his bullshit I take it," Eric mused as he pulled out a run sheet and began to fill in their information.

"Nope, not at all," she said, spotting Greg running out of the coffee shop and heading for the ambulance.

When she stopped she heard the backdoor open. It slammed shut as she pulled onto the road. She didn't even bothering waiting for Greg to buckle up, but headed for the nursing home. It wasn't her job to wait for him. If he wanted to do this job then he needed to be prepared to drop everything that he was doing when a call came in and he really needed to drop his attitude while he was at it.

"The next time you ignore a call I'm writing you up," Eric drawled lazily as he continued to fill in their information.

Greg didn't say anything and she wasn't exactly surprised. Eric might appear to be calm and relaxed, but she knew that he was truly pissed and Greg must have picked up on that as well. This call might have been called in as a non-emergency medical transport, but they'd learned a long time ago that that status could quickly change so they didn't drag their feet doing the call. It also didn't hurt that they'd probably get their asses chewed out by a nurse or a family member if they took their sweet time getting to the call.

Ten minutes later she pulled the ambulance up and around the circle drive to the front door and parked behind a chair car, a van decked out to transport people in wheelchair and sometimes those who could walk but needed an extra hand. The only thing a chair car driver needed was a license and a valid CPR card, other than that it was basically a cab.

She called them on scene, turned off the ambulance and pocketed the keys. By the time she made it to the back of the ambulance Eric was already pulling their stretcher out and gesturing for Greg to move his ass.

"Can I drive?" Greg asked as he hopped out of the ambulance.

"No," she said with absolutely no hesitation.

"Driving is part of the job. How can I do my job if you won't let me drive?" he pointed out with irritation.

"Because you haven't learned to do the most important part of the job yet," Eric explained.

"What's that?" Greg said, moving to walk past the stretcher.

Eric pushed the stretcher in his direction, cutting him off. When Greg only frowned, Eric gestured to the stretcher. With a glare, Greg grabbed the front metal handle and gave it a pull in the direction of the double doors.

"You need to learn how to deal with patients and run a call. If you can't do that then there's no point in learning how to drive an ambulance because you won't be working here," Eric explained as he took the rear position of the stretcher, leaving her with nothing to do but shut the doors and follow after them.

"I know how to handle a call," Greg argued. "I've been doing it for several weeks now."

"No, you haven't. The only thing you've managed to do is ride along and puke," Eric pointed out as he pressed the call button by the front door to be buzzed in.

"I was sick," Greg argued, lying and further irritating the hell out of her. He'd get so much further if he just admitted he was nervous and ask for help, but he was too damn worried about his pride and that was going to be his downfall.

"I don't really care what the problem was. Just do your goddamn job so that we can do ours," Eric said as they were buzzed in. Greg's face turned red, but he didn't say anything else as they walked inside.

Since Eric was the tech for the call she let him do all the talking.

"Good morning, ladies. Who do you have for me today?" he asked charmingly as he set his clipboard on the nurse's station counter. She noted that several of the nurses blushed and she had to bite back a smile. Eric really had no idea how devastating that bad boy charm of his was or he would have used it on her last night to get her to give him that half hour back massage that he demanded for making her dinner. In the end she'd slapped some scented oil in his hand and he'd given her a body massage to die for, all while grumbling and bitching of course.

"Beverly needs to go the emergency room to have her central line replaced," Margaret, a nurse, said as she placed Beverly's inch think medical file on the counter for Eric.

With a murmured "thank you" he opened the file and began to fill in their run sheet with Beverly's medical and insurance information. She was about to suggest that he have Greg do it when she spotted the man in question lounging lazily in a chair by the nurses' station.

Great. Just what they needed, another Teddy to deal with, she thought dryly as she grabbed the stretcher by the safety bar and headed for Beverly's room. She didn't need to ask where it was. After five years of picking Beverly up for this and that she knew exactly where the woman's room was.

She was a favorite patient of theirs and every time they had to return a patient here they stopped by to check on her. Beverly was black, barely five foot nothing, and was one of the sweetest women Joe had ever met. If Joe could, she'd adopt the woman as her grandmother.

"Joe!" Beverly said, grinning hugely when she spotted her. Joe smiled in return, pushing the stretcher to the side in the small room before she walked over to help Beverly gather the things on her lap and move them to the nightstand.

"Are you here for me?" the older woman asked, smiling sweetly up at Joe.

"I'm here for you, darling. Joe's just tagging along," Eric announced as he walked into the room. He tossed the clipboard on the straight basket beneath the head of the stretcher and walked over to Beverly. He took both the old woman's frail hands into his. "Are you ready to run away with me yet, sweetheart? Just say the word and we can be in Vegas in hours making our love legal."

With a soft laugh Beverly playfully swatted Eric's hands away.

"Is this your way of denying our love once again?" Eric asked, pouting.

"I'm afraid so," Beverly said matter-of-factly as she grabbed her reading glasses and a paperback novel and hugged them to her chest.

"What if I beg?" Eric asked, lowering the bed's side rails.

"You already have," Beverly pointed out with a smile.

Eric sighed heavily. "It's because you want a younger man, isn't it? I've grown past my prime and now you're done with me."

Beverly nodded solemnly. "I'm afraid that's it."

"I don't think I'll ever recover," Eric said, sighing as he leaned over and scooped Beverly up into his arms. Normally they would have placed the stretcher against the bed and worked together to shift Beverly onto the stretcher, but she barely weighed a hundred pounds. Plus, they both knew she got a kick out of being swept off her feet by a handsome man.

"Probably not," Beverly agreed as Eric gently placed her on the stretcher and began strapping her in.

"Where's Greg?" Joe asked when the other man didn't walk into the room by the time Beverly was all loaded up and ready to go.

Eric's lips twitched as he said, "He went for a walk."

Chapter 27

"Are you going to tell me where Greg is yet?" Joe asked as she perused the vending machine selection in the EMS room of Shamrock Hospital's ER. It was a place set up for EMTs to fill out their paperwork as well as swap out equipment. Some hospitals didn't have any designated areas for EMTs so they knew they were fortunate that the hospital gave them a room to work out of.

It made it a hell of a lot easier filling out paperwork in a designated area than trying to hunt down some counter space, or worse, using the stretcher. As long as they kept this room clean the hospital was happy to let them use it.

"I might if you buy me a Coke," he said, filling in the narrative section on the run sheet.

"You drive a hard bargain," she said, sighing as she purchased a twenty ounce bottle of Coke and placed it in front of him. "Okay, spill. What happened to our third rider?"

He opened the bottle and took a sip as Joe sat on his left leg and put her arm around his neck. His arm automatically went around her waist as he considered how to answer her question.

"I believe I mentioned that he went for a walk," he said, feeling his lips twitch from the memory.

"Yes, you said that," she agreed as she stole his soda and took a sip.

"Did I mention that I discovered the reason why he was acting so damn cocky?" he asked offhandedly as he took the soda back from her and took a sip.

"No," she said, pursing up her lips in thought. "I'm pretty sure I would have remembered that part."

"Do you remember USG Ambulance?" he asked, knowing that she already did.

"That ambulance company you interviewed with a few years ago?" she asked, shifting to get more comfortable on his leg.

"Well, it seems that he interviewed with them last week and had his uncle put in a good word for him. It seems that he was just waiting for their call," he said absently as he ran his eyes over her, appreciating the way her uniform fit her.

"I'm guessing he got it while I was talking to Beverly," she surmised, giving him a sexy little smile even as she gently cupped his chin and forced his eyes up.

"Apparently they're convinced that he only needs to do their two day requirement of ride along before they put him to work," he said, wondering if she'd be up to hunting down an empty hall closet and fulfilling another one of his fantasies.

"So he just walked out?" she asked, frowning in adorable confusion.

"More or less," Eric admitted with a mumble.

Her eyes narrowed on him. "What did you do?"

He blinked innocently. "I didn't do anything," he lied.

"Uh huh," she said, obviously not believing him as she stood up and stole his soda and walked back over to the vending machine to pick out a snack.

"Did somebody at least call dispatch and let them know that he quit?" she asked as she counted out enough change for a package of peanut butter cups.

"He called Bill," Eric said, not mentioning that the little bastard demanded that Joe and he bring him back to the station. He calmed the little prick down by arranging a ride for him. One that took him to the middle of nowhere and forced the little prick to walk ten miles to the nearest gas station, but he decided it was best not to mention that or the fact that the guys may have decided to give Greg a farewell gift by making it easy for him to return his uniform. So the asshole was probably walking along Madison Road at this very moment in his boxers and boots.

But Joe really didn't need to know about *that*.

He finished up his report and headed for the door, pausing only long enough to give her a quick kiss and swipe the candy bar out of her hand. When she swatted him on the ass he simply ignored it as he finished off her chocolate. Why did the food he stole from Joe always taste so damn good? he wondered as he reached out and stole back his soda. He ignored her muttered promises to kick his ass and dropped his run sheet off at the nurse's station on his way out to the ambulance bay.

"I'll clear us with dispatch since you're still enjoying my snack," she said, shooting him a look that promised all kinds of pain for his poor wallet.

If he wasn't head over heels in love with this woman he'd consider dropping her for her gold digging ways. But he did love her so he was probably going to have to suck it up and treat her to the dollar menu at McDonalds.

* * * *

"Did you call 911?" Joe asked as she bent down to look into the adorable little boy's face.

"Yes," he said, nodding.

"Is someone hurt?" she asked, looking around the front porch and yard and not seeing anyone. Eric walked past her and looked through the window.

"Yes," the little boy who couldn't be older than five said, gesturing towards the backyard.

With a slight nod, Eric jumped over the porch railing and headed into the backyard.

"Can you tell me what happened?" she asked the little boy, deciding it was best to keep him here until Eric let her know what they were dealing with. If it was something this little boy shouldn't be seeing she was going to have to call over one of the neighbors that were now watching them to come over and watch him until they could get the police to come and handle the boy.

"Roger hurt Toby really bad," the little boy said with his little chin wobbling.

"Where's your mommy and daddy, buddy?" she asked soothingly.

"They're out. I was s'posed to be with Uncle Charlie, but I didn't like leaving Roger and Toby by themselves so I came back," he admitted, shuffling his feet nervously.

"Does your Uncle Charlie know where you are?" she asked, guessing it wouldn't be very long before the man in question showed up or the police did.

The little boy shook his head stubbornly. "No, he doesn't want me to play with Roger. He thinks Roger is bad."

"What's your name?" she asked, already noting the name Henderson on the mailbox.

"Caleb."

"Okay, Caleb. I need to call my dispatcher and have him call your uncle. Do you know your uncle's phone number?"

He nodded.

"What is it?'

He squished up his face in thought. "It has a five in it."

Okay.......

"Do you know where your uncle lives?"

"Uh huh," he said, wiping his nose on the back of his arm.

"Can you tell me?" she asked patiently as she pulled her cell phone out and started to scroll down until she found dispatch's phone number.

"That way," Caleb said, pointing in no particular direction that really helped her.

Biting back a sigh she dialed dispatch.

"Dispatch," Hank said in way of answer. If she'd called the emergency line he would have told her that the line was being recorded, but thankfully she didn't have to deal with that.

"Hey, Hank, it's Joe. Um, I have a Caleb Henderson at that call you sent us on. Has anyone by chance called looking for him?" she asked, wondering what was taking Eric so long. He should have at least given her a head's up by now.

She heard him sigh in relief. "We have police and fire scouring the town for him. Is the call his home address?"

"Yes."

"There should be a police unit there soon. Is the boy hurt?"

"Doesn't appear to be. He called for his friends. Eric's checking now I should-"

"*Holy shit*!" Eric suddenly shouted, startling the hell out of her. Seconds later he came running back around towards the front of the house. He paused in his mad dash only long enough to throw Caleb over his shoulder and grab her by the hand and drag her towards the ambulance.

"Joe? What the hell is going on?" Hank demanded, sounding nervous, which was good because that meant that she wasn't the only one.

"Is that dispatch?" Eric asked as he ushered her and Caleb into the back of the ambulance.

"Yes."

He didn't say anything else to her as he grabbed the phone from her. "Hank? Call animal control," she heard him say as he paced in front of the ambulance, but thankfully didn't close the doors.

"I think Roger is going to be in trouble," Caleb said sullenly.

A sneaking suspicion crawled up her back. "Caleb, who is Roger?"

"He hurt Toby," Caleb mumbled sadly.

"Is Toby a dog?" Eric asked, still pacing as he kept an eye on the house.

Caleb nodded. "He's big."

"That's what I figured," Eric said, turning his back to talk quietly into the phone.

Sick of being left out of the loop, she climbed out of the ambulance, motioning for Caleb to stay where he was and walked towards the back of the house. She hated not knowing what the hell was going on.

Eric knew that and she had a sneaking suspicion that he was going a little overboard with trying to protect her. If he was still hell bent on getting her off the truck after everything they'd gone through in the past week she was going to......going to.........

Why was that really thick yellow and white hose moving? she wondered.

More importantly why was it coming towards her? she wondered as she registered Eric's hand on her arm as he yanked her away and pulled her into a run.

She swallowed hard as they ran towards the ambulance. "Was that a *snake*?" she asked, unable to hide the disgust in her tone. She hated snakes, absolutely hated them, which was probably why Eric didn't tell her what it was. He knew she'd freak out.

"Yup. Looks like a twenty foot python and that large lump is probably Toby," he said, giving her a gentle push to get her to climb back into the ambulance.

"I see." She nodded hollowly as she reached out and pulled one of the back doors shut.

"You want to stay in here until it's captured?" he asked, moving to shut the other door for her.

She gave him a "duh" look that had him wincing as he shut the other door. Joe wasted no time in locking them. Then she scrambled over Caleb who was frowning to lock the side doors as well.

"I don't think Roger will hurt you," he said.

"Really? Why not?" she asked absently as she kept watch through the side window. She swore if she saw anything yellow or white move towards the ambulance that she was driving off and never looking back.

"Cause I don't think he can fit you and Toby in his tummy," Caleb explained, probably thinking that he was helping.

He wasn't.

Even if they weren't dating she knew that she'd be making Eric sleep with her for the next week or so. They'd be using the same drill as the time she found that large black spider crawling across her kitchen floor at two in the morning. Only this time he would also have to check around the property too before checking every room in her house and doing a double check of her room. He would also be responsible for getting up and checking her room and bathroom when she woke up during the night and needed to pee as well as checking the kitchen when she needed a drink.

At least she didn't have to worry about him planting fake snakes around her house since she was pretty sure that he learned his lesson from hiding that fake spider in her cereal the last time. He may have thought it was funny at first, but when she accidentally kicked him in the balls he'd learned his lesson rather quickly.

Granted, she wouldn't have kicked him between his legs if he hadn't fallen to the ground laughing his ass off at her the same time the fake spider was knocked to the ground. Okay, so kick might be an understatement. It might have been more like a stomping or two..........five times.

In her defense she had been a little too freaked out to notice his screams of agony.

Chapter 28

"Wow, I'm impressed," Jeff said and Eric knew the man wasn't talking about the way he was washing the ambulance.

He looked up at the small group of men who had gathered in front of him as he dunked the brush in the soapy water. "Impressed with what?" he asked, knowing that they'd keep bugging the shit out of him until he bit.

"Three months and she hasn't killed you yet," Jeff said, shaking his head in wonder. "I'm shocked."

He was too.

Three months, easily the longest relationship he'd ever had in his life. If at all possible he loved her more today than the day she took a chance on him. She was everything to him, his partner, his best friend, his lover and his soul and he had fucked it all up

He knew this day would come, but he'd been so damned sure that he could do this with her, but he'd been wrong. He'd obviously done something really stupid, because she was pissed at him. Well, he was pretty sure that she was pissed at him since she hadn't said more than a few words to him since their overtime shift ended last night.

When he showed up at her door last night to take her out she mumbled an excuse, gave him a quick kiss on the cheek and sent him on his way. This morning he came in a bit early, anxious to see her. Since they came together three months ago they hadn't spent a single night apart and he hated not holding her in his arms last night. She was pulling away from him and he didn't know why.

Sure, he'd screwed up along the way and pissed her off. They fought and they practically made up before they were done arguing. She made him unbelievably happy and he couldn't for the life of him figure out how he'd fucked up. Last night while he ignored his brother's bitching about their mother's latest setup, he'd paced his living room, taxing his brain and tried to pinpoint exactly how he'd messed everything up. He was sure that he'd done something to piss her off, but after twelve hours of racking his brain he couldn't figure out what that was.

This morning he'd come up with a plan. Since he didn't know what he'd done he was just going to focus on making it up to her and hope that it was enough. He was going to do all the things that he knew she liked and a few dozen that he'd seen his brother do for women over the years. If by the end of their shift she hadn't forgiven him then he was going to have to apologize and promise never to do it again and hope that she dropped a hint about what he did. If that didn't work then he'd have to send Nathan over to her house with a half dozen of those milk shakes that she loved and hope that she told his brother what he did so that he could fix this before it was too late.

"Uh oh, someone's in the dog house," one of guys crooned.

Frowning, he looked up in time to see Joe climb into the back of the ambulance without a word to anyone. Thankfully the guys lost interest after a few minutes of busting his balls and walked off, giving him a chance to set his plan into motion.

He finished rinsing off the ambulance the same time Joe finished checking out the ambulance. When she jumped out and shut the doors he walked to the front of the ambulance and grabbed the large white pastry box that he hid from the guys.

"Good morning, Joe," he said, holding the box out to her and feeling like an idiot when she only stared at it. "I got you breakfast."

"Oh," she said distractedly as she accepted the box and looked around the garage. "Thanks. Do you mind getting on the road a little early I want to pick something up for breakfast," she explained, still not looking at him.

Feeling his lips twitch, he gestured to the box. "I picked breakfast up for you," he said, trying not to laugh since he knew that would only make things worse.

"Oh," she said, frowning down at the box. "Then I need to grab a coffee."

"Got one in the truck for you," he said, feeling quite proud of himself for meeting all her needs this morning.

"Thanks," she mumbled, looking lost.

It was then that he realized he'd gone beyond fucking up. It was over. She was dumping him and he was helpless to stop it. He didn't know what he should say or do, but he knew that he didn't want this to go down in front of the guys. If she was going to break his heart then he wanted it done in private.

"Let's go for a ride," he said, gesturing to the ambulance.

With a nod she walked around the front of the ambulance and climbed into the passenger seat. After a slight pause he followed. He called them on the air, half praying that dispatch had a call for them so that they could put this off for a little longer, but they didn't. They were posted to the south side and he thought that maybe that was for the best.

For ten minutes they rode in silence as Joe absently toyed with a corner of the cardboard box. His hands tightened around the steering wheel as he wondered how something that hadn't even happened yet could hurt so damn much. His chest ached and he felt sick to his stomach. Any other woman and he would have beat her to the punch line and dropped her before she could drop him, but this was Joe.

His Joe.

He needed to hear it from her lips. He needed to know that this was what she wanted. He'd give her a chance to explain all the ways he'd fucked up and then he'd use that newfound knowledge to fix their relationship and beg her to take him back. She had to know that he couldn't live without her and that he loved her. That had to mean something.

"Echo seventeen on south side," he said into the mike as he threw the ambulance into park.

"*Echo seventeen, received.*"

For a moment they sat there in silence as he did his best to prepare for what was about to happen. What he hadn't been prepared for was Joe suddenly unbuckling her seatbelt and scrambling over the middle console to climb onto his lap and wrap her arms around him as she buried her face against his neck.

"Joe? Baby, what's wrong?" he asked, wondering if he should feel relieved that she was clinging to him so tightly. If she was ending things between them he didn't think she'd be reacting this way.

At least he hoped not.

It was a little concerning that after three months he still didn't have this relationship shit down. Then again being with Joe was nothing like dating those other women. With her he was calm, relaxed and happy. He didn't have to try hard to impress her like he'd done with the other women and he'd only done that to get them in bed just to get off. Things weren't like that with Joe. He touched her and did things for her because he enjoyed being with her, not because he wanted something from her.

"Nothing," she mumbled against his skin.

"Nothing, huh?"

"No."

"Then why are you on my lap?" he asked, wrapping his arms around her and pressing a kiss to the top of her head.

"Because you're comfy," she mumbled, snuggling deeper into his arms.

"What's wrong, Joe?" he asked softly, hating to see her upset. He almost wished that she was mad at him, which he was eighty percent sure at the moment that she wasn't, just so he could apologize and fix it.

"Why do you think something's wrong?" she mumbled, repositioning herself until she was sitting across his lap with her back against his door. She laid her head against his shoulder while she absently played with the buttons on his shirt.

"Besides the fact that you canceled our date at the last minute last night and you aren't devouring the pastries I bought you?" he asked dryly.

She shrugged. "I could have had a better offer last night."

"And how would that explain you turning down free pastries?" he asked, feeling himself relax.

"Because he fed me breakfast in bed," she answered, turning her attention to tracing shapes on his shirt.

"Was he good?" he asked, leaning his head back to look down at her.

She let out a long suffering sigh. "I've had better."

"I'm sorry to hear that," he said, smiling as he leaned down to press a kiss to her forehead.

"So was I. I had such high hopes for him, too," she muttered, giving up her idle movements to simply snuggle in his arms.

He looked around the abandoned parking lot, noting a few private ambulances also stationed in the area. Normally he wouldn't mind shooting the breeze with any of them to pass the time, but today he was glad that they weren't parked close to them and the other EMTs didn't look like they were going to come over and chat anytime soon. He pressed a kiss to Joe's head as he looked across the street at the convenient store, wondering if he should get her some chocolate since it always seemed to make her feel better.

"Isn't that Greg?" she suddenly asked.

Curious, he followed her gaze and sure enough there was Greg. They'd had several third riders before and after him, but not one of them had pissed them off more than that guy and he was counting the guy he'd knocked out.

"Oh my god..........," Joe breathed, sounding as shocked as he probably looked.

"They have a third rider training with him?" he asked, shaking his head in disbelief.

"Looks like it," she said as they watched a timid young woman step out of the back of the ambulance, wearing a dull gray uniform that matched Greg's. She walked over to join Greg and his partner at the front of the ambulance where they stood talking.

He knew a lot could happen in three months and Greg could have grown up and did his damndest to learn the job, but he knew that wasn't the case. They had several run-ins with the jackass over the past three months and seen his skills first hand. It was more than obvious that he didn't belong on a truck. He was still a cocky arrogant little jerk who mouthed off to nurses and didn't know shit when it came to simple care for a patient. There were more important things to focus on, he reminded himself. Like the woman in his arms who was obviously upset.

"What's going on, Joe?" he asked softly.

"Promise you won't get mad?"

"I promise," he agreed even as he wondered what she could possibly tell him that would upset him. Then a thought occurred to him, a rather frightening thought.

Could she be pregnant?

They'd been having unprotected sex for three months and even though she was on birth control that was still a risk they should have considered. Birth control wasn't a hundred percent and accidents happened. A baby with Joe? Hell, yeah, but not now.

Not yet.

He wasn't ready to be a daddy yet. He wanted to focus on Joe for a little longer before they moved ahead. Hell, he wanted to be a paramedic by the time they had a baby just so he could make more money so that she wouldn't have to work.

But if she was pregnant now he wouldn't have a choice. He'd have to man up and do the right thing by her. If she was pregnant now that also meant that he'd have to wait a few years to do the paramedic course. He loved his job, but they would need the money. He'd have to take as much overtime as he could get his hands on and hope she didn't kill him because that would leave her to watch the baby by herself most of the time. He wouldn't be happy about it, but he would do it for her.

"Bill called me last night," she said, shooting him a look as she nibbled on her bottom lip.

"And?" he prompted when it looked as though she was going to drag this out.

"You remember when we signed up for the paramedic training list?" she asked, sounding hesitant.

"Yes." They'd signed up six years ago with the knowledge that they would probably never make it up the list before they decided to go to school.

Every two years the city came up with enough money to send two city EMTs to train as paramedics. It was a long list and more importantly it would save whoever won the spot fifteen grand. It also meant those selected wouldn't have to worry about losing their jobs while they attended training. As great as it would have been to be selected they'd known the chances of that were slim and had been saving money every year to pay for school and to cover bills while they trained. He estimated that they had another year or two of saving before they could do it.

"We got it this year," she announced quietly.

It took a moment for her words to sink in and when they did he couldn't help smiling. "We got it?" he asked excitedly.

She swallowed nervously as she nodded. "Bill called me on my way home. I told him that I would tell you," she explained.

"We got it?" he asked, barely able to believe it. When she nodded he leaned down and kissed her, unable to help himself. This was great. This was beyond fucking great. Not only did they now have a serious chunk of change in the bank to keep, but their training would be paid for and they had guaranteed jobs at the end.

It also meant that they could move forward, something he'd been toying with since they got together. They'd known each other for over twenty years and he knew he wanted to be with her for the rest of his life.

"You got it," she mumbled against his mouth.

"What?" he asked, sure he misheard her as he pulled back.

"I said," she said, licking her lips nervously, "that you got it. I turned my spot down."

He could only stare in wonder at her for a moment before he blurted, "Why the hell did you do that?"

Chapter 29

"You promised not to get mad," she said, trying to climb off his lap, but the damn man pulled her back down and wrapped his arms around her, keeping her right where he wanted her.

"That's before I found out that you did something insanely stupid," he snapped. "I'm calling Bill and telling him that you changed your mind," he said, shifting her in his lap to get at his phone.

She snatched the phone out of his hand before he could make the call and tossed it on her seat where he couldn't get it. She knew he'd be mad about this, but she couldn't force herself to go through with something that wouldn't make her happy.

Six months ago she would have been ecstatic to get a free ride to paramedic school, but now.......

Now she wanted different things in life. Thanks to Eric's over protectiveness she'd discovered that she loved other aspects of this job. She worked two shifts a week as a dispatcher and as much as it pained her to say this, she loved doing that a little more than working on the truck. She also loved teaching.

Several times a month she taught CPR and first aid and a few weeks ago she helped teach the EMT course at the community college and she loved it. She'd never grow rich doing these things, but she really enjoyed doing them. Somehow they went from being her backup plans when she couldn't work on the truck any longer to what she wanted to do now.

She still loved working on the truck, but wanted to do that part time now. She could still work with Eric while he attended school. Once he was working full time as a medic she fully planned on picking up an overtime shift with him once or twice a month. Thankfully she'd taken the course required for basics to work with medics last year so she was all set.

"Give me the phone, Joe," he said, trying to move her off his lap so he could grab the phone.

"It's not what I want anymore, Eric," she said, trying to figure out how the hell she went from wanting this so badly to turning it down flat to take a new direction in life.

"Explain," he said tightly as he sat back and shifted her on his lap so that he was once again looking at her.

"It's all your fault," she said, deciding that was the best way to go. When his eyes narrowed on her she hastily rethought that plan and went with another approach.

She reached up and ran her fingers through his hair as she thought over all the reasons that stopped her from accepting what used to be her dream. Finally she decided on the truth.

"I love working on the truck, Eric. I love working with you, but....."

"But?" he said quietly when she hesitated.

"But I want to try other things. I still plan on keeping my ticket and working with you part time, but I've really been enjoying working in dispatch and teaching and I want to give that a try," she explained, holding back the main reason for her decision since she had no idea where he stood on the matter.

Before she used to imagine her life working side by side with him, more than happy to have at least that much. Since they came together she'd started to have other ideas for her life, things that she fought so hard not to want, but she did. She wanted a life with Eric. She wanted to get married and if that was still too much for him then she would settle for him moving in with her and she wanted a family. Not yet, but soon and she wanted that with him.

"I need to know if I'm part of the reason that you turned this down," he said quietly.

"And if you are?" she asked, not really sure that he'd be happy that she wanted something that he may not be able to give her. The fact that he was able to handle a real relationship with her should have been good enough, but she wanted more.

"Am I part of the reason, Joe?" he asked again.

She looked up and met his eyes and shrugged like it was no big deal even though the thought of him telling her that he couldn't give her anymore scared the living hell out of her. Honestly, she didn't know what she would do if he didn't want anything more than what they had now. This should be more than enough for her, she knew that, but it wasn't. She wanted to fall asleep in his arms every night and wake up the same way every morning. She wanted to fight with him over the remote, manipulate backrubs out of him every week and know that he was hers.

He pressed his lips against her forehead. "Please tell me I'm the reason, Joe."

"Why?" she asked, unable to hide her surprise. Never in a million years would she have thought, prayed yes, that Eric wanted more with her.

"Because I want to know that you want me as much as I want you," he said against her forehead.

"And if I do?" she asked, smiling as she relaxed in his arms.

His hold around her tightened as he let out a little growl that curled her toes. "I wish like hell that we weren't having this conversation at work."

"Me too," she said, sighing softly as she reached up and cupped his jaw. "I love you, Eric."

"I love you too, Joe," he said, pressing another kiss to her forehead before moving back. He reached up and cupped her face. "You know I want to marry you, don't you?" he asked as uncertainty flickered across his features.

"Now I do," she said, leaning in to brush her lips against his, but just like it usually did, the kiss quickly got out of hand.

Although they'd fooled around in the ambulance before they'd never done it in front of an audience and she had no plans on doing it now, but the second their shift was over she was tying him to her bed and using him until they both passed out.

"We have to stop," Eric said, gasping as he pulled back. She nodded her agreement as she climbed off his lap and willed her shaky legs not to give out.

She sat down in her seat and ran her hands down her face, willing her body to cool down and doing her best to resist the urge to jump him. Her eyes landed on the pastry box and sighed in relief, thankful to have something to focus on besides the sudden ache between her legs.

Without a word she handed the apple fritter over to Eric and grabbed the chocolate frosted coffee roll for herself. She took a bite and tried to focus on anything but Eric, but it was difficult being this close to him and not thinking about him or wanting to touch him. For a few minutes they sat there silently as they ate until Eric broke the silence.

"I don't want you to quit for me, Joe," he said softly, surprising her.

Frowning, she looked over at him to find him staring down at his half-eaten fritter. "That's what you wanted a few months ago."

"I know," he said, shaking his head as he sighed heavily, "but I don't want you to give up something that you love because of me, Joe. I don't want you to have any regrets later."

She reached out and took his large hand into hers. "I won't, Eric. I'm not giving it up entirely. I love dispatching and teaching and I would love to focus on that for a while. If it doesn't work out I plan on coming back to work on the truck and going to school," she explained. Of course if she went to paramedic school later on she doubted the city would pay for it.

"I only want you to be happy, Joe," he said, bringing their entwined hands to his lips. He pressed a soft kiss to the back of her hand.

"I am happy," she promised before giving him an impish little grin. "But, I'd be happier with an orange juice."

Chuckling, he shook his head as he started the ambulance. "Little gold digger."

"That's me," she agreed.

Loud sirens caught their attention. Joe looked to her right to see Greg speed across the large empty parking lot with his lights going and his sirens blaring.

"What a fucking idiot," Eric said, following after him at a much slower pace.

She couldn't agree more, especially when he peeled out in front of an SUV and raced down the street. They watched the ambulance as it rode down the middle of the road, forcing cars to pull off to the side or get hit.

* * * *

"Remind me to have Bill give OEMS a call about that little prick," Eric said, voicing her thoughts at the moment. He really didn't belong working in an ambulance and he sure as hell didn't belong behind the wheel.

"Oh shit," Eric snapped, turning on the emergency lights and grabbing the mike as she watched in horror as Greg ran through a red light and was slammed into by a tractor trailer that hadn't been given an ounce of warning to stop.

"Echo seventeen to dispatch," Eric said as they sped through the parking lot, watching as the ambulance rolled over several times until if finally landed on its hood only to have the truck slam into it as the sound of screeching breaks broke through the sounds of metal being crushed.

"*Echo seventeen.*"

"We are onsite at an MVA involving an ambulance and a tractor trailer at Washington and Paramount. Requesting assistance from fire and ambulance," Eric said, smoothly turning onto Washington.

"*Received Echo seventeen, MVA at Washington and Paramount.*"

"That fucking idiot," Eric growled out as he moved through traffic, switching the sirens as he requested the right away.

Once they reached the scene of the accident he pulled up and blocked the road that the destroyed ambulance occupied. He left the emergency lights on as he jumped out, glad to see the other ambulances that were stationed alongside of them earlier heading towards the accident.

When he got his hands on the little bastard he was going to kill him, he decided as he and Joe worked quickly to pull their stretcher out, load it with oxygen, a trauma bag and the long board. Just as he was about to push the stretcher towards the overturned ambulance Joe jumped back into the ambulance. Seconds later she was jumping out with a fire blanket in her arms.

"Glass," was all she said. With a nod of understanding they headed towards the ambulance.

As soon as the scent of gasoline hit his nose he shot a look towards Joe and mumbled a few curses that she thankfully missed over the sounds of sirens drawing near. He didn't want her anywhere near this accident, but he didn't have much of a choice. They had three patients inside the fucked up ambulance and were going to need as many hands as they could get to get them all out of there before the damn thing caught fire.

It was probably selfish, but he was glad that Joe was moving on and finding other things that interested her. He wanted her safe and happy. He knew accidents could happen anywhere probably better than most people and that she could just as easily get hit by a bus than get hurt working on an ambulance, but it made him feel a hell of a lot better to know that she wouldn't be in a position to take risks soon.

Well, she wouldn't be taking risks fulltime anymore and when she did he would be there to keep her safe. He'd still worry, but for her he'd deal with it. As long as she was happy he would deal with anything even if that meant she stayed on the truck fulltime. He wouldn't like it, but he would accept it for her.

"Eric," Joe said, her voice breaking.

"What?" he asked, shaking his head clear and forcing himself to focus. It was only then that he realized that they'd stop pushing the stretcher and Joe was kneeling next to the mutilated driver's side door.

"He's dead," she said hollowly.

Praying that she was wrong, he moved to kneel next to her and tilted his head to look at the bloody mess. When his eyes landed on Greg's vacant expression and the severe damage to his head and neck he knew the man was gone.

Legally they weren't allowed to pronounce someone dead and were technically supposed to do whatever they could for Greg but there really was nothing they could for him. They also had multiple patients and as the first EMTs on the scene it was their job to access the damage. Without a word they stood up and hurried over to the passenger side to find Greg's partner in the same condition.

"The third rider," Joe said flatly as she got to her feet and moved to the side doors of the patient compartment.

When she couldn't get the doors to budge he helped, but it was more than obvious that the doors weren't going to open without the help of the Jaws of Life. They quickly moved to the back of the ambulance and he let out a sigh of relief when the doors opened and he heard the young woman sobbing.

"We need a neck collar and the long board," Eric said.

With a nod, Joe took off to grab the stretcher while he inspected the scene inside the ambulance. The stretcher had come out of its hold and was on the floor, or rather ceiling. He grabbed it and pulled it out, giving it a good shove away from the ambulance so they had room to get the woman and get the hell out.

He noted the broken glass and medical supplies scattered on the floor before moving his eyes to the woman hanging upside down in the tech seat. Blood dripped off her as she struggled to free herself.

"Hold still. We're going to get you out," he said, crouching low as he walked towards her.

"I-I c-can smell gas!" she cried.

"I know," he said soothingly. "We're going to get you out as fast we can and get the hell out of here, but I need you to do exactly what I tell you to do, okay?"

"O-okay," she agreed, forcing herself to remain still even as she trembled with fear.

He heard broken glass being crushed behind him and wasn't surprised when Joe and Justin, an EMT that worked for a large private ambulance company, moved in behind him. He damn near sighed with relief. Justin was a large guy, but most importantly he knew his shit and would help get the woman the hell out of here. More importantly he'd work fast so that he could get Joe the hell out of here.

"I'll secure her neck if you two gentlemen and I use that term loosely," Joe said, forcing herself to get into the rhythm of things and keep everyone calm as she moved towards the patient, "would be so kind as to get her down and out of here."

"Sounds good," Justin said, shifting to Eric's left.

They both donned gloves as Joe carefully worked the collar around the woman's neck. Eric reached over and held the woman's head still as Joe secured the neck collar. When she was done he removed his hands and Joe got into a position where she could hold the woman's head still and stay clear of the area while they worked.

He knew from experience that job was extremely uncomfortable and sometimes had to be held for a long time while crews worked around the patient, but that wouldn't be the case today. They needed to get the hell out of here. He hoped that Fire was on its way since they'd take care of the gas problem quickly.

"If I cut her down do you think you could grab her?" Eric asked Justin.

With a firm nod, the man got his hands into position, ready to hold the woman where she was until Eric could help move her. He'd love a few extra hands, but there wasn't enough room or time for that. Shooting a nervous glance at Joe he grabbed his trauma shears out of pants and cut the lap belt off the woman.

"I-it was a-a priority three call," the woman said softly as tears rolled down her cheeks, surprising the hell out of them.

Priority three calls were not allowed to use the emergency lights or sirens. Those were the calls for patients who were in absolutely no danger and therefore the State decided that that the crews operating the ambulances and people on the road would not be put in harm's way as a result. A priority three patient was supposed to get a nice, calm ride to the hospital.

"Mark told him to shut down the lights, b-but he wouldn't listen," the woman said, sobbing softly.

"Shhh, it's okay," Joe said, trying to give the woman what little comfort she could.

"I didn't want to ride with him," the woman admitted softly and Eric didn't blame her one bit. Not that he voiced that opinion, but he shared a look with Joe that communicated exactly how he felt.

"On my count," he said, drawing back their attention to getting the hell out of there as he prepared to cut her shoulder belt. "One, two......three."

When the belt gave way he dropped his shears and reached up to grab the woman and gently guided her down. Carefully, but quickly, the three of them managed to keep her neck stabilized and moved her to the long board. Justin moved to the doors and picked up the foot of the backboard while he picked up the head. Joe kept her hold on the woman's head as they moved out.

They didn't bother with straps at the moment since it was more important to get the hell out of there before it blew up. As Eric reached the backdoors he smelled the unmistakable scent of smoke.

"Fire," he yelled.

Thankfully Joe and Justin reacted quickly as did the EMTs waiting outside the ambulance to help. Several men grabbed the side of the backboard and together they hauled ass towards their ambulance and not a moment too soon.

Immense heat flashed behind him with a loud explosion sent him stumbling, but thankfully they didn't drop the patient. As soon as they were safely behind their ambulance they placed the backboard on the ground and worked together to secure her. Since their stretcher was now consumed in flames one of the other crews took their patient.

"Let's get the hell out of here," Joe said after she finished giving her statement to the police. Knowing that she needed to get the hell out of there he nodded as he took her hand and gave it a squeeze as they headed for their ambulance.

Chapter 30

"Echo twelve is on scene."

"Echo twelve is on scene at 16:22," Joe said, shooting a glance at her monitor's clock as she put the crew on scene.

"I'm sorry I'm late," Derek said as he hurried to her side.

"Don't worry about it," Joe said, waving it off as she got to her feet and stepped away from the call center station so that Derek could sit down and take over.

"I meant to pick up a coffee for you on the way here to celebrate your first official day, but Lindsey and the baby were sick. I really appreciate you covering for me," Derek said, pulling on the headphones that she'd just pulled off.

"There's always tomorrow," she said with a wink as she headed for the door of the dark room. They kept the room dark to help block distractions and help the dispatchers focus on the monitors. It took a while for her to get used it. Once she started to work unofficially full time as a dispatcher she'd quickly acclimated to her new surroundings.

She'd been working as a dispatcher fulltime now for about a month, but today was her first official day as a fulltime dispatcher, something that made her both happy and miserable. She was happy with the job. She loved it in fact and was glad when a fulltime opening unofficially became available after the accident.

As much as she hated to admit this that accident freaked her out pretty badly and she had desperately needed a break. She was glad when the dispatching position became available, but she felt guilty leaving Eric before he started school. He said he was fine with it even when he got stuck with Teddy for two weeks straight, but that didn't make her feel any better. She felt like she'd abandoned him, but she honestly couldn't have kept working on the truck.

She'd burned out and she knew it and he probably did as well. It happened and she was just glad that she had her dispatcher training to fall back on. Not that she had to worry about money, for a while at least. She had her paramedic nest egg which she decided to use to splurge on a tropical vacation for her and Eric before he started school, which would happen in three months. Of course it didn't hurt that Eric had moved in pretty much the night of the accident and decided that he would take over the bills, something they constantly argued about.

It was nice having him around even if it was unofficial. She liked having him there at night and in the morning. Loved having him around to spoil her. She just plain loved the man.

"Have a good night, Derek," she called out as she opened the door and stepped into the brightly lit hall.

"You too!" Derek said, sounding amused as she squinted against the sudden brightness. When her vision cleared she felt her brows arch clear to her hairline at the site that greeted her.

"Hey, Joe," Jeff said with an evil grin that didn't bode well for her as he lazily waved around a folded strap. "We just thought we'd give you an official goodbye from the station," he said, gesturing to the dozen or so firefighters and EMTs that blocked both sides of the hall.

Oh, damn.......

Why hadn't she considered this? She really should have considered this happening since she was usually part of the official goodbye party for anyone that left their station. With a forced smile she reached back to open the call room door only to find it locked. She swore she heard Derek laughing his ass off but she wasn't sure.

"That's, um, real nice of you guys, but I'm kind of running behind as it is. Perhaps another time?" she asked, sounding hopeful as she discretely shifted towards the left, but the men simply closed in on her, grinning.

"I think now is a great time. What do you think, guys?" Jeff asked.

"Sounds good to me," Rick, a large firefighter that she may have helped shaved from head to toe when he joined their station five years ago, agreed.

"I guess that leaves me with no choice but to run," she said solemnly seconds before she tried to make her escape.

Unfortunately for her she wasn't fast enough and was soon strapped tightly to a backboard and hoisted up in the air. She had to bite her lip to stop herself from begging them not to shave her head, dye her skin or strip her only because she didn't want to give them any ideas.

Why the hell hadn't she accepted Eric's offer to pick her up after work? Because she was a moron that's why. She wanted to go home, freshen up and look beautiful for him since he was taking her out to celebrate her first official day. Now thanks to her damn vanity she was facing a future without hair or being purple.

"Maybe we can talk about this? Guys?" she said, hoping they'd let her go, but of course they wouldn't. She decided to ignore their laughs and jokes as she tried to break free from her restraints, but unfortunately for her they knew how to do their damn jobs.

When they brought her outside she tried not to squirm and draw attention to herself, but of course that was pointless. The building that housed dispatch was right next to city hall and across the street from a strip mall. She prayed that they would keep this little display of insanity private and throw her ass in an ambulance and take her back to the station, but of course they didn't.

They decided to stand her up and lean her back against the black iron fence that cut across the front of town hall. She couldn't see past the thick wall of men that suddenly surrounded her, but she was pretty damn sure that a crowd was forming and that some of them were taking pictures. She tried to ignore them as she renewed her struggles to break free, but there was no give.

"Guys, don't do this!"

Jeff merely shrugged. "Sorry, but it's for your own good, Joe," he said with a wink before they all stepped back as one and Joe felt her heart skip a beat as her eyes landed on Eric.

She swallowed hard as she looked him over and felt herself melt against her restraints. He looked incredible in his dress uniform as he walked towards her.

"Joe," he said in way of greeting as he neared her.

"What's going on, Eric?" she asked, shooting nervous glances towards the men grinning hugely at her side and the large crowd gathering around them.

"The guys wanted to give you a proper sendoff," he explained.

"And you?" she asked, hating the way her voice trembled.

With that bad boy smile that she loved, Eric dropped down to one knee in front of her and pulled out a small velvet box. "Wanted to know if you would marry me?"

She opened her mouth, but no words came out. She swallowed and tried again, but the only sound that came out was a little sob. Mortified, she tried to hold the next one back, but it broke free the second she realized that hot liquid was running down her cheeks.

Not hot liquid, she realized with dread, but tears. She was *crying*, she thought with disgust. She never cried, no matter what. It was a useless waste of energy and something she never allowed, but now in front of all the guys she'd worked with for twelve years and half the town by the looks of it, she was crying.

"Oh shit," one of the men breathed, "he broke Joe."

Joe ignored him and the rest of the comments as she struggled to break free and hide her face as the damn burst. She hadn't cried in years, not since she was a little girl and now it seemed that all those tears she'd saved up wanted out. It was so embarrassing.

"Shhh, Joe, shhhh. It's okay, baby," Eric said softly as he stood up and cupped her face, gently wiping her tears away with his thumbs, but that only cleared the way for more to come.

"Don't cry, Joe," he said, sounding like his heart was breaking.

"I'm not crying!" she snapped, but she was. Oh god, she was crying and people were taking pictures! She would never live this down.

"Then what would you call the tears running down your beautiful face?" he asked, cracking a smile as he brushed his lips against hers.

"Rain?" she suggested.

That earned a chuckle from him as he kissed her again. "Are you planning on putting me out of my misery anytime soon?"

"What?" she asked, wishing that she could shut off the damn tears, but there didn't seem to be a shut off valve.

"I asked you to marry me, Joe," he said, smiling sheepishly. "In front of all these people and you're leaving me hanging here."

She sniffled, further adding to her humiliation. "Untie me and I'll give you an answer."

He pursed his lips up in thought and looked like he was thinking it over. "No, I'm sorry. That's just not going to work for me, Joe. I'm afraid I'm going to need an answer."

"What if I give you the wrong answer?" she asked, feeling her lips twitch.

"Then I guess I'll just have to keep you strapped to that board until you give me the right one," he said, cupping her face in his hands.

"Oh? And what's the right answer?"

"That you'll marry me and make me whole, Joe," he said on a reverent whisper.

"And if I don't?" she asked, her voice breaking as joy like nothing she'd ever known before surged through her body.

He shrugged even as he brushed his lips against hers. "Then I'll just have to stuff worms down your shirt until you say yes."

"I'll just make you eat them," she pointed out, smiling even as more embarrassing tears streamed down her face.

He chuckled softly against her mouth. "Marry me or I'll have my big brother beat you up."

"He's a pushover," she felt obligated to point out.

"Fine," he said, smiling. "Marry me and I'll finally get you that steak dinner I promised you."

She pretended to think it over for a minute before asking, "Can I have an appetizer with it?"

"Will you give me children?"

"Maybe," she said coyly, trying not to grin hugely at the thought of having his babies.

"Then mabye," he conceded slowly.

"And dessert?"

He sighed heavily as he pulled back to look in her eyes. "Will you put out at least five times a week if I do?"

She nodded. "I'll put out twenty times a week if I can have ice cream with it."

"Then you can have ice cream, you little gold digger," he said with a putout sigh.

"Then my answer is yes," she said, not even caring that she was crying anymore as he leaned in and kissed her. She was happy, but more importantly she was his.

Epilogue

Four years later.......

"He's going to kill her," Joe felt obligated to point out as they watched in fascination as Nathan's eyes darted from his butter knife to the latest harpy Alice tried to set him up with.

"But it will entertain us and really that's all that matters," he said as Emily, their two year old rambunctious daughter, climbed onto his lap.

Eric adjusted her on his lap so that she was sitting on his knee and close enough to steal his dessert without falling. He kept one hand pressed against his little girl's tummy as he returned his arm to lie across the back of Joe's chair. She shifted uncomfortably on the chair as she rubbed her large stomach.

"Are you okay?" he asked for probably the hundredth time since he got off work and picked her and Emily up.

"I'm fine," she said, giving him a tight smile.

He moved his arm from the back of her chair to place his hand on her stomach. "Is he giving you problems?" he asked, rubbing his hand soothingly over her stomach, chuckling when his little boy decided to follow the moves with little kicks that his mother probably didn't appreciate.

"He's just really active today," she said, pushing her plate of triple fudge cake towards Emily only to have it snatched up.

Eric watched in amusement as his brother dug into the cake. "I need it more than she does," Nathan grumbled and Eric couldn't agree more. The woman was an annoying pain in the ass and Eric had to wonder where the hell his mother kept finding these women. Seriously, after all these years she should have run out of available annoying woman, but not yet.

Of course he also knew that if their mother didn't have a strict no drinking policy when Emily was in the house that Nathan would probably be drunk off his ass by now.

"What is it that you said you did again?" the woman, whom he didn't even bother learning her name, demanded suddenly.

It wasn't until he looked away from his brother pouting that he realized that she was speaking to him. She was a beautiful woman, of course she had nothing on his Joe, but she was stuck up and rude in his opinion at least. She hadn't felt the need to acknowledge him or Joe with more than a murmured hello two hours ago. Instead she spent the entire time giving Nathan as much attitude as she could muster while their mother fretted around the kitchen nervously.

"Drug lord," Eric answered, chuckling when Joe poked him in the ribs. Nathan smiled for the first time since this dinner from hell started and their mother even cracked a smile, but not the ice princess. She simply glared at him.

"He's a paramedic for the city," his mother felt obligated to explain. "He's also a field supervisor," she said proudly, making him roll his eyes. The woman did love to brag.

"But I'm still his boss," his beautiful wife pointed out teasingly.

The woman shifted her eyes over to Joe and blinked as if she'd just realized his wife was there. How she could have missed Joe with that huge stomach he'd never know, but she looked genuinely surprised to see her. Then again most women took one look at his wife and easily dismissed her. They were all idiots. His wife was fucking hot and he knew it and so did most of the guys much to his horror.

It was one thing being married to the hottest woman on earth, but it was quite another for other guys to notice as well. Even after four years of marriage it still pissed him off when he caught some asshole checking her out, not that he could blame them, but still......

"She's a supervising dispatcher for the city," his mother said proudly as she sent Joe a fond smile.

"Oh," the woman said, not sounding too impressed. Not that he was a snob or anything, but he really didn't think a woman who worked at the mall customer service counter had any business looking down her nose at anyone.

"Grandma?" Emily said, drawing his mother's attention.

"Yes, pumpkin?" she asked, giving Emily the smile reserved solely for her.

Emily pointed accusingly at Nathan. "He took my cake," she said, pouting.

"Nathan Parish!" their mother said in shocked outrage as she reached over and took back the half eaten slice of cake and placed it in front of Emily, who happily attacked the frosting.

"Tattletale," Nathan grumbled even as he sent his niece a wink that made her giggle.

"Alice? I'm not trying to be rude or anything," the woman started and he seriously doubted that. She'd been incredibly rude throughout the entire meal. "But, I think you have a leak or something," the woman said, gesturing to the floor as she stood up and walked away from the table.

"What?" Alice asked, looking confused as she peered down at the floor.

"Not a leak," Joe said, gasping. "My water just broke."

"Shit," Nathan gasped as Eric stood up and passed his daughter over to him.

"Let's get you to the couch, Joe," Eric said calmly as he reached down and scooped her up into his arms.

"I don't think you should be doing that," the woman pointed out. "You could hurt the baby!"

He sent his mother a glare for inviting the woman as he walked towards the living room. A talk was long overdue about the woman's unwanted dating services. Judging by her reluctant nod she knew what was coming.

"More cake?" Emily asked sweetly.

"You sure can," he heard Nathan say as he walked into the living room.

He wasn't too surprised when his brother walked in a minute later, talking on the phone while he handed Eric a pile of white towels and blankets.

"Is that 911?" Eric asked.

When Nathan nodded Eric held out his hand and took the phone. Nathan quickly sat down by Joe's side and put his arm around her as he offered her his hand to squeeze. That actually surprised Eric since the last time the man did that Joe ended up breaking three of his fingers during a rather nasty contraction.

"What's the address?" he heard Roger, a dispatcher of two years ask.

"Hey, Roger, it's Eric."

Roger chuckled. "Let me guess, Joe's the one ready to burst?"

"Oh yeah," he said, watching as his wife squeezed Nathan's hand as she bit back a scream. Nathan didn't fare so well. He dropped to his knees on the floor, whimpering but he never pulled his hand away.

"Only give her two fingers so she doesn't break your damn hand," he said in exasperation as his brother struggled through another contraction.

With a sigh of relief his brother pulled his hand away and offered only two fingers. Joe grabbed onto his hand as she bit back another scream. He didn't need to look to know that his little boy was going to be making his appearance soon. This was her second child and that usually meant a quicker delivery and judging by the space between her screams it was going to be real soon.

"What's the address?" Roger asked.

"458 Cranberry Road," he answered.

"Okay, I'm sending them now. Good luck, Eric."

"Thanks," he said before hanging up.

He placed the phone on the coffee table and knelt in front of Joe. "Baby, I think we should get you set up on the floor. What do you think?" he suggested, brushing her beautiful long hair out of her face.

"I think," she said, glaring at him with murderous intent, "that if you or that damn battering ram you have the nerve to call a dick ever comes near me again so help me I will- *Aaaaaagggggghhhhh*!" she broke off her beautiful words of love to scream.

"Time to get you on the floor," he said, ignoring Nathan's amused chuckles as he gently helped Joe lie on the freshly polished floor.

"Get behind her and let her sit back against you," he said, thankful that Nathan did what he asked without complaint.

"Um, what are you doing?" the woman he'd forgotten about suddenly demanded.

"Dinner appears to be over. You might want to leave before this gets messy," he said, not bothering to take his eyes off his wife as he carefully pushed up the soft flowery cotton maternity dress that she hated so much.

"I don't think you should be doing that," the woman said, ignoring his polite way of telling her to get the fuck out.

"It's fine. I really need you to go now," he said as he gently gripped Joe's wet pink panties and pulled them off. When he saw what was waiting for him he nearly groaned.

"Look, you shouldn't be doing that. I'm going to call an ambulance for her," the stubborn woman said, obviously refusing to leave.

Eric liked to think he was a patient man, but his wife was in pain and from the looks of it his son was crowing and ready to make his appearance. "Look, *sweetheart*, this is a family moment and you're not family so you can either haul your ass out of here or I can throw you out. It's your choice," he snapped, moving to do just that.

"Fine, you didn't have to be so rude about it," she snapped, placing her phone in her purse and she practically stormed out of the house. "Don't bother calling me," she bit out, probably to Nathan, he decided as he placed a towel on the floor between Joe's legs.

"Where the hell does she keep finding women like that?" Joe bit out tightly between panting.

"I don't know, but I really wish she'd stop looking," Nathan grumbled.

"You know what you have to do if you want that to happen," Eric said conversationally as he placed his hands between his wife's legs.

"Not until I find the one," Nathan grumbled and Eric just barely stopped himself from bitch slapping his brother upside the head.

The man wanted the perfect woman and he didn't realize that Eric already had her. He was too damn picky and stubborn to realize that any of the dozen or so women he'd dated in the last five years would have made him a very happy man. It was a mistake that he was afraid was going to cost him.

"Anyone home?" a familiar voice called from the front door.

"Come on in!" he yelled.

"Oh god," Joe muttered and he knew she was going to be embarrassed to have the guys from work witness this, but there really was no choice in the matter. Their little guy was coming whether she was ready or not.

He heard people piling into the living room, more than he should have and risked a glance back and had to laugh. It seemed all the guys on duty decided to come help, even Teddy. That didn't surprise him as much as it would have a few years ago.

After the accident Teddy became more somber and serious at work. For a while people were placing bets on how long it would take the old Teddy to come back. So far no one had won that bet.

It was one of the good things that had come as a result of the senseless tragedy. Almost overnight every ambulance service in the county changed their ride along time. The company that Greg had worked for changed the time from two days to a week. Not that it mattered since the company went out of business. It probably didn't help that the third rider in that accident had sued and won, pushing the company into bankruptcy.

"Hey, Joe," Teddy said as he knelt beside Eric.

"Hey, Teddy," Joe nearly cried.

"Getting ready to have another beautiful baby I see," Teddy said as he pulled open an OB kit, a birthing kit every ambulance carried for such an occasion.

Joe nodded weakly as Nathan used a towel to wipe sweat off her face. She looked so damn beautiful. All he wanted to do was take her into his arms and tell her how much he loved her, but he knew she'd kick his ass if he let anyone else do this.

"I need you to push now, Joe," he said, accepting the sanitized towel Teddy handed him.

"And I need to kick your ass for doing this to me!" she snapped even as she pushed.

Nathan grunted in pain as she squeezed his hand. Teddy reached over and took Joe's free hand into his, manfully taking the abuse that she dished out as she began push.

"Suction," Eric said when the head popped out. Teddy thankfully was ready and handed him the rubber bulb. He quickly cleared out his son's airway before handing the bulb back.

"Push," he said, gently holding his son's head as he slowly came out.

"You push, you bastard!" she yelled, earning several nervous chuckles from the guys.

"Oh, you're all here!" he heard his mother say. "Why don't some of you boys come help me make coffee and cut some cake," his mother thankfully suggested. He knew the guys were anxious for Joe, but he really didn't need witnesses when she went for his balls.

"Yes, ma'am," he heard Jeff say.

"Here we go," Eric said as the baby's shoulders cleared. He caught hold of his wiggling son as Teddy swooped in and wrapped the screaming infant up in a swaddle.

He smiled down at his son as Teddy quickly moved to tie off the cord and cut it. Jonathan, a fire fighter and part time EMT moved in to help wipe the baby down. Not once did his baby stop screaming and Eric couldn't have been prouder. He didn't think it was possible to be happier than he was at that moment. Of course Joe just had to go and wreck his moment of bliss.

"You are so buying me a steak dinner for this," she bit out.

His eyes shot to his brother who simply shook his head with pity. "Little gold digger," they both grumbled, earning a killing glare from the woman he absolutely adored.

Life really couldn't get any better, he decided as he placed his screaming child in Joe's arms and leaned over to kiss her, narrowly missing her shot to his balls.

"I love you, you little gold digger," he whispered against her lips.

The End.......

Made in the USA
Middletown, DE
07 August 2021